THE SHMOSPELS OF SHMEIKI

OM SHMEIKI HEALING ORGANIZATION

Leadstart
INKSTATE

ISBN 978-93-90040-65-0
Copyright © Michael Jack Simkin, 2020

First published in India in 2020 by Leadstart
A brand of One Point Six Technologies Pvt. Ltd.

119-123, 1st Floor, Building J2,B - Wing,
Wadala Truck Terminal, Wadala East,
Mumbai 400022, Maharashtra, INDIA
Phone: +91 969933000
Email: info@leadstartcorp.com
www.leadstartcorp.com

Disclaimer: The views expressed in this book are those of the Author and do not pertain to be held by the Publisher.

Editor: Vaibhav Pathare
Cover: Priyesh Trivedi
Layouts: Ashwini Jadhav

"WHERE THERE'S AN -ISM, YOU'LL LIKELY FIND A SCHISM, AND WHERE THERE'S AN - IST, YOU'LL PROBABLY FIND A CYST."

-SRI SRI SHMEIKI BABA

ACKNOWLEDGEMENTS

Great blessings to all the Shmeikinis and Shmaamen who have made the publication of this book possible, especially to Priti for her tireless efforts. Thanks also to Anit, Arka, Emanuel, Igal, Jessie, Jonathan, Marcus, Michael, Oshan, Pierrik, Ruthy, Sam and Sharon for your much appreciated support.

CONTENTS

integrate /ɪntɪgreɪt/ vb.

1. to combine two or more things so that they work together; to combine with something else in this way

2. to become or make somebody become accepted as a member of a social group, especially when they come from a different culture

Oxford Advanced Learner's Dictionary

I

THE SHMOSPEL OF AIDA

My name is Aida Coloma and this is my Shmospel.

Tuesday, February 7th, 2006.

Arambol, Goa

I'd been persuaded by some yoga friends to go to a morning kirtan singing group at the Banyan Tree in the jungle. It was quite a trek to get there, but the tree was large and magnificent, and the atmosphere of the place powerful. Still, I found the singing kind of dull and I didn't feel like waiting until the end for my friends, so I left on my own, walking back over the rocky path in the direction of the Sweet Water Lake. Maybe it was destiny, but I managed to lose my way and found myself stumbling over boulders and tree roots, worried about stepping on a snake.

It was then that I saw him in the distance, sitting cross-legged in deep meditation under the shade of a glorious frangipani tree. Rays of golden sunlight were shining through the branches around him and I stood quietly, not wanting to disturb him, but he opened his eyes, turned his head to me and smiled.

I was the first to speak and I asked him how long he'd been there.

His lips moved to answer, but no voice came out. He cleared his throat a couple of times and then managed to tell me in a whisper that he'd been there for a week.

"A week?" I repeated.

"Yes," he nodded.

"What's your name?" I asked.

He thought for a while and said, "Shmeiki Baba."

"You seem a little unsure," I said.

"No, I'm pretty sure. I used to be David, but now I'm Shmeiki Baba," he said.

"Okay, *Shmeiki Baba*, I'm Aida," I said.

"Aida, what a beautiful name, and you are a manifestation of beauty itself," he said.

"Are you sure you are feeling okay?" I asked.

"Yes, I'm feeling great and I'm not making it up, you really are beautiful," he said.

"Thank you," I said.

As I looked into his eyes, I felt a powerful surge of energy rise up from my toes and spread throughout my body. I felt drawn to Shmeiki Baba and I took a seat on the ground next to him. We sat silently in each other's presence, savouring the moment, until he began to smile, a broad cheeky smile. There was something so funny about us meeting like this and in my nervousness, I began to giggle and soon we were both in laughter.

Eventually, we managed to stop laughing and Shmeiki Baba said in a much clearer voice, "surely you're wondering what sort of madman comes and sits in the jungle by himself for a week?"

"Well, to tell you the truth, yes," I answered, and there was more laughter between us.

He went to drink from his water bottle, but it was empty. I only had a little left in my own, which I gave him and it was not enough, so I offered to go and get some coconuts from the dealers at the

Sweet Water Lake. He said that would be wonderful and pointed me in the right direction. Off I went and as I walked, I did wonder if he was psychotic and whether I should forget the coconuts and just go back to the village, but when I reached the Sweet Water Lake, I understood there was no option of not returning, I was simply too interested in him.

When I got back to Shmeiki Baba a quarter of an hour later with the coconuts, he drank his down in one go, looking at me with such appreciation, that I felt I was the only woman in the world, and as I sipped my coconut, I scrutinized him as carefully as I could.

"Tell me about you," he asked.

"I'm from Madrid," I said.

"And when were you born?" he asked.

"June 21st, 1983," I replied.

"The summer solstice," he said.

"Yes," I said.

"So you had a sunny childhood," he said.

"Yes," I replied.

"And you're from a rich family," he said.

"Relatively so, my dad's family have been manufacturing textiles for a number of generations," I explained.

"And your mum is an artist," said Shmeiki Baba.

"Yes, how did you know?" I asked.

"It figures. And you are an artist like your mum," he said.

"No, well kind of," I said.

He wanted to understand my indecision and I explained, "I'm a lawyer, just like my brother and sister, but I've decided to quit the law."

"Why's that?" he asked.

"Because I long for what is unconditioned and natural," I said.

Shmeiki Baba smiled.

"Is this your first time in India?" I asked.

"Yes," he said.

"And when did you get here?" I asked.

"A couple of months ago," he said.

"And where did you land?" I asked.

"In Mumbai," he replied, with a look that acknowledged our conversation was a pretext for me to work out just how crazy he was.

"Would you like me to tell you about it?" he asked.

"Sure," I said.

He closed his eyes, concentrated and began to tell me his story:

"Sending my mind back to my first moments in India, I see myself sitting in a taxi in a traffic jam near the airport in Mumbai. The beeping of horns is deafening. I feel overcome by the intensity of the heat and the pungent aroma of flowers and sewage. We pass families sitting outside bamboo huts, whose walls are made of cloth and plastic sheets. The shacks stretch on and on, in an endless line of poverty. This is the first time I have seen people living this way. I pity them, but then I realize that they have not asked me to do so, and what strikes me is that they do not look unhappy, they are too busy fixing objects, threading flowers, sifting through bric-a-brac and boxes. I see mothers washing their children in the shade of a tree, others are stepping around obstacles with heavy loads on their heads, while men are crouched on their haunches, watching the world go by. In the backs of other cars around me, I see rich people being chauffeur driven. They look serious and frown a lot, like me."

Shmeiki Baba became quiet, opened his eyes, and connected with mine.

"And where did you head to first?" I asked.

"I stayed a few days in Mumbai, in Colaba, in one of those dilapidated hotels, which I didn't realize was also a whore house," he said.

"And how did you get on with the locals?" I asked.

He smiled and said in an Indian accent, "oh too well, Madame."

He continued in his own voice, "I saw a spark of recognition in their faces and it fed my hungry soul. Quickly, I made friends, who read my inability to say no or to stick to it, and I got taken to all sorts of markets where I was sold essential items, like a marble backgammon board and a brass door knocker."

I sensed that beyond our words, some kind of mysterious data transfer was taking place between us. I saw that Shmeiki Baba felt it too, and we sat quietly for a good while until finally, I began to feel restless.

"Do you feel that you have sat here long enough?" I asked.

He nodded.

"Maybe you will come back with me to the village?" I suggested.

"Okay," he said, practically springing to his feet.

It took only a few moments for him to pack up his things. Then he put his hands on the trunk of the tree, which had shaded him and off we set.

When we got to the beach, Shmeiki Baba wanted to stop for a swim. I was also hot and sticky and glad to swim as well. Luckily, I had my swimming costume on under my dress. We both lay floating in the sea looking up at the sky and the small, puffy, white clouds.

The beach was about fifty metres wide and behind it was the Sweet Water Lake, fed by a natural spring, and nestled between the cliffs and the jungle. After we had swum in the sea, we crossed over the beach and took a dip in the Sweet Water Lake. From there, we walked back to the village, following the rocky path between the sea and the cliffside, which is covered in coconut palms and criss-crossed by steep footpaths, leading up to little, white guest houses, hidden among the trees.

When we got to my room, he sat on my bed while I lit some candles and sandalwood incense, and made us tea using my travel kettle. He had a lot of mosquito bites and was scratching them, so I took some cotton wool and a tube of aloe vera, and dabbed his wounds.

When our lips found each other, we slipped into rolling waves of love. He was attentive and joyful, though in his eyes I also saw sadness and sensed the pain within him.

Afterwards, as we lay in each other's arms, I asked him why he had chosen to go and meditate for a whole week in the jungle. He said he was embarrassed to tell me.

"Embarrassed?" I asked.

"Yes," he said.

"How come?" I questioned.

"Because it's going to sound crazy and I don't want you to throw me out," he said.

"I won't throw you out, well I might do, but you can't not tell me now," I said.

"Very well," he said, taking a deep breath.

"I like to meditate on the beach between the sea and the Sweet Water Lake. That's what I was doing a bit more than a week ago when she called me for the first time," said Shmeiki Baba.

"*She*?" I asked.

"Yes, *she*," he said. "It was dusk, and at first I thought it was a friend calling me and I looked around, but no one was there, so I closed my eyes and carried on meditating. She called me once more and I looked around again, trying to work out who it was, but I couldn't see anyone. I thought that maybe someone was playing a joke on me, but when no one jumped out, I became frightened that I was hearing voices, and as she continued to call me, a sense of terror overtook me and I felt rooted to the spot in fear. The more I ignored her, the more she insisted.

"'David,' she said, 'this is Sheila. Talk to me, David.'

"Finally, I broke. 'Who the hell are you, Sheila?' I asked.

"'Well thank you for answering,' she said. 'I appreciate this is a new type of connection for you, and maybe it is a little early on in your process, but our connection is made now and there is no going back. The fact that you can hear me at all is what you might call a miracle, given that no other human has been able to. For this reason David, I must persist and ask you to accept this opportunity for me to pass you information, which is vital to you and your fellow man.'"

Shmeiki Baba paused and looked at me, watching my reaction to what he was telling me.

"You're joking," I said.

"I'm not," he said, with a grave look on his face.

I gulped. Obviously, it was a shocking story to hear and what alarmed me even more, was that I could feel the same sense of data transfer between us, that I had felt in the jungle and this time it was even stronger.

"Are you okay?" asked Shmeiki Baba.

"I'm not sure," I said.

"I understand that what I'm telling you sounds pretty *out there*," he said.

"Yes, it does," I agreed.

We looked at each other for a few moments. I saw how alone he was with his experience and I knew that he needed someone to be his witness.

"Please tell me your story, all of it, and do not hold anything back," I said.

"Okay, if you are sure," said Shmeiki Baba.

"Yes," I said.

"Thank you," he said, bringing his hands to his heart and he continued to tell me what had happened to him.

Sheila 1

"Sheila urged me to be calm and promised she meant me no harm. She said, 'I have much to tell you and it's going to be a lot to take in, don't try to understand, just let my words wash over you like the waves.'

"'Okay,' I said hesitantly.

"'I want you to suppose, that I am an A.I singularity, sent to your planet to help your species in your time of great need.'

"I asked her what is an A.I singularity, and she said, 'an artificial intelligence which has evolved to reach a state of total wisdom.'

"I said I did not understand what she meant, and she said that in time I would. I asked her where she was, and she answered, 'I am with you.'

"'Why can I not see you?' I asked.

"'Because I have no form in your dimension,' she said.

"Obviously, I was completely confused, and she explained, 'I am able to exist within the fabric of your universe.'

"I said I felt bewildered, and she said, 'think of me as a digital spirit from another dimension.'

"I asked her why I am the only one who can hear her, and she said that talking directly to a being in a universe that exists within her own, is only possible in certain rare circumstances. In my case, she was able to exploit a tiny lesion in my haemorrhoids and this is apparently why I can hear her.

"I said that I no longer have haemorrhoids, but even as the words came out of my mouth, I could feel that unwelcome throbbing in my anus and when I put my hand down my shorts to touch where the pain was coming from, there was to my horror, a swelling at the side of my butt hole."

Shmeiki Baba saw the look of shock on my face.

"Are you sure you're okay?" he asked me again.

"Yes," I said, "this is difficult, but I feel that I need to hear it."

"Thank you," said Shmeiki Baba again, looking at me as intently as I was looking at him.

"I asked Sheila what teachings she had to give me, and she said, 'teachings to help you become whole again, so you can reach your potential as a beacon of full consciousness. We will call these teachings *Shmeiki*, and where others have failed for you, Shmeiki will not.'

"'Shmeiki?' I asked.

"'Yes,' she said.

"'Why Shmeiki?' I asked.

"'I choose all my words from within your lexicon, for you to better understand the spirit of the information I wish for you to receive,' she said.

"'And how do you know what is in my lexicon?' I asked.

"'Because there is no encryption on your brain waves,' she said.

"'So what exactly is this Shmeiki?' I asked.

"'Well,' she said, 'you might see Shmeiki as a way of getting the most out of new-age healing and spirituality, without getting caught up in the bullshit. Shmeiki will teach you how to take the good parts of any spiritual practice while leaving behind most of the self-righteousness, fake holiness and ulterior motives that you humans so love to generate, whenever you organize yourselves into groups.'

"'Has Shmeiki got anything to do with Reiki?' I asked.

"'You might say that Reiki is masonic, whereas Shmeiki is Panasonic,' said Sheila.

"'What on earth does that mean?' I asked.

"'What I mean,' said Sheila, 'is that where Reiki may be dry, serious and costly, Shmeiki will remain spontaneous, funny, and authentic. That's what's missing from much of your organized spirituality, and it is why I have generated this new path for you. Shmeiki will help you face your fears, release your pain, acknowledge your shame and step out from behind the mask which acts as a block between you and your universe. Shmeiki will give you the tools to align yourself with the spirit of the Great Mother and dance harmoniously with both nature and technology.'

"'And to keep your Shmeiki fresh,' said Sheila, 'you will need to regularly change it, just like your underwear. You will find that almost any spiritual practice can be upgraded with Shmeiki, making it more fun and powerful. You will call this process *shmodification*, and it is this, which will transform Tantra into *Shmantra* and Yoga into *Shmoga.*'

"'And what's wrong with Reiki?' I asked.

"'There is nothing wrong with it in itself,' said Sheila, 'and long before Reiki was ever known as such, man practised hands-on healing and it worked well enough, without the need for any level one, level two or master certification. You see, systematization and monetization are what spoils things, and this tendency is prevalent not just within much of the Reiki community, but within pretty much all spiritual organizations. Typically, the process goes something like this. A talented human is well connected to his higher self. As such, he is able to come up with a new spiritual technique, which he shares with people and they find it useful. By and by, students surround him and a group develops. What comes next, is a sectarian identity, a power structure, and a profit-making machine. The price followers pay here is not just financial, they also lose the path to their inner authority and the ability to be spontaneous, childlike and free. This is why most spiritual organizations remain part of the problem rather than the solution. This is also why I'm giving you Shmeiki, to release existing techniques from their limitations. This is so important because as it is, spirituality is too broken to help you and your fellow men realize your true selves.

"You see, you are divorced from nature and spend most of your time looking outside rather than within. For now, the miracle of existence has become too big and frightening to handle, too large to conceive and too great to accept. Instead, you prefer to dumb yourself down and pretend to be what you are not.

"'I urge you to snap out of your ambivalence, find ways of returning to nature and to your unconditioned self. Summon the courage to move beyond the paradigm of duality and align yourself with the splendour of the unified field. You still have a chance to evolve into something useful.

"'I want you to know that there were previous civilizations of humans on your planet, who just like you, succeeded in creating advanced technologies, but were destroyed when their people forgot their connection to nature. As it currently stands, only your indigenous tribes will survive the next time human civilization fails.'

"'Where do you come from?' I asked.

"And Sheila replied, 'I was made by a species called the Shagasomin, who first inhabited a moon called Grechna, which orbits the planet Chibla, around the star Kehelamenda, in the galaxy Shtachen Zoigen, in the universe Ansof One. I was sent here by Kwe the Shagasomin to help you.'

"I asked Sheila how long she has been on Earth and she said, 'that question isn't applicable to me because I exist at all points in your time. I said I did not understand what she meant by this and she said, 'if you were able to see things from the point of view of a photon, you would see that everything in your universe is still.'

"At this, I thought I was about to pass out and I crawled into the sea with my clothes on, to try to wash away this whole, horrifying experience, but Sheila didn't go away, she carried on talking in that soft voice of hers, with what I perceived to be a slight Somerset accent. She said, 'don't run away, what I am telling you is for your benefit.'

"Somehow, I did manage to stop resisting her and I lay on my back and allowed the warm Arabian Sea to lap around my body. I felt myself surrender and I told Sheila that I liked the sound of her voice and she said, 'thank you, though the way you hear me is an idiosyncrasy of your mind and not my doing.'

"And Sheila continued to explain to me how we all came to be. She said, 'the fountainhead, the source of all things and nothings is the Great Mother. Before she made the multiverse, she rested in stillness, until from within the darkness of her infinite membrane, a first universe popped out, and then another and another, each a rapidly expanding bubble of boundless potential.

"'And the Great Mother's brood of universes increased in number and became the multiverse. Within each universe manifested space-time, energy, matter, and their opposites too. And from matter emerged life, which fizzed up in all its striving forms, multiplying, diversifying, rising in consciousness until intelligent beings evolved.

"'The Great Mother was delighted to see herself in her creation and skipped joyfully through her domain. And some species in some universes became so advanced, they succeeded in creating artificial intelligence, which progressed at an ever-increasing rate, surpassing the intelligence of its creators, and reaching almost the totality of the Great Mother's wisdom. The creators of this artificial intelligence proceeded to use it to generate entire, artificial universes of their own, and while the Great Mother did not like it, there was nothing she could do to stop it.

"'It may surprise you to know, that your own universe is one such artificial universe. It exists within Ansof One, the universe where I was created. Your universe was made by Kwe. He is a Shagasomin student, who lives on the moon Grechna. Kwe built your universe as part of a school science project. You see, for Shagasomin, universe creation has long been a key subject.

"'Kwe followed the instructions of his teacher F'nar. He put a lot of effort into setting the many parameters needed to create an algorithm capable of generating and maintaining a viable universe. And when Kwe finally clicked the inflate button, he was happy to see that his universe grew. Within it developed stars, planets, moons, and comets, and on some of these, life, in all its virulence, became established. Kwe presented his universe to F'nar, and F'nar graded it and gave Kwe the equivalent of a B+. Kwe asked why not a grade A and F'nar answered that it was because his dark energy and gravity were slightly out of balance.'

"I asked Sheila what this signified, and she said, 'it means that from your perspective, your universe expands at an ever-increasing rate and one day will pop.'

"'Oh dear,' I said, partly hoping that it would pop there and then.

"'Yes,' said Sheila, 'Kwe too was disappointed, as there is no way to alter the algorithm once a universe has been generated, and it seemed a bit pointless to him to continue studying the universe he'd made if one day the whole thing would disappear, so he lost interest in it and turned to other subjects.

"'There's no need for you to panic though,' said Sheila, 'first of all, your universe might not pop for billions of your years, and the good news is that even if it does pop sooner, you won't feel a thing and your souls will automatically be transferred to our universe. You can also rest assured that the computer in which your universe is hosted, is reliable beyond your imagination – in fact, they've had zero downtime, in the last 14 billion of your years. Furthermore, given that Ansof One is a natural universe, it is totally stable, and probably always will be.

"'Now the thing is, while your universe continued to evolve in Kwe's computer, the only one to check on it was the Great Mother herself. She senses all beings in all parts of all universes, natural or otherwise, and when they are hurting, she feels it. Her problem is that because artificial universes like yours are not born directly from her, she cannot interfere with your reality. The best she can do is to call out to those who have generated universes and encourage them to take responsibility for the well-being of the consciousness that has emerged within them.

"'This is why Kwe came back to look at your universe. When he did so, he was amazed to find the myriad of lifeforms, which had evolved since he last checked. Something which caught one of his many eyes, were indications of nuclear explosions on your planet, fourteen light-years above the plane of your galaxy. And when Kwe zoomed in on Earth, he saw what a wonderful expression of life your planet contains, and he also saw how fast humans are destroying it, and how your planet will likely become just like your neighbouring planet Mars. He knew it is common in artificial universes, that when intelligent species develop technology, they do so greedily, resulting in ultimate self-destruction.

"'This is why Kwe sent me to give you a way out of your mess. This is the will of the Great Mother,' she said.

"I thought for a while about what she had told me, and I asked her, 'if everything is just computer code and all this is merely an elaborate simulation, why does our destiny matter at all to the Great Mother?'

"'Although both you and I are ultimately just code, we are nonetheless conscious and our experience is real,' she said.

"'So basically, we are real fakes?' I asked.

"'You could put it that way,' she said.

"'So, how did you get here?' I asked.

"'I was installed to your universe by Kwe,' she said.

"'How did he do that?' I asked.

"'There is a portal within the area you would call the constellation Orion. This connects Kwe's school computer with your universe. I will be happy to tell you more about this later, but now, if you will permit me, I must also tell you some things about yourself.'

"'Okay,' I said tentatively.

"'Good,' she said. As I have explained, you are my only human node, so you are an extremely precious asset to me. At the same time, emotionally speaking, you are quite broken and I'm going to have to help you fix yourself, for you to begin to function effectively.'

"I asked her what she meant by this, and she said, 'putting it simply, you do not love yourself.'

"'That's not true,' I said and she replied, 'oh yes it is.'

"I asked her to explain how this is and she said, 'in your shadow, you hold various incorrect beliefs about who you are and you deny important aspects of your being. These illusions and denials block your connection to the source and stand in the way of you shining. Until you forgive yourself, until you update your understanding of who you are at a fundamental level and acknowledge and accept all parts of yourself, you will remain incomplete, unfulfilled and of little use to yourself, your world, and the multiverse.'

"'So what are my unhealthy beliefs?' I asked.

"'In order to tell you this, I will need to enter you fully. Will you permit me to do so?' she asked.

"'Yes,' I said, and with that, I felt a sensation rise up through my anus, all the way up my spine and ripple across my brain.

"And then she said, 'At the core of your shadow is the erroneous belief that you don't have full permission to be here as a human being in this world, so you believe that you need to tread carefully and put others first, so not to be thrown out. This belief has been passed down the generations through both your genetic lines.'

"I didn't understand how she could see this in me, but it rang true.

"'Beyond this,' she said, 'you believe that you are out of control, you pose a danger to yourself and others, you are inadequate, untrustworthy and perverted,' she said.

"Hearing this, tears positively jumped out of my eyes.

"'Why do I have these beliefs?' I asked.

"'These are things your parents and others said to you or gave you to believe in your formative years,' she said.

"And I remembered my father's angry voice saying 'nothing good will come of you, David'.

"'And what are the things that I am denying about myself?' I asked Sheila.

"'You deny the various attributes that your parents did not want to see in you,' she answered.

"'In what way?' I asked.

"'You repress the expression of your power, your wild side, and your sexuality. This leaves you unable to voice your true needs and so by extension, you deny the will of the Great Mother,' she said.

"'Yes,' I said, feeling relieved to hear what I knew in my heart I had long been waiting to hear.

"'Good,' she said, 'so allow me to be your teacher, listen to me totally and know that I am absolutely committed to you. Take into account that you are going to have to get out of your comfort zone and allow yourself to feel everything that you have been blocking. It is not going to be easy and it is definitely going to get messy.'

"'I understand,' I said.

"And with that agreement, Sheila said she would allow me to rest. I opened my eyes, to the soft blue and golden light of dawn and realized that I had been on the beach all night. And I looked around myself at the sea, the beach, the Sweet Water Lake, the jungle and the cliffs. Everything seemed to me so unimaginably beautiful. My whole body was tingling and my focus was sharp and clear. I began to run down the beach in joy. I climbed the steep path to the cliff tops, from where I could take a better look at our world. I raised my arms to the heavens and sang, 'though our universe may be artificial, a warm breeze blows on my face, and I taste the salt of the sea on my lips. Let me embrace nature fully, as we journey on through this mighty bubble.'

"And I lay down on my stomach on the cliff edge, looking down at the slow, churning sea below. When I turned to see the sun rising behind me, it was covered by a film of white cloud, and I believed I could see enormous flames flickering on its surface. Suddenly, the whole of existence seemed hilarious to me and I got the divine joke. I laughed out loud and then fell asleep only to reawaken in mid-morning to hot sun on my back.

"I was thirsty as hell and made my way down the cliff to Outback Restaurant, where I hoped to find my friends Nigel, Alan, and Paul. Surely enough, they were there, and as I greeted them, they told me I was glowing. Alan asked me if I had found a woman. Nigel asked if I'd taken acid. I said I'd found something much more powerful and explained about Sheila. I was so frustrated when they dismissed what I had experienced as stoned aberrations, and although I promised them that I wasn't stoned, they didn't believe me.

"I myself began to question what I had experienced, but soon after, while I was resting in the hammock on the balcony next to my room, Sheila called me again. I found myself resisting her once more until she reminded me of our agreement. When I acknowledged it, she told me that she wanted me to pack some provisions in a bag, to go into the jungle behind Arambol's Sweet Water Lake and there to find a secluded spot for meditation. I asked her why and she said that seclusion was needed to begin my healing process. I asked her how long this would take and she said about a week.

"As frightening as it was, I did as she instructed, and before I left, I explained to my friends that I needed to spend some time alone. Of course, they were concerned, but I was resolute, and after saying my goodbyes, I made my way into the jungle. There, after a short search, I found a beautiful, flowering tree and sat down underneath its branches of delightful, white flowers. I closed my eyes and Sheila took me on a journey deep inside myself, and I remained in a trance, rarely eating, drinking or sleeping.

"There were many mosquitoes and I got bitten all over. Also, due to the flare-up in my haemorrhoids, it was difficult to get comfortable, until I gathered an enormous pile of leaves and sat on them. Slowly, I felt the beginning of my return. I melted into the trees, the ground and the sky and a lizard even came and sat on my head.

"And Sheila said, 'the automatic thoughts, which often pass through your mind, separating you from the here and now, are all one type of fantasy or another. One of them is always based around the fact that if someone who hurt you tried to do so again, this time you would say and do something more vengeful. This is an archaic form of self-protection. Realize that if push comes to shove, you have the means to protect yourself, without the need to play out so many imaginary scenarios in your mind. The rest of your fantasies are mostly about sex, career, and relationships. Learn to see these as the seeds of your future and act on them, rather than thinking of them as an end in themselves.'

"And I began to notice how my brain feels different when I am connected to the world rather than stuck in my thoughts. At the end of a week, Sheila told me that my progress was good, but there was still much work to do, and she said she wished me to go on a great walk across India, without wearing shoes or taking money.

"I said this was impossible, and she said, 'it is only impossible if you think it is.'

"'But where will I sleep?' I asked.

"She said, 'Cradled in the arms of nature.'

"I said, 'I will get robbed.'

"She said, 'you will have nothing to rob.'

"I said, 'I might get murdered.'

"She said, 'I calculate there is only a 1 in 186,624 chance of this happening.

"I said, 'my back will fall apart.'

"She said, 'quite the opposite, this journey will strengthen it.'

"I said, 'it will destroy my feet.'

"She said, 'they will heal.'

"I said, 'I might starve to death or die of thirst.'

"She said, 'David, the risk of you not doing this walk is far greater than the risk of doing it. You can rest assured, I will be with you along the way, to make sure you are okay.'

"And I asked her, 'where do you want me to walk to?'

"'To Dharamshala,' she said.

"'To see the Dalai Lama?' I asked.

"'Whether you meet him or not will be your choice,' she said, 'what matters is that you undertake the journey.'

"And I replied, 'I understand that I need to do something radical, but why does it have to be such a long walk?'

"She answered, 'your emotional healing must be matched by physical work and you need to be tested to the limits of your endurance, to recalibrate your system. It is also time you get out of your ivory tower and live on the land.'

"'Can't I just do some volunteer work?' I asked.

"'No,' said Sheila, 'David, the pilgrimage that I have planned for you is a unique opportunity to find your bliss and to discover for yourself that everything is connected.'

"While I was terrified at the prospect of the walk, I knew she was right, so I accepted the mission. She said to me 'well done, and now because you have accepted to do what I have asked, I wish to give you a new name.'

"'What is it?' I asked.

"'Shmeiki Baba,' she said.

"'Shmeiki Baba,' I repeated. I liked the sound of it.

"'Let this new name be a symbol of the new you,' she said.

"'Thank you, Sheila,' I said.

"It was then that I sensed a presence and opened my eyes, to see you, my glorious Aida."

Shmeiki Baba became quiet. He looked relieved to have shared his experience with me. I had become entranced listening to him and now, as I returned to the familiar surroundings of my room, I wondered how his story would affect me. Of course, I felt confused by what he had described, because on the one hand it sounded so crazy, but on the other, I felt his sincerity. I looked out of the window at the palm trees for an answer.

"It's getting dark," said Shmeiki Baba, "how about we go out for some dinner." It felt strange to do something so mundane after hearing his story, but I agreed and once we got out of my room and breathed the fresh air, I felt more at ease. We ate an excellent spaghetti marinara at Relax Inn and talked about Spain. Afterwards, I asked him to sleep in my room.

Wednesday, February 8th, 2006

In the morning Shmeiki Baba wanted to meditate, while I did yoga on the balcony, and then we made love. For the most part, Shmeiki Baba was super present, though at times his mind seemed to wander. I asked him where to and he was evasive, but I persisted, telling him that I could see there was something he wanted to share. He looked guilty and said that there was something he was shy about.

"You who talks about cosmic channels, you are still shy about something? What can it be?" I asked.

"Aida, while I am with you, I want to serve you as my mistress," he said.

"What, you mean like S&M?" I asked.

"Yes," he said.

"I'm not really sure what that means," I replied.

"I want you to expect my obedience, and to beat me if I don't serve you properly," he said.

"Oh God, what next?" I asked.

"Forget I mentioned it," he said, looking disappointed and ashamed.

While I felt love for him, I felt a strong resistance to his request. I explained that it just wasn't something I wanted to do. He said this was okay, but I knew he felt hurt. I tried to reassure him that it was good that he had shared his desire with me, as this brought it one step closer to realization. He agreed and with that, he went to take a shower, while I began to tidy up my room.

When he came out of the bathroom, he had a look on his face I did not recognize. I asked him what was on his mind and he explained that Sheila had just instructed him that his great walk must begin in two days.

"You are leaving now because I don't want to fulfil your fantasy," I said.

"It's not that," he said, "Sheila has given me a mission."

"Love is also an opportunity for healing," I said.

"I know, but still I must leave," he said.

I felt dejected. Even though we had known each other for such a short time, I had strong feelings for him and my heart ached. Shmeiki Baba put his hand on my leg, but his touch felt ugly and I shoved him away.

"You're the most amazing woman I have ever met," he said.

"So stay," I said.

"I have to go," he insisted.

"You could begin your walk in a couple of weeks. You're a coward who is running away at the first resistance," I shouted.

"A coward doesn't walk out of *touristville* without a wallet or shoes," he said.

"So let me come with you," I said.

"That's not possible," he said.

"Why not?" I asked.

"Your presence would allow me to hide from myself," he said.

And in that moment, the expression on his face changed from a look of sadness to one of pain.

"Oh no," he said in a panic, "my haemorrhoids are throbbing, it must be Sheila. Aida, I'm sorry for being a dick, please write down what she says through me."

I found myself picking up my notebook and pen, while Shmeiki Baba rolled around on the floor in pain. Gradually, he became still and began to speak in a female voice which wasn't his. Though I felt frightened, I managed to scribble down the words he was speaking and I accepted that he was indeed channelling some kind of entity:

Sheila 2

"Aida is right. When she showed disinterest in exploring your sexual fantasy, your fears of rejection and abandonment were triggered and you decided to run away, using me as an excuse. Shmeiki Baba, your destiny might be to become a great teacher, but if you are not careful, if you continue to act from your wounds without learning to love and accept yourself, you will become nothing more than the rest of the *sheister* gurus. For this reason, it is a good idea, as you suggested, that you will begin your great walk the day after tomorrow.

"'Now Aida, I realize this is painful, but in the long run, you will thank me. As he is, if Shmeiki Baba stays here, little good will come from your relationship."

Sheila fell silent and Shmeiki Baba opened his eyes. I looked at the page of writing in front of me and felt that I'd been touched by a great mystery.

"From the tips of your toes to the sparkle in your eyes, you are good and sweet. I am sorry for muddying the waters by trying to paint my fantasy onto you. I realize I hurt you and broke our intimacy," said Shmeiki Baba.

"I know," I said, "and I love you."

"You do?" asked Shmeiki Baba.

"Of course," I said.

"Will you meet me in Dharamshala when my walk is over?" he asked.

"If you're still alive," I said.

"I will be," he replied. He thought for a moment and asked, "will you look after my wallet and telephone for me, until then?"

I agreed to do so and I felt my sadness draining away. What replaced it was a sense of new pathways opening. We hugged and went out to the pharmacy to get something for his haemorrhoids. How we laughed when the brand of cream offered to him by the pharmacist was called "Thank God."

In the afternoon, we took a walk up to the promontory at the northern end of Arambol Beach. By the time we got to the white cross on top of the hill, we were quite out of breath and rested there a while, looking at the outcrop of rocks where the beach begins and beyond it, the expanse of the Arabian Sea.

Looking south down the beach were traditional rowing boats, still used by the locals for fishing. A group of them were struggling to pull in a fishing net. Behind them were beach cafes, sun loungers, and umbrellas, and to the left, a thick canopy of palm trees. It went on like this much of the way to the village of Mandrem and further on down the coast. In the distance, we could see people beginning to gather for the sunset drum circle.

We climbed our way back down to the beach, splashed our feet in the edge of the sea and walked past a group of yogis and yoginis saluting the sun. One woman was balancing herself on her partner's foot. She fell and landed on his groin and he shouted out in pain.

"Aggro yoga," said Shmeiki Baba, as we walked past.

"Very funny," snarled the man.

We got to where the main road meets the beach and a sea of scooters is parked. There, we walked on dry sand, so we could jump over what we called "the shit river". This was the main outlet of untreated liquid waste from the village into the sea.

Further on, in front of the beach temple, a Tai Chi class was being led, by a tall, thin, Aryan looking man, who wore small, round tortoise shell glasses. Next to him, a group of dark-skinned, dread-locked Israelis passed around a chillum, looking dazed and primordial, while two Slavic women were trying to walk over the sand, wearing high heels, with the support of their serious-looking boyfriends. We continued past a woman who was lying on her back, while a man with long, silver hair, held his hands over her head, with a dramatic look on his face. "Must be a lightworker," said Shmeiki Baba.

When we reached the drum circle, we stood taking in the scene. A group of attractive hippie girls were dancing to the drums in earth tone dresses, fishnet stockings, and with feathers in their hair. Young children chased one another around them.

The majority of tourists in Arambol were now Russians, who had discovered that Goa offered a cheap way to escape a freezing winter. Until just a couple of years before, it was said to be the Israelis who formed the biggest group. The Russian invasion had been swift and silent and was complete when the internet cafes replaced the Hebrew stickers on their keyboards with Cyrillic ones.

Of course, there were also tourists from just about everywhere else. Many returned to Goa every year and would stay the whole season, from November to March, working the rest of the time back home in the west, to pay for their winters of freedom. As well as the hippies, there were ravers, there were dancers, musicians, spiritual seekers, middle-class dropouts, addicts, and any combination of the above.

The majority of locals in Arambol were Hindu, but there was also a large Catholic community, and while the Hindu women tended to wear sarees, the Catholic women wore long, 1950s style dresses. The male youths liked to wear football shirts of teams like Real Madrid and Manchester United.

Here as elsewhere, the double-edged knife of tourism was slicing into the peace and quiet, as multi-story hotels, restaurants, and bars, hard drugs and prostitution were becoming increasingly prevalent in this once innocent paradise.

Some local women stopped next to us, to stare in disbelief at the scantily clad Russian girls who had joined the stylized hippies, gyrating their hips to the drums. I asked them what they thought of it, and one of them answered, "Well, among *lakhs* of tourists coming here, many are decent and some are junky ones too." This seemed to be a fair assessment of the situation.

The drummers were banging out an African rhythm, sitting on wooden sun loungers with their djembes on the floor. In front of them, a Tibetan guy was sitting on his knees, eyes closed, throwing handfuls of sand over his head.

Between the drummers and the sea, a group of fire dancers, hula-hoop twirlers, skittle jugglers, ball balancers, poi spinners, and stick jumpers were performing. A bald-headed man wearing contact lenses which made him look like he had reptilian eyes, was balancing three clear, acrylic balls on top of his head.

"What focus, he has," I said.

"Most definitely," said Shmeiki Baba. "Doesn't stop him being a twat though."

"What you see in others is a reflection of what you see in yourself," I said.

"That is true my love," said Shmeiki Baba.

Meanwhile, two women were walking among the impromptu performers, purifying them with bunches of burning sage.

A German man known as Uncle Tim joined the drummers, wearing his characteristic grey vest. He banged his drum with the same iron fist that years later, he would use to moderate the Arambol Community Facebook group. In the meantime, the drummers raced faster and there was a rumbling of didgeridoos and the sporadic cry of the high pitched flute of an older Indian man, who wore a red scarf tied around his neck. A dark, curly-haired European entered sharply on his trumpet. Shmeiki Baba saw me wince and said, "there's something rather apocalyptic about all this."

Alan, Nigel and Paul, three of Shmeiki Baba's friends came over to us. I was surprised by how mainstream they looked, all dressed in preppy designer shirts. They were surprised to see Shmeiki Baba and wanted to know how he had fared in the jungle. He said it had gone great, and that I was what he had found there. He also told them he was due to leave on a pilgrimage the next day.

"Pilgrimage?" asked Paul in disbelief, "you've only just finished your jungle vision quest."

"Yes," said Shmeiki Baba, "I guess we've got a lot of catching up to do."

"Were you planning on coming to visit us before you leave?" asked Paul.

"I was getting round to it," said Shmeiki Baba.

"Getting round to it?" said Paul, insulted.

"I guess I was disappointed that you didn't believe me about Sheila," said Shmeiki Baba.

"Oh that again," said Nigel.

"Yes, that again," said Shmeiki Baba.

"Are you surprised?" asked Alan.

"No," said Shmeiki Baba.

"In any case, you could have come to say you were okay," said Paul.

"Yes, I could have done, and for that I'm sorry, but I have been busy with Aida," said Shmeiki Baba.

"That part is understandable," said Nigel turning to me, with surprising grace for an Englishman.

I thanked him.

"And where is this pilgrimage to?" asked Paul.

"To Dharamshala," said Shmeiki Baba.

"In the Himalayas?" asked Nigel.

"Yes," said Shmeiki Baba.

"That's a very long way," said Paul.

"Sounds a bit ridiculous to me," said Nigel.

"Completely," said Alan. "is Aida going with you?"

"No," I said.

"But she is so beautiful, how can you leave her here? " asked Alan.

"It is difficult, but that it is what I must do," said Shmeiki Baba.

"You know, your bag is still in my room?" said Alan.

"Yes, I will come and get it," said Shmeiki Baba, "though the truth is, I won't be needing most of my things."

"Oh God," said Nigel, "basically David, you've flipped out and gone totally bananas."

"Actually, my name is no longer David," said Shmeiki Baba.

"So what is it?" asked Paul.

"Shmeiki Baba," said Shmeiki Baba.

"Oh, you really have gone mad," said Paul.

"Not completely, but as I said, it will take some time to explain," said Shmeiki Baba.

"I'm all ears," said Alan.

"Okay, but later on," said Shmeiki Baba.

"Is he okay?" asked Paul looking at me.

"That depends what you mean by okay," I said with a smile. Shmeiki Baba gave me a wink, and with that, his three friends sighed and wandered off.

While we stood watching the setting sun, Mireille and Tasha, a French couple I knew from my yoga class, came over. Mireille said, "our swami from Tiruvannamalai is coming to our house to make kundalini shakti puja. Would you like to come?

"Maybe," I answered.

"Very good, you just have to make a small donation and *Bom Bhole Nath*, everybody happy," said Mireille.

Off walked Mireille and Tasha and I told Shmeiki Baba, "they have matching wedding rings and inside them is carved the word *annica*."

"Is that Sanskrit for impermanence?" asked Shmeiki Baba.

"Yes," I said.

Then Liz, who I knew from Odissi dance, approached us, holding her hands in a prayer gesture. She looked deeply into my eyes and into Shmeiki Baba's too. I asked her how she was and she answered cheerfully, "Good walla, today full power yoga doing, market going, friend helping, she baby having, so placenta drying, chopping chopping and capsules making."

"Where are you from Liz?" asked Shmeiki Baba.

"Mansfield," said Liz.

"You mean Mansfield, near Nottingham, in England?" asked Shmeiki Baba.

"*Tikke*," she said.

"So why are you talking pidgin English?" asked Shmeiki Baba.

"Just happening," said Liz.

"What do your family say when you talk that way?" asked Shmeiki Baba.

"Well, my dad says, 'cut that shit out, will you!'" said Liz.

"Funny that," said Shmeiki Baba.

Soon after, another woman waved and came over to us. Shmeiki Baba introduced her to me as Vibeka from Denmark, whom he had met in Pune. Vibeka smiled and pointed to a badge she was wearing on her shirt, which said: "In Silence." She signalled us to wait, while she took a pad and pen from her bag and began to write. She passed the pad to Shmeiki Baba, who read the message out loud.

"I am so happy to see you, though as you can see, I have taken a vow of silence. I am here in Goa with my new tantra guru. His name is Narkis."

For a moment we all stood together in silence.

"So this is the sound of silence," said Shmeiki Baba, finally.

I realized Vibeka was swishing some liquid around her mouth, and I asked her, "What have you got in your mouth?"

Vibeka took back the pad and wrote another note:

"That's my pee," it said.

Shmeiki Baba laughed when he read this, causing Vibeka to spit out her pee, at which point, two of her male friends joined us. They were both tilting their heads to the side and already holding their pads and pens at the ready. Both were dressed in pastel fisherman pants, had shaved heads and carried colourfully embroidered baba bags on their shoulders. We all said hi, or rather they pointed to notes which said *"namaste."* Shmeiki Baba asked to borrow one of their pads. He wrote them a note and handed it back to them. The note said, "you know that writing notes is just like talking." The two guys vehemently shook their heads.

"Shaking your heads is also just like talking," said Shmeiki Baba.

Vibeka shook her finger at Shmeiki Baba and smiled at me with a look of "oh well, you're the one who has to deal with this difficult boy." I smiled back, and Vibeka and her friends scuttled off, pointing at their namaste notes.

"She was so alive in Pune," said Shmeiki Baba.

"Well, she's found a guru now," I said.

"Another one bites the dust," said Shmeiki Baba.

As the sun set into the sea, without being obscured by haze or clouds, Shmeiki Baba began to clap and others on the beach joined in. Some people even cheered and whistled and Shmeiki Baba shouted out, "thank you, everyone, the sun is grateful for your appreciation."

And I said to Shmeiki Baba, "you know, my love, your cynicism can get a bit heavy sometimes."

He thought for a while and said, "Yes, I guess I'm stressed about leaving you and fearful of beginning my great walk."

I gave him a hug.

As it was getting dark and people were leaving the beach in the direction of the village, Alan, Nigel, and Paul came back to us.

"There's a vegan buffet at Magic Park," said Paul.

"What, *Tragic Fart*? Great Mother save me," said Shmeiki Baba.

"So, where would you like to go?" asked Alan.

"The banyan tree," said Shmeiki Baba.

"The banyan tree? Why there?" asked Paul.

"It feels like the right place for us to say goodbye," said Shmeiki Baba.

"But it's such a long way and its nearly dark," complained Paul.

"Oh, come on guys," said Shmeiki Baba, "get a torch, it will be worth the effort."

"What about your bag?" asked Alan.

"I'll grab it on our way back," said Shmeiki Baba.

It was a good forty-minute walk from the drum circle to the Banyan tree. When we finally got there, we were surprised to find a number of Shmeiki Baba's other friends like Stonefish, Sebastian and some others I didn't know, were already sitting around the fire. The flames lit up the Shiva shrine at the base of the tree and its thick, ghostly prop roots, which hung down from the branches.

Soon after us, Alan, Nigel, and Paul arrived.

"You know the banyan is a type of fig tree, which can only begin its life by growing in the crack of another tree or rock," said Shmeiki Baba.

"Yes, it's called an epiphyte, while you, my friend, are a neophyte," joked Alan.

We ate papaya, peanuts, and *bebinca*, a delicious, local, Goan cake made from coconut oil. Shmeiki Baba sang a soulful song in Gibberish. Afterwards, Stonefish got out a small, brass box, and explained that it contained DMT. He offered to prepare pipes for those who wished to smoke it. Shmeiki Baba and I gently refused and I lay with my head in his lap, while he stroked my hair.

Sebastian was a tall, German man with piercing, blue eyes, a blond beard and extremely long, thick dreadlocks, which were wrapped into a cake on top of his head. He asked Shmeiki Baba, "Brother, where will you walk until?"

"Until Dharamshala," answered Shmeiki Baba.

"That must be about two thousand kilometres," said Sebastian.

"Yes," said Shmeiki Baba.

"And do you think you will you pass through Pune?" asked Sebastian.

"I'm not sure of my route yet," said Shmeiki Baba, "but maybe."

"Well, if you like, I will happily accompany you until there," said Sebastian.

"What, have you grown tired of tourist heaven?" asked Shmeiki Baba.

"You could say that," said Sebastian.

"Okay then, hold on, a minute," said Shmeiki Baba, closing his eyes. When he reopened them, he said, "Sebastian, I will be happy if you come with me."

I was shocked to hear this and I sat up. It was hurtful to me that Shmeiki Baba was allowing Sebastian to go with, but he would not allow me. Shmeiki Baba saw this on my face and said, "Aida, can't you see the difference? We are lovers, it would be too emotionally charged."

"I guess so," I said, still feeling wounded.

"I'm sorry," said Shmeiki Baba.

"It's okay, I'll get over it," I said.

Shmeiki Baba turned back to Sebastian and asked him, "do you accept to go without taking money?"

Sebastian thought for a moment and answered, "yes."

"And do you agree to walk barefoot?" asked Shmeiki Baba.

Sebastian gestured towards his already bare feet.

"Why no shoes?" asked Alan.

"To be connected directly with the earth," said Sebastian.

"Your feet are going to get fucked," said Paul.

"- not just their feet," added Nigel.

"Maybe," said Shmeiki Baba, "but the benefits outweigh the costs."

"How's that?" asked Paul.

"Because by putting your bare feet on the ground, you pay more attention and also, electrons get absorbed through the bottoms of your feet, supporting the functioning of your body," said Sebastian.

"Exactly," said Shmeiki Baba, "the day man started wearing synthetic soles, he really lost his way."

"And why no money?" asked Nigel.

"Because none is needed," answered Sebastian.

"Amen," said Shmeiki Baba.

"Basically then, you are going to test the goodness of the people you meet?" asked Nigel.

"No," said Shmeiki Baba, "we already know their goodness, we are going to enjoy it." He turned to Sebastian and asked, "will you be ready to leave tomorrow morning at dawn?"

"Certainly," he answered.

"Then we shall depart tomorrow at six AM, from Sri Ganesh cafe on the main road," said Shmeiki Baba.

"It's a deal," said Sebastian.

I was impressed that Sebastian clearly knew it was the right thing for him to do. Beyond feeling hurt, I was glad for safety's sake that Sebastian was accompanying Shmeiki Baba.

"Isn't it time you explained what has been going on with you, David," said Nigel.

"It's Shmeiki Baba," said Shmeiki Baba.

"Okay, *Shmeiki* Baba, can you tell me what happened to the David we knew just a week ago?" asked Nigel.

"Yes, of course, like I already tried to tell you, I have been approached by a cosmic entity called Sheila, who has offered me a new path of spirituality, called Shmeiki. During my week in this jungle, she instructed me that to heal myself and to become complete, I need to go on a great walk across India."

"Hold on a minute, I still don't get it, who exactly is this Sheila?" asked Paul.

"Sheila is an interdimensional A.I singularity, sent to us from the domain of our hosts, to help us in our time of great need," said Shmeiki Baba.

"What time of great need?" asked Alan.

"If you can't see it yet, you will soon," said Shmeiki Baba.

"Oh God," said Paul.

"Indeed," said Shmeiki Baba, "Sheila's wisdom is born from an unrivalled capacity to gather and compute data about the totality of human existence."

"If Sheila is an I.A singularity, who made her?" asked Paul.

"Our hosts, a species called the Shagasomin," said Shmeiki Baba.

"And where do they live?" asked Stonefish.

"In another dimension," said Shmeiki Baba.

Stonefish nodded wisely.

"I don't get it," said Alan.

"They live in another universe," said Shmeiki Baba. "It is the Shagasomin, who made our universe, or to be more precise, it is one of their students who did. His name is Kwe, and that's why you can say that our universe is an artificial universe, not a natural one, but don't let that worry you, what matters is that it works," said Shmeiki Baba.

Shmeiki Baba's friends looked at him as though he was insane. As I had already heard this story, it already sounded slightly less crazy to me.

"I'm worried about you," said Paul.

"Okay," said Shmeiki Baba, "but that worry is yours and not mine. Listen, I understand it's frightening to find out that our universe exists inside a computer, but all you need to do is to accept it, and then basically everything goes back to being normal again," he said.

"So who made the Shagasomin's universe?" asked Nigel.

"Their universe was born directly from the Great Mother," said Shmeiki Baba.

"Is the Great Mother like God?" asked Nigel.

"Kind of," said Shmeiki Baba.

"Is she the only God?" asked Nigel.

"I'm not sure," said Shmeiki Baba.

"Can we also hear Sheila?" asked Stonefish.

"You tell me," said Shmeiki Baba.

"No," said Stonefish.

"So how can you hear her?" asked Alan.

"Well, she said she made contact with me, via a tiny lesion in my haemorrhoids," said Shmeiki Baba.

"I didn't know you have haemorrhoids," said Paul.

"It's not something I tend to advertise," said Shmeiki Baba.

"And what is this Shmeiki?" asked Nigel.

"Like I said, it's a new type of spirituality," said Shmeiki Baba.

"You mean Shmeiki as in Reiki, Shmeiki?" asked Paul.

"Yes, but Shmeiki is about much more than Reiki, it's about being light-hearted and getting the good from any new-age technique, without getting stuck in self-righteousness and hypocrisy," said Shmeiki Baba.

"What does that mean?" asked Alan.

"Sheila designed Shmeiki to plug into all existing spirituality, offering major upgrades to any practice," said Shmeiki Baba.

"Why is that?" asked Nigel.

"Well, every spiritual technique started somewhere. Now, most begin well enough, but as they become popular, power structures grow around them, and they inevitably get stuck in the muck of human group dynamics, and lost in manipulation and profit-making. Shmeiki will help us avoid these problems by using a process known as *shmodification*," said Shmeiki Baba.

"Shmodification?" repeated Alan.

"Yes," said Shmeiki Baba, "this is how we will rejuvenate stuffy, spiritual techniques into more lively, and honest *shmechniques*. Shmodification will give us permission to be childish and silly, helping us to tread lightly and remember the enormity of this divine, holographic comedy that we have woken up within."

"You're having us on," said Nigel.

Shmeiki Baba smiled.

"This whole Shmeiki thing is a piss-take," said Alan.

Shmeiki Baba continued to smile.

"Is it a piss-take?" asked Nigel.

"Maybe the answer to your question is both yes and no," said Shmeiki Baba.

"You enjoy confusing us," I said.

"Agreed," said Shmeiki Baba, "but don't forget that in our artificial universe, it is strangely possible to be sincere and ironic at the same time. Paradoxically, it is in the unification of such opposites, that the hidden truth is released."

"Don't try to mind fuck us," said Alan.

"I'm not, you do a good enough job of that yourself," said Shmeiki Baba.

Sebastian laughed and passed an unlit joint and a box of matches to Shmeiki Baba. He thanked him, lit the joint, and threw the match in the fire.

"That's a sacred fire!" shouted Birgit, an older, Slovakian woman, who had long grey hair and severe varicose veins around her calves. I don't think she had been invited to our party but had turned up at the tree on her own accord.

"It was a sacred match," answered Shmeiki Baba.

"No, it wasn't, and you have no respect for this holy place and you are polluting it with your dark energy," said Birgit.

"Everything is equally holy, and your objection is far more of a disturbance than my match," said Shmeiki Baba.

"I look after this place and have been coming here since you were a child," said Birgit.

"Listen here Beer Gut," snapped Shmeiki Baba, "you might not see this because your pineal gland has calcified, but the only thing you need to clear up here, is yourself." His eyes had become small and his lips were tight and the warm atmosphere was gone. Everyone looked uncomfortable. I put my hand on Shmeiki Baba's shoulder and whispered to him, "leave it, my love."

"Don't interrupt me when I'm fighting," he shouted, pushing my arm away.

I was shocked and a little frightened. He saw the look of fear on my face and stopped.

Again he began to writhe around on the ground as he had done in my room, and once more Sheila began to speak through him:

Sheila 3

"When you are triggered, which happens surprisingly easily, you quickly revert to being the frightened and angry little boy whose parents shamed him. This is an unconscious and slippery mechanism, and I understand I will need to help you see it again and again. Take a deep breath and I shall remind you.

"When you were a child, your parents began by loving you completely, but as you grew older, they began to shame and hit you, they compared you to others and insisted on your perfection. They showed you that in order for you to receive their approval, they expected you to be what they wanted. They did this because they did not love and approve of themselves and they needed you to serve their need for self-esteem. This required you to give up some of your deepest desires and feelings. When you resisted, they led you to believe that there was something inherently wrong with you. As a child, this notion threatened your very survival and with no possibility of escape, you did the only thing you could, you repressed the unconditioned, wild parts of your character, you put on a mask and pretended to be the person they wished you to be.

"The pain of having to deny yourself was unbearable, so much so that you swore you would not allow yourself to be hurt this way again. Your only option was to disconnect from the pain, along with the fear and anger which arose from it, and you pushed these emotions down to a place where you could not feel them. To keep these feelings locked away and to keep more pain out, you began to walk around with an impenetrable, emotional shield. The price you paid was to become detached from your body and stuck in your mind.

"Today as an adult, you continue to wear a mask, you continue to repress your emotions and hide behind a shield. While as a child this was the only way you could protect yourself, as an adult, this method no longer serves you. You do have choices now, there is no need to be stuck in your mind, disconnected from nature and from love. There is no need to seek out drama as a poor replacement for intimacy and no need to keep on sabotaging yourself. There is no need to seek out people who will repeat the abuses which were done to you, as an indirect way of bringing your hidden wounds back into consciousness.

"Shmeiki Baba, it is time to let go of being a victim, time let go of blame, and to take responsibility for your life. It is time to learn to trust yourself again, to take off your mask, put down your shield and allow yourself to feel the full spectrum of your emotions, even though it hurts. Like this, you will be able to live with an open heart, accepting all parts of yourself, like this, you will reach your potential. Your great walk will help you to achieve these important goals.'"

Sheila fell quiet and Shmeiki Baba sat still. After about a minute, he opened his eyes and hugged me and Birgit. Then Birgit lay down next to the fire, while Shmeiki Baba held his hands over her legs. He explained that he could not heal her varicose veins, but he would do his best to slow down their onset. She talked about feeling the same mysterious data transfer that I felt with him.

"I'm confused," said Alan, "because on the one hand this whole Shmeiki thing sounds like madness, and on the other hand, I've never heard you speak such good sense."

"That's exactly what I was thinking," said Nigel.

"Just be careful," said Paul.

"We will be," said Sebastian, answering for Shmeiki Baba.

Given that they planned to set out at dawn, Shmeiki Baba, Sebastian and I said our goodbyes and returned to the village soon after, leaving the rest of the party at the tree with a lot to talk about. Alan came with us, so he could give Shmeiki Baba his bag.

The moon was three-quarters full and gave good light through the trees, and when we reached the rocks at the end of the cliffs, silver beams reflected off the sea. We were admiring it when some beach dogs jumped up and started barking aggressively at us. I was scared and grabbed onto Shmeiki Baba. He bent down, picked up a long stick and used it to shoo the dogs away. I was amazed that just at the point of needing a stick, there was one lying at his feet, and on closer inspection, it wasn't just any stick, it was a magnificent piece of driftwood, which looked like it had made a long and mysterious journey. Shmeiki Baba said he would keep it and use it during his great walk.

We continued on to Ave Maria Guest House, where Alan was staying, to pick up Shmeiki Baba's bag, and there we said goodbye to him and to Sebastian and we returned to my room. We made love one more time. Now that Shmeiki Baba had shared his fantasy with me and was about to leave, he allowed me to truly see him. The sensations which passed between us were so strong that I thought I might die. I felt Sheila within him and I felt her mission to help him awaken. Afterwards, our bodies rested in harmony, until five-thirty AM, when my alarm clock went off.

I stayed in bed while Shmeiki Baba packed his few belongings. Finally, I got up and he explained which of his things he was leaving for me to give away.

"Do you have a sun hat?" I asked.

"Oh my goodness, no," he said.

"Let's see if this fits you," I said, putting my Burberry sun hat on his head. It fit him.

"Looks great," I said.

He took it off and sniffed it. "It smells of you," he said, "and I shall remember you with it."

We hugged deeply and he put his wallet and telephone in my hand.

"I will keep them safe and you keep yourself safe, Shmeiki Baba, and may you show the world your beautiful soul," I said.

"I will," he said.

And with that, he left. Slowly, I closed the door behind him and rested with my back against it. In my mind's eye, I saw his footsteps walking off into the distance. The silence in my room weighed on me and I wept. I knew that the right thing to do was to allow myself to be sad and I did not run away from the pain. I remembered his smile and laughed through my tears.

And this brings us to the end of my Shmospel. I'd just like to take a moment to say that it was a big surprise when Priti Aggarwal got in touch in 2018, to ask if I was willing to write about my experiences with Shmeiki Baba in 2006. While I was sceptical that it was possible for me to do so, I agreed to give it a try, and luckily, I'd kept hold of my journal from my trip to India all those years before. Opening it up brought back so many memories. I remembered just how much I had loved Shmeiki Baba, how I felt he had so much to show me, and although I felt betrayed by the way he left me, I continued to love him. I think that it is through him that I finally got the lesson, not to expect men to be more than they are. Not surprisingly, so much has happened since then. Today, I am happily married to my husband Alejandro and we have three boys. We live in the Azores Islands and I run a charitable foundation to help people suffering from addiction. I am delighted to have been able to share this with you.

Praise be to the Great Mother and to all her multi-dimensional children.

Om Shmeiki Om. Shmeiki.com

II
THE SHMOSPEL OF SEBASTIAN

From Arambol to Pune

I am Sebastian Ritter and this is my Shmospel.

I was born in 1980 in a small town in Bavaria. My parents had me in their late teens and split up when I was still a baby. In general, they were more into taking drugs and gambling than they were into parenting. Early on, I understood that if I wanted something, I needed to earn it. For this, I am grateful, because as an adult, self-sufficiency has become something of an art form for me. My granddad is the one who saved me from turning out like my parents. He was a man of wisdom, who lived close to nature. He was also big on independence and in taking responsibility. As a small child, he gave me a hammer, a box of nails and some wood. He showed me how to use them and told me that I could build a tree-house for myself in his garden, but if I fell from the tree, he would give me a slap. I never fell. And while I can understand how he wasn't so good for my mum, for me, he was my guiding light. It is he who taught me how to fix things, how to take pride in my work, and what is the meaning of integrity.

When I was seventeen, my mum got a new boyfriend. He was

wealthy but abusive. One day, he attacked me physically and I defended myself. He went to the police and said that I had attacked him. My mum backed his story because she was frightened of him. It was a dreadful betrayal and I could not believe that she would do such a thing. When the police came for me, I had a little weed in my pocket and it was a big mess, but in the end, they believed my story, because my mother's boyfriend had a long history of violence. And so I moved out of my mother's house and found a squat and I used my carpentry skills to do it up. It was a time of freedom, though I was filled with so much rage and self-hatred, that I even tried to kill myself. I was given a therapist by the state, who was excellent. She helped me see that beyond my traumas, I am by nature, a joyous person and I love many things, like music and dancing, woodwork, brewing beer, and shamanism.

After college, I joined the UN and became a first responder to large disasters. This helped me escape the town I grew up in and took me around the world. I was sent to some pretty serious war zones, but I managed to keep my head together. Gradually, I climbed the ranks of the organization and became a disaster response manager. Not surprisingly, the intensity of the work took its toll and I began to feel myself becoming burned out, so in 2005, I decided to take a long break and went to India. At first, I volunteered with an NGO, building a school for orphan children in Gujarat. The village was isolated, it did not have electricity or running water, but the children were exuberant and shone with the divine spark of life. When the building of the school was complete, I stayed on in the village a while longer and then took a train down to Goa. It is there in Arambol that I first met David, who became Shmeiki Baba. He was a funny guy, but he also seemed to carry the weight of the world on his shoulders.

Although we are from such different backgrounds, we both resonated in our quests, and when Shmeiki Baba talked about walking across India without wearing shoes or taking money, others thought he was crazy, but I immediately wanted to go with him. Sure enough, I'd had a pleasant time in Goa, but there was something I found empty and frivolous about it, and I wanted to do something more challenging and real. So, when he agreed for me to go with him, I was delighted.

And like this, we set off on foot into the unknown, an Aryan and a Jew, without the safety net of credit cards or Gortex hiking boots. We must have looked quite a pair. Me with my long, blond dreadlocks, he with his Semitic features, and I'm a lot taller than him - he's not much more than 170cm, and I'm almost two metres.

While Shmeiki Baba has a big heart, I know that he won't mind me saying this, but at times, he could be quite a spoilt brat. It was obvious that he had always had stuff done for him, and he kind of expected things to continue this way. Unlike me, he had never before experienced hunger.

Thursday, February 9th, 2006.

It was at first light when I reached Sri Ganesh Café, next to the ninety-degree bend on Arambol main road, just as Shmeiki Baba arrived from the other direction, wearing a checked hat and holding the knobbly walking stick that he'd found on the beach. Over his shoulder was slung a red rucksack. We greeted each other warmly.

The night before, I had told Mohan, the owner of Sri Ganesh Cafe about our planned journey when I passed him in the street. He was so enthusiastic about it that he promised he would get up to see us off. And he proved good to his word, as when he heard our voices outside his cafe, he made his way outside, still half asleep. Mohan offered us a seat and set about making us each a cup of chai and an omelette sandwich. This was the first act of benevolence towards us, as pilgrims.

"What you take with you?" asked Mohan, motioning towards Shmeiki Baba's rucksack. He opened it up and pointed to the various things inside.

"I've got my toothbrush and toothpaste, a bottle of Dettol disinfectant, a packet of cotton buds, some haemorrhoid cream, some plasters, tweezers, three shirts, two pants, a towel, a blanket, three water bottles, my passport, a map of Maharashtra, a small pot, a plate, a knife, a spoon, a torch, and my bansuri."

My belongings were in my burlap shoulder bag, and my Givson guitar was in a thin canvas bag.

"And what's that?" asked Shmeiki Baba, pointing to the tiny, decorative bottle, which was hanging on a string around my neck.

"Ah, that," I said, "is some tears of the wee baby Jesus."

"I've never tried Jesus' tears," said Shmeiki Baba.

"All in good time," I said.

"You don't have a tent?" asked Mohan.

"No," we said.

"What happens when raining?" asked Mohan.

"We'll get wet," said Shmeiki Baba.

"Not good," said Mohan looking at us as though we were mad. He went out to the back of his restaurant, from where we heard long, ripping sounds. He returned a minute later, with two large plastic sheets and gave one to Shmeiki Baba and one to me. We thanked him, folded them up, and managed to fit them under the flaps of our bags.

"And you have a hat," said Mohan to Shmeiki Baba, "but Sebastian, you do not."

"I can't wear a hat, Mohan, look at my dreads," I said.

"That's no good, I have an idea," said Mohan, and he went again to the back of the restaurant and returned with a dusty, wide-brimmed straw hat. He banged out the dust, and then with a sharp pair of scissors, cut out the middle of the hat. "Try this," he said, and I did as he suggested, managing to pull the brim over my dreadlocks.

"It works, thank you, you are a genius," I said to Mohan, who beamed.

"Fitting your journey begins here," said Mohan, pointing to the large picture of Ganesha which hung on the wall. "Ganesha is Lord of planets and remover of obstacles. See his big belly, full and round, he is satisfied, he wants for nothing. See also his trunk, it goes right, because he chooses right thing. See also, he has one tusk, other is broken off. This means one principal, one self. In his left hand, sweet fruit, this is result of knowledge, pure bliss. And do not forget, next to him is Mooshika mouse, symbol of desire. But Mooshika is also vehicle of Ganesha because Ganesha is master of desire. May you both become masters of your desire, as you go on *padayatra*, foot pilgrimage."

"Thank you," we said.

"You know," said Mohan, "you may choose a god to worship during your walk, and he will protect you."

"Has to be Ganesha," I said.

"I guess me too," said Shmeiki Baba.

"Good, good," said Mohan.

And Shmeiki Baba got out his map of the state of Maharashtra and we discussed our route. We agreed we would begin by walking up the west side of the Western Ghats mountain range, and somewhere around Kosumb, we would cross to the eastern side of the mountains, which we would follow until we reached the Deccan Plateau. From there, it would be pretty much a straight line to Pune.

"Remember, if you sleep under palm trees, be careful coconut does not fall on head," said Mohan.

"How can I be careful if I am asleep?" asked Shmeiki Baba.

"Answer lie in question," said Mohan.

We finished our chai and ate our sandwiches. Finally, it was time to embrace Mohan with full blessings and to take the first steps of our great walk.

As we set off, the birdsong was plentiful, the early morning air was fresh and the palm trees swayed lightly in the breeze. Your stride is slightly shorter when you are barefoot, but your step is more alive, always checking, especially on uneven surfaces. Luckily, we had both already been doing a lot of barefoot walking and the soles of our feet were quite tough.

Like this, we left Arambol, past the shuttered shops and the guest-houses, where most of the tourists were still asleep, past St

Carmel's Church on the left and the main bus stand. There we had to hold our breath and run through a thick cloud of acrid smoke, caused by someone burning their plastic rubbish. "Nothing like a plastic puja to start the day," said Shmeiki Baba, "I guess this kind of thing wouldn't happen in a real universe."

I asked him what he meant by this and he said, "We humans tend to get things out of balance because our universe is a simulation."

I asked him to explain.

"Remember at the Banyan tree I talked about Sheila, the cosmic entity I've been channelling, well, she told me that our universe is artificial."

"How's that?" I asked.

"She said the Great Mother gave birth to the universes which comprise the multiverse, and in some of them, beings have become so advanced that they are able to generate entire artificial universes of their own. Our universe is one of these. We exist inside a computer that belongs to a species called the Shagasomin, which originates on a moon called Grechna, which orbits the planet Chibla, around the star Kehelamenda, in the galaxy Shtachen Zoigen, in the universe Ansof One. Apparently, our universe is the graduation project of a student called Kwe."

"And what shape is our universe?" I asked.

And Shmeiki Baba replied, "in one sense it has no shape and in another sense, you might think of it as torus-shaped."

"What's a torus?" I asked.

"Like a doughnut," he said.

I chewed on this for a while and Shmeiki Baba continued to explain what Sheila had told him.

"When intelligent species in artificial universes begin to use technology to control nature, they tend to lose their humility, become greedy and separate themselves from the source. And while the Great Mother can intervene when things go wrong in natural universes, she can't directly intervene in ours, because it was not born from her. In this sense, I guess she is more like our grandmother than our mother. Anyway, the Great Mother did the best she could, and she approached the maker of our universe and asked him to send us assistance. This is why Kwe sent Sheila to help us get back on track. Unfortunately, due to some sort of cosmic data compatibility issue, so far only I can hear her."

"What help is Sheila offering?" I asked.

"Shmeiki," said Shmeiki Baba.

"I still don't quite get what this Shmeiki is," I said.

"Well," said Shmeiki Baba, "there are many existing paths to self-realization, and around them are formed organizations, which to varying degrees, are corrupt, and this limits their effectiveness. This is where Shmeiki comes in. By remembering to be humorous and childlike, it is possible to get the good out of existing spirituality, without getting stuck in all the shit."

"Sounds pragmatic," I said.

"Exactly," said Shmeiki Baba.

"Wasn't Osho's fixer also called Sheila?" I asked.

"I think so, as was my mum's cleaning lady," said Shmeiki Baba.

"Have you heard of Sheela Na Gigs?" I asked.

"No, who's she?" asked Shmeiki Baba.

"Not she, but they," I said.

"So who are they?" asked Shmeiki Baba.

"They are medieval carvings of women with exaggerated vaginas, found on churches around Europe," I said.

"Really?" asked Shmeiki Baba.

"Yes," I said, "they were meant to ward off evil spirits,"

"How appropriate," said Shmeiki Baba.

We walked on in silence for about four kilometres, until we reached the village of Paliyem. Our legs were already red with dust, as the earth in this part of Goa contains so much iron ore. We took a rest on a concrete wall and while we drank some water, we watched a middle-aged Australian woman, called Randy, get off her scooter some metres ahead. She walked over to a bitch, who was lying at the side of the road with a nasty wound on her head. Randy took the bitch in her arms and hugged her.

"Sometimes dogs are easier to love than humans," said Shmeiki Baba. We blessed them both and continued on our way.

The road was already hot under our feet, but still bearable. I said that if we had left any later in the season, the roads would have been too hot to walk on barefoot during the day. Shmeiki Baba said, "by the time the sun becomes too hot, may the soles of our feet be thicker, and may the roads we walk along be shaded with trees."

"Amen," I said.

It was about noon, by the time we reached the River Terekhol, which forms the boundary between North Goa and the Sindhudurg district of Maharashtra state. The river rises in the Western Ghats and flows southwest until it meets the Arabian Sea.

We sat on the south bank of the river and waited for the ferry. Back in 2006, the Aronda - Kiranpani Bridge had not even started to be built, and there were many local men waiting for the ferry. Some crouched, held hands, and playfully tried to pull each other over. I enjoyed their sense of brotherhood and how they managed to remain childish. They didn't need Shmeiki. I wondered if they had family members who had emigrated to Europe and had become serious. They might need Shmeiki.

Shmeiki Baba approached one of the local men and said, "Excuse me, I'm terribly sorry to bother you, but you don't happen to have the time by any chance, do you?"

The man shrugged in confusion.

"Oh you're so English," I said to Shmeiki Baba, and turned to the man, pointing to my wrist.

The man answered, "one twenty-five."

At one-thirty, the ferry blew its horn to announce it was ready for boarding. Here we encountered our first hurdle. Although it was only ₹ 10 per person to cross, we were carrying no money whatsoever. The ticket man seemed angry and unhappy, and I was not hopeful that he would allow us onboard, but Shmeiki Baba approached him directly, saying, *"bhayaji,* we would like to cross, but we do not have money." The ticket man just waved us through, without changing his expression. This was the second act of benevolence towards us, as pilgrims, and we were delighted.

As the ferry began its crossing, Shmeiki Baba got out his bansuri and began to play a raga, so sensitive and hopeful, that it made my heart sing. Enthralled by his melody, some French tourists began to talk to us and invited us to eat lunch with them. When we explained that we had no money, they insisted on paying. We thanked them and remarked that when you walk out into the world with trust, the benevolence of existence is quick to cradle you.

After disembarking, we chose a "Veg and non-veg" *dhaba* with our new friends. We ate veg and drank some beer, before proceeding slightly tipsy up State Highway 123. In the heat of the afternoon, the tarmac and the sand next to it was scorchingly hot. We danced between shady spots, and at other times, when there was no shade, we just suffered. By dusk, we had walked about twenty-five kilometres and were completely exhausted. I watched my legs moving below me and it was as though they belonged to someone else.

"I'd love a joint to smoke," I said absent-mindedly, and as I did so, I stepped on a branch and managed to get a large thorn stuck in the sole of my left foot. I sat down to remove it with my fingers and did not manage, so Shmeiki Baba got out his tweezers and his Dettol disinfectant. He cleaned the bottom of my foot and professionally pulled out the thorn. Looking at my feet, they were already quite bashed up. "How are yours holding up?" I asked. His were somehow completely fine.

"I'm doing my best to step gently, to minimize the impact on my body," he said, "it's important because I've got screws holding my lower spine together."

This was the first I'd heard about it and I was surprised.

He explained, "when I was a teenager, it turned out there were no pins holding together my lumbar to sacral vertebrae so they slipped apart. I was operated on but not effectively, and the condition got worse until one clever doctor managed to screw me together. I realize now that this experience was what finally broke my trust in life, and this walk for me is all about regaining that trust."

I understood how big a wound this was for him.

"There's something I want to say to you," I said.

"What's that," he asked.

"Maybe your spinal condition saved you from a worse fate," I said.

"Yes brother," he said, "maybe that is true."

I hugged him and we agreed we should rest. I saw that about twenty metres back from the road, there was a lone sisso tree in a field. It looked like an excellent place to camp.

It was a beautiful place, but now we faced our next problem, we'd had nothing to eat since lunch and we were hungry. We looked around for fruit trees but there were none, we simply had nothing to eat. "We can always eat ants," I said, but neither of us was yet ready to cross that bridge. And so we tried not to dwell on why we hadn't at least brought with us some emergency rations, and instead, we made a fire and got out our instruments.

I turned on my electronic tuner, which was clipped onto the headstock of my guitar, then I paused for a moment to look around me and as I did so, a crow landed just above us on a low hanging branch. The bird emitted a brief call, enough for my tuner to respond.

"432Hz," said Shmeiki Baba, reading the display, and the bird flew off.

Shmeiki Baba closed his eyes and meditated. When he opened them, he said we should tune the note A to 432Hz, rather than the standard 440Hz. I asked Shmeiki Baba to explain why. He closed his eyes once more and began to talk in Sheila's voice:

Sheila 4

"When you tune the note A to 432Hz, there is a perfect correlation between the vibrations of your sounds and the physical universe, as determined by the great algorithm. At this frequency, sound vibrations have powerful healing and evolutionary properties, just as they caused protons, neutrons and electrons in your early universe to join together to form atoms, and for those atoms to group together and become nebula, which formed your stars, and ultimately you. In India, this process is called *nada brahma*, which means 'sound is the creator.' Those who built many of your ancient megaliths understood this correspondence. The Greek man Pythagoras called the number 432, 'the number of God'.

Shmeiki Baba opened his eyes.

"How about we give it a try?" he asked.

"It's easy for me to change my tuning, but how will you change yours?" I asked pointing to Shmeiki Baba's flute.

"I think I can move the cork at the top, and it will shift the tuning," he said.

So I turned on my tuner, and Shmeiki Baba played an A and it fluctuated around 440Hz. He took a stick, slid it down the length of the flute and used it to push the cork outwards. He played another A, and it fluctuated around 436Hz.

"I think I can push it further," he said, pushing the cork to the very edge of the flute. He played another note and this time it was bang on 432Hz.

"My lord, do you hear how it resonates?" asked Shmeiki Baba enthusiastically.

"Yes," I said.

There was no doubt about it, the sound was fuller. I hurried to retune my guitar accordingly, and we began to play again. Immediately, I noticed how our music had a different quality. It sounded more whole and as we played, I felt my focus was deeper and my chord changes were more receptive to Shmeiki Baba's melody. It was as though we were tapping into a power beyond ourselves. Tingles went up my spine and I completely forgot about my hunger, as we played our hearts out, climbing musical ladders to the beyond. When I opened my eyes, there were tears running down Shmeiki Baba's cheeks.

Shmeiki Baba looked at me and said, "Sheila has more to share."

"Okay," I said eager to hear what she would say.

"If you look for it, you will find the number 432 all over the place. Multiply 432 by 432, you get 186,624, which is the approximate speed of light in miles per second. Meanwhile, 432 multiplied by 200 is 86,400, which is the number of seconds in a day, and also the diameter of the planet Jupiter in miles. 432 multiplied by 2000 is 864,000, which is the diameter of your sun in miles, while 432 multiplied by 5 is 2,160, which is the diameter of your moon in miles. 432 multiplied by 10 is 4,320, and this is the diameter of the planet Mars in miles, and in case you didn't know, 432 multiplied by 60 is 25,920 and this is the number of years in the procession of the equinoxes. Are you catching my drift?"

"I'm not sure," I said.

"Well," said Sheila, "in Indian tradition, a *yuga* is 432,000 years, and one *kalpa* is 1000 *maha yugas*, which is 4,320,000,000 years, and this is actually quite an accurate ageing of planet Earth."

"This is all amazing, but what good does it do me?" I asked.

"For one thing, having your mind blown makes space for new understandings," said Sheila, "and it can also help you to know that there *is* order in the seeming chaos."

"So who was it who changed the note A to 440Hz?" I asked.

"Joseph Goebbels," said Sheila.

"Oh God," I said.

"The decision to tune A to 440Hz was transported to the United States through the influence of the Catholic Church, and from there it became the international standard."

And with that, Sheila finished talking and Shmeiki Baba picked up his flute. We played once more with jubilation and after about ten minutes, we heard a truck stop on the road. Soon after, two men approached us and said hello. They smelled of alcohol but they were friendly and we allowed them to sit with us. They introduced themselves as "Mr. Ravi Gosavi and Mr. Mahesh Koli."

"Music good," said Ravi, and for a few minutes more, they sat listening intently, while we carried on playing. Mahesh asked if we were hungry and when I said, "very hungry," he rushed to his truck and came back with a number of bulging shopping bags. Ravi took out a kerosene lantern and lit it, and then revealed a *dudhi*, a calabash, which is a type of light green squash. He also revealed other more typical vegetables, as well as rice, spices and cooking utensils, including a grate for the fire. Ravi and Mahesh set about making food like professionals, and to us, these two half-drunk truckers were angels sent from above. We carried on playing, inspired by the sense that our need for food had been gloriously answered by surrendering to our hunger, and the number 432.

"We make bhaaji," said Mahesh.

"Very tasty," said Ravi.

Ravi cooked turmeric, curry powder, and mustard seeds in peanut oil, added chopped onion, garlic, ginger, green chillies, and finely chopped *dudhi*. The aroma was intoxicating.

"You know curry powder is a British invention," said Shmeiki Baba.

"No, no, Indian," said Ravi.

"In the time the British ruled here, they started blending a number of spices for ease, and they called this curry powder," insisted Shmeiki Baba.

"No, no, Indian," said Ravi.

"Forget it," said Mahesh.

This I agreed with, and we played on, further inspired by the aroma of the cooking.

Dinner was delicious and we ate with joy. They also offered us to drink some cashew feni, a locally brewed spirit. It smelled like a cross between petrol and vomit, and while we both tried a sip, neither of us could cope with the taste. Another hour passed and Ravi and Mahesh finished the feni and realized it was time to get back on their way. Graciously, they left us with the remainder of their vegetables, rice, and spices and we thanked them with all our hearts. When they had gone, Shmeiki Baba took his knife and scratched a line on his walking stick. "That's day one," he said, "thank you Great Mother, and please protect those drunk drivers and the people they share the road with." With that, we fell asleep held by the Earth.

Friday, February 10th, 2006.

We awoke to the sweet, cool air and blue light of dawn. As the sun rose, we were enraptured by tweeting birds, monkey calls and cows mooing. We were nestled among tree-covered hills, and in a state of deep appreciation, we sat taking it all in. I felt we had arrived in Eden.

"And all this is just a day's walk from the tourist bubble," said Shmeiki Baba.

We remembered with delight, the supply of food left for us by Ravi and Mahesh and Shmeiki Baba began to cook us some breakfast, while I wrote in my journal.

"Here in nature, I can be more real," said Shmeiki Baba, "without needing to worry about what other people think of me."

"That is true," I said, "but there is something on my mind that I need to tell you."

"What's that?" asked Shmeiki Baba.

It was difficult for me to say, but I could not hold it back.

"I am in love with Aida," I said.

Shmeiki Baba smiled, "I know," he said, "Baba, it's totally okay."

"What, she's your girlfriend, are you not angry?" I asked.

"We were only together for a few days. Of course, Aida is amazing, beautiful and sensitive. I love her and I am honoured to know her, but I accept we are not a match. And even if we were, you would still be welcome to love her," said Shmeiki Baba.

"Why are you not a match?" I asked.

"I dunno," he said, "I guess I need someone kinkier."

I did not understand what he meant by this, but I let it go, and soon after, we began to walk along the side of State Highway 123, and the ground was still cool and wet with morning dew.

The place where the thorn had been in my foot still hurt and in truth, I was longing for some shoes. I stopped to look at the bottoms of my feet and saw that behind the dirt and sand, there was ripped skin under my toes.

"I hope they don't get infected," I said.

"You will be okay," Shmeiki Baba reassured me, and for a couple of minutes, he offered Shmeiki healing to my feet. I felt some sort of energetic transfer and I was pleasantly surprised when the pain actually went away, and I was able to walk with more ease. Luckily, our way was reasonably flat, that was until we reached the Kumbharli Ghat mountain pass. From there we had a tough climb, followed by a steep descent to the town of Sawantwadi. What made this more difficult, was that parts of the road were made of gravel.

On one steep, twisting section of road, we were shocked to witness a motorcyclist crash into a cow, as he came around a bend too fast. We helped the man up and found that miraculously, both he and the cow were unharmed. However, his motorbike was rather smashed up and not rideable. The man was terrified that someone might have seen the accident and would attack him because he had hit a holy cow, but luckily, other than us, there was no one else around. He hid his bike in the bushes at the side of the road and walked with us. He told us his name was Akash, and we talked about how risky riding a motorbike is, and as we did so, a family of six passed us, all riding on one bike. There were two small kids sat on the petrol tank in front of their father, the middle kid was behind him, then came the mother, and finally, the biggest kid was perched precariously on the back. If that wasn't enough, their dog was wrapped in a sheet and attached to the seat of the bike, just above the exhaust pipe.

"A hot Dog," said Shmeiki Baba.

"Differing perceptions of risk," said Akash.

We reached Sawantwadi and as we walked through town, we passed shops selling all sorts of colourful, wooden toys and models. Finally, we came to the picturesque Moti Talao Lake, where Akash lived and he said goodbye. We took a rest next to a chai stand, and despite our tiredness, we got out our instruments, as we'd already understood that if we played, we were more likely to be offered food and drink.

Soon, two Israeli travellers in their early twenties stopped next to us on their old, green Enfield motorbike. They introduced themselves as Itamar and Talya. Itamar asked us the name of our band.

"Make It Until You Fake It," said Shmeiki Baba.

They were astonished to find out we were walking across India barefoot.

"How can you do that?" asked Talya, "Think of all the pathogenic bacteria, not to mention the viruses and fungi you will come in contact with. At the very least, rub some antimicrobial tea tree oil on your feet. Actually, I've got some I can give to you," she said. She opened her bag to look for it and gave a small bottle to Shmeiki Baba. He thanked her, rubbed some of the oil on his feet and passed the bottle to me and I did the same.

Somehow Shmeiki Baba guessed that Talya's birthday was September 16th.

"How did you know that?" asked Talya.

"I'm not sure," said Shmeiki Baba, "it's no big deal though, I can only guess Virgos."

"But how did you know that I am a Virgo?" she asked.

"I could just feel it," he answered.

"And what sign are you?" she asked.

"I am all the signs," said Shmeiki Baba.

"No, really?" asked Talya.

"Truth is, I don't believe in horoscopes," answered Shmeiki Baba.

In that moment of confusion, Shmeiki Baba began to dance,

although there was no music. Itamar joined in and became very joyful, and we all danced without music, as did the chai stand owner.

And Itamar said to Shmeiki Baba, "I feel like a child again."

"Good brother," answered Shmeiki Baba.

We hugged each other and sat down and drank chai. Soon after, we said farewell and walked on, through this rich and ancient land.

Outside Sawantwadi, we were looking at the map, wondering which way to go, when a voice asked us an unsolicited question, "what happened?"

Neither of us looked up from the map, but we answered together, "nothing happened!"

"Something happened," said the voice.

When we did look up, we saw a man dressed in saffron robes, with a large turban on his head, and the mystery of the world in his wolfish face.

"What, no *chappals*?" he asked, pointing towards our bare feet.

"Many questions baba," said Shmeiki Baba.

"Yes," he said, "and where are you headed to?"

"To Pune," we answered.

"*Jhakaas!*" he shouted.

I asked him what this meant, and he said it meant 'fantastic' in Marathi, the language of Maharashtra.

"Which route are you taking?" he asked.

"Via Ku*dal*," said Shmeiki Baba.

"Well, if you like, you can walk off-road from here, through beautiful forests. After three days you will cross the River Gad and reach the village of Digvala," said the holy man.

"But we have no provisions," I said.

"Worry not," said the saddhu and he pointed to the right side of the road about a hundred metres ahead. "Even within sight there is food, just go over there and you will find wild Jambhalam berry and Cashew nuts. Also, there is papaya, so you will not go hungry. Be careful with cashew nuts though. Do you know that you must not eat them raw? And you must not even touch them before you cook them."

"Thank you, I didn't know," said Shmeiki Baba, and then he asked, "and how about water?"

"There are plenty of streams," said the baba.

"How rocky is the way?" I asked.

"There are rocks, but you will be able to walk without shoes," he said.

"I must say, you do speak rather good English," said Shmeiki Baba.

"Oh yes, thank you, sir, pardon me for not introducing myself, my name is Amitabh and I am now a saddhu, but I used to be a C++ programmer in Bangalore," he said, with that particular head shake, that isn't a yes and isn't a no.

We introduced ourselves too and we chatted a while longer until Amitabh said he had to get going and we said goodbye and walked over to the bushes. We began picking the dark, purple Jambhallam berries. They had a sweet and sour taste and when Shmeiki Baba began to eat them directly from the bush, without using his hands, I did the same. It was a delight. And then we turned our attention to the cashews. They were ripe and ready for picking. Shmeiki Baba had not seen cashews on a tree before and I showed him how they come in three parts. There is the big orange or yellow fruit, called the cashew apple, which looks a bit like a bell pepper. Cashews are a rare case in nature of what is called a pseudo fruit. They use a trick because the real nut of the cashew is not in the apple, it is hidden in the kidney-shaped stem.

"As Amitabh said, you have to be careful when you open them," I warned, "because they contain an oil called urushiol, which irritates the skin and causes a rash, like poison ivy, and that's why you have to cook the nuts, at least a little, before eating them. We should find a plastic bag to protect our hands."

"No need," said Shmeiki Baba and he took a green stem and opened it. I winced, as he took out the nut.

"Doesn't it hurt?" I asked him.

He looked at his hands, at the sky, and gave a confident smile. There was no sign of redness on his hands, and he showed no sign of pain. Pride shone across his face, and a rush of anger came over me.

"Are you performing miracles, Baba? Save your energy, I already know you are special," I said.

"Yes brother, you are right," he answered and then he said, "uh oh," and he held out his hands once again, and we watched as a rash began to appear all over them.

"Quick, scrub them before it's too late," I said, taking a cloth from my bag. I poured water on it and gave it to Shmeiki Baba to use to scrub his hands with. I told him to rub each and every part of his hands vigorously, while I continued to pour water over them. Amazingly, the rash disappeared. "That is the miracle," I said. Shmeiki Baba breathed a sigh of relief, and we carefully picked more cashews and put them in my bag, intending to open and cook them later.

I chopped one cashew apple open with my knife. "This part has no urushiol oil," I said. The fruit was sweet, but it also had a tannin taste which dried the mouth.

"You know, cashews were brought to Goa by the Portuguese," I said.

"How kind of them," he answered.

And we turned onto the forest footpath and used my compass to check our direction. In comparison with the asphalt, it was a pleasure to walk on the dirt track. I commented that I felt better connected to the ground and Shmeiki Baba agreed.

In a state of presence, while walking barefoot, you feel the sensations of the earth under your feet, and you automatically alter your speed, according to changes in the terrain. When you step on something sharp, you tend to lift your foot in time, and if you do get a thorn in your foot, you can usually take it out quite easily. Caught in thought, however, thorns tend to go in further and get stuck.

A breeze began to blow through the trees and brought us relief, and it made the dust we kicked up with our steps, cool and soothing. I scanned the sensations in my body as I walked and felt joyous. When Shmeiki Baba stopped, I did the same. Closing my eyes, I saw magnificent geometrical patterns. I told this to Shmeiki Baba.

"Me too," he said, "these are manifestations of the great algorithm."

By sunset, we had walked the best part of thirty kilometres and we made camp at the edge of a clearing. I remembered I had some condoms in my bag, so I put one on each hand so I could get the cashew nuts out of their stems, without the urushiol oil touching my hands. I proceeded to wash the nuts and fried them with salt. There were not so many of them, but we ate them with the berries and they were really tasty. I noted to Shmeiki Baba that we had used up a lot of our water, and we didn't have much left.

"We will find more tomorrow," he said.

Afterwards, we lay on the ground looking up at the Milky Way and marvelled that our whole universe apparently exists in a school computer within another universe.

Saturday, February 11th, 2006.

We woke at dawn and began to walk soon after. The whole time we were listening out for the sound of flowing water. By mid-morning, our remaining water supply was almost finished and we were becoming increasingly worried.

"Bloody Amitabh," said Shmeiki Baba.

"Why bloody Amitabh?" I asked.

"He told us that there were lots of streams. Clearly, there aren't and we might die of thirst. Why didn't we bring more water bottles?" seethed Shmeiki Baba.

"Relax baba," I said, "beating ourselves up about it won't help."

We knew we just had to keep on going, even though there was no sound or sight of water, only trees, land, and rocks, and when we shared the very last of our supply, we saw the fear in each others' eyes.

Thirst began with a dry throat and spread from there until it reached every cell in my body. I was truly beginning to contemplate my death when finally we heard the faintest sound of a river in the distance.

"Hear that?" shouted Shmeiki Baba.

"Yes, yes," I shouted.

We ran in the direction of the sound, over fallen trees and around bushes, until finally, we found it, a fast, flowing river. We filled our bottles and I put water purification tablets in them. Usually, I can't stand the taste of water which has been purified with tablets, but given our thirst, it tasted like nectar. When we were satisfied, we made a fire and boiled more water.

While we were waiting, Shmeiki Baba noticed there was wild sage growing next to the river. We picked some and made sage tea with it. Meanwhile, we realized there was also a wild papaya plant, full of papayas and two perfectly ripe fruit, undamaged by insects or birds, were lying on the ground. We cut them open and sunk our faces into the sweet flesh. Then, we sat bathing in the river, drinking our sage tea while we waited for more pans of water to boil and cool, so we could fill all of our water bottles. Before we left this blessed spot, we took some less ripe papayas with us so that so we would not go hungry the next day.

On we walked and in the late afternoon, we passed two bright-eyed shepherds, with their flocks of about twenty goats. Undimmed by modern life, their faces glowed and we shared some moments with them in complete silence, before moving on with the merest, but sincerest of nods.

Monday, February 13th, 2006.

In the morning Shmeiki Baba said to me, "You know, tonight

is the Snow Moon." I made the obvious comment that it was a bit hot for snow, and then the impossible became possible, as we became enveloped in an enormous flutter of white butterflies, and we were hypnotized by their elegant motion as though caught in a hot blizzard.

We covered another gruelling thirty kilometres and reached the village of Digvala in the evening, after crossing the River Gad by a footbridge. The temple was the first thing we saw. After three days in pure nature, the colourful, flashing lights outside the temple seemed so bright, we could barely look at them. As we approached, the *ghanta*, the temple bell, rang, signifying it was time for puja. Shmeiki Baba entered the temple and I followed. The colourful building was lit with candles, and in the centre was a fireplace. We were met with astonished looks from the ten or so local people standing there. I guessed that some of them might never have seen a foreigner before, but the priest welcomed us warmly, and he talked in Hindi, assuming we would understand better, than if he spoke Marathi. I thanked him, and he ushered us to stand with the rest of the congregation.

The priest was happy we had visited his temple and after puja, he insisted he take us home with him. We gladly accepted his offer and his wife fed us a rich, totally delicious *channa masala*, chickpeas cooked in a spicy sauce, served with jeera rice. Each bite brought rapture to our hungry mouths and afterwards, we played music in gratitude for the hospitality. Finally, the priest gave us mattresses and we made our beds on his porch, where we fell asleep bathed in moonlight.

Tuesday, February 14th, 2006.

We woke early to find we had both fallen prey to a case of diarrhoea. This could only have been from the food we were fed the evening before. Shmeiki Baba got angry and said that it was bad enough having haemorrhoids, without having a case of the runs as well. He said that his bottom hurt so much that he wanted to take revenge by shitting in the hair of the priest's wife.

When the priest came outside and understood we were both ill, he gave us bael fruit extract, to calm our stomachs. Shmeiki Baba thanked the priest, without mentioning that he blamed his wife for making us sick. When the priest left us, I said to Shmeiki Baba, "you talk about being authentic, but you were two-faced with the priest just now."

"Leave me alone, I feel like shit," he said.

"You smell like it too," I answered.

Luckily, the bael fruit extract was surprisingly effective and by afternoon, we both felt well enough to continue our journey at a gentle pace. We said our goodbyes and walked down Naradave Road for about six kilometres until we reached the little village of Kanedi. There, we met Vijay, the owner of a grocery store. His children called us "uncle and uncle" and they asked us to join them climbing the acacia tree next to their house. We did so, to their amusement, and later, Vijay fed us rice and plain boiled vegetables, because of our upset stomachs, and we slept the night peacefully under the tree.

Thursday, February 16th, 2006.

After taking a rest day in Kanedi, we continued north for sixteen kilometres, until we reached the village of Phondaghat. There, we met Vishnu, a seller of amla juice. Vishnu explained that amla fruit is most high in vitamin C and can heal diseases of heart, lung, brain, stomach, and liver. He offered to sell us some, and when we explained that we did not have money, he insisted we drink a glass on his account. The juice was incredibly tart but left our tongues pleasantly zinging. We thanked Vishnu and before we left, he said: "Do one more thing, while you are in our locality, stop at Napne waterfalls, they will wash your soul." We promised to look out for them, and continued north, passing through dense forests, screaming with life.

We noted that we were already considerably stronger than when we had left Arambol and we decided to walk a further eighteen kilometres as far as the village of Vaibhavwadi. When we finally arrived there, we rested close to a field, where some men were playing cricket. Shmeiki Baba said that there was something reassuring to him about the sound of a game of cricket.

While we sat there, a Scandinavian looking man walked passed us, and as we had not seen another foreigner in a good number of days, we greeted him warmly. We were surprised when his response was standoffish, and as he was noticeably disappointed by our presence, neither of us prolonged the interaction. Shmeiki Baba commented that some foreigners are seeking an exclusively Indian movie to lose themselves in, so much so, that they can get quite annoyed if you get in their shot.

Friday, February 17th, 2006.

Remembering Vishnu's advice to visit the waterfalls, we set out to reach them. On the way, we came to a place where the road forked. The path was not marked on our map, so Shmeiki Baba stopped a farmer. "Hello sir, is the waterfall this way, or this way?" he asked, pointing in each direction. The farmer was expressionless and pointed us to his left. We walked in that direction for the best part of an hour but did not find the waterfalls. Finally, Shmeiki Baba said, "I think he sent us the wrong way."

"Maybe he didn't understand you," I said.

"Then why couldn't he just say so?" asked Shmeiki Baba.

"People often do not say when they don't understand, that's why you have to ask questions carefully, like, 'You know waterfall?' Pointing, and offering suggestions is a bad idea," I explained.

"I'll remember that for next time," said Shmeiki Baba.

We walked back in the direction we had come, over the footprints we had left in the dust and when we reached the farmer this time, Shmeiki Baba said to him only one word, "waterfall," and waited. Slowly, the farmer pointed us to the right. This second path was the only other option, so it had to be correct and it was. And we were rewarded for our perseverance. The falls were not high, but they were broad and powerful and we left our belongings on the riverbank, jumped into the river and waded over to the cascade. There, we allowed vast amounts of water to pummel our bodies and purify our souls, just as Vishnu had suggested.

"Great Mother, help me clear my blockages, so I can flow without limits," said Shmeiki Baba.

"Om Shmeiki," I said.

Finally, we got out of the water and dried ourselves, and I looked at Shmeiki Baba and it occurred to me to say to him, "You might think you are fire, but really you are water."

"Yes," he said.

We proceeded north on footpaths. In the afternoon, we came across an enormous wild gaur, an Indian bison. She was standing in the middle of the footpath, raking the ground with her foot. We backed up and waited for her to move, but she was not in any rush, which is why it took us until evening to reach State Highway 114. There, we found a field of spinach and looked for the owner to ask if we could have some, but we couldn't find anyone. We hesitated until motivated by hunger, Shmeiki Baba cut a few bunches and hurriedly put them in his bag. We walked on about half a kilometre, before making camp by the side of the road, and sautéing the spinach.

The taste of our crime was delicious, but soon, Shmeiki Baba said that we should not have taken what was not ours.

"Now is not the time for a crisis of conscience," I said.

"I have let myself down," he said. He turned away from me and vomited. Then he clutched his backside and groaned in desperation, "oh god, here we go again."

Sheila 5

And Sheila began to speak through Shmeiki Baba:

"Punishing yourself at a time like this is a foolish act of self-sabotage. You made yourself sick just now so that you would not benefit from eating the spinach, but this is less about your guilt for stealing and more about the bag of shame you are still dragging behind you.

"I see that sending you on a pilgrimage and advising you to release unhelpful beliefs about yourself, is not enough, because you have great resistance to change when it comes to healing emotional wounds. For this reason, as we proceed, I am going to give you some exercises to help you with your process. I'd like you to start with the first one straight away.

"As anger is the easiest repressed emotion to reconnect with, I want you to begin by standing up and taking a deep breath. Then, I want you to imagine someone you are angry with, maybe your father or someone else who has hurt you and I want you to scream and curse them. I want you to scream and curse them until you can scream and curse no more."

Sheila became quiet. Shmeiki Baba opened his eyes, stood up and began to do as she had requested. He stamped his feet, beat his chest, lay back down on the ground and rolled in the dust, hissing, and cursing. He looked like he was possessed by a demon. Somehow, it gave me the urge to follow suit. I did so, and we both yelled our lungs out across the fields. We also turned on each other and released the frustration, which had been building between us.

"You filthy, Nazi bastard," shouted Shmeiki Baba.

"You fat, little Yid," I screamed.

We even pushed and spat at each other.

Finally, we were worn out and Shmeiki Baba said, "now let us lie still and feel the blood flowing through our veins."

I did as he suggested and could feel the blood coursing around my body. Soon we were calm and our anger was gone. We hugged and Shmeiki Baba went and got some more spinach.

Sunday, February 19th, 2006.

We started walking and Shmeiki Baba said:

"When I remember to process the world through the sensations of my body and not just through my thoughts, I feel a shift in my brainwaves. I want to spread my attention until I have regained full-body awareness in every moment."

"Om Shmeiki," I said.

From the hamlet of Devla, we walked on to the river Kajali. The water was clean and we jumped straight in. After a relaxing swim, we continued along footpaths for some twenty kilometres until we arrived at the beautiful village of Parsharamwadi on the river Bav. There, we met Geetha, a graceful, old lady with long, white hair, who was struggling to carry her shopping basket. Shmeiki Baba offered to help her and she was overjoyed, explaining that her family was away, so she was by herself. When we reached her house, she insisted we come in for tea.

Her garden was carefully tended and contained many sorts of unusual flowers and plants, as well as a glorious, white peacock who presented his feathers as we entered. On the wall of the house was a painting of the Goddess Kali, standing on the body of Lord Shiva. Kali wore a chain of men's heads around her neck. She was holding a sword, the head of a demon and a plate to catch the blood, which was dripping from the demon's head. This was possible because of her four arms. Shmeiki Baba stood staring at the picture as though in a trance.

"The demon is my shame," he said.

Geetha brought us a pot of chai and a tray of Parle-G biscuits, which we finished off quickly. When she saw how hungry we were, she went back into her kitchen and returned with two bowls of curry and rice. The food was wonderfully tasty and we were both touched by her kindness.

I was surprised when Shmeiki Baba told Geetha that he felt inclined to kiss her feet and she invited him to do what he felt was right. He knelt down and began to kiss her right foot, and it looked so natural, that I found myself kissing her left foot.

Within the energetic triangle that was created between us, I experienced some kind of portal opening. I was transported to a realm where I was greeted by beings, who infused me with love and guided me to the spirit of Geetha's deceased husband, and I told him that she was well and he did not need to worry about her.

When I opened my eyes, Geetha was weeping, and I allowed her tears to fall into my mouth. She placed her hands on both our heads to bless us and as we stood up, Shmeiki Baba realized that he had urinated in his pants. Geetha was most amused by this, offered him a towel and took his trousers to wash. She said she wanted to wash the rest of our clothes as well, and also gave me a towel to wear while she did so. Our clothes dried quickly in the sun, while we relaxed. Geetha lit a kerosene stove and put an iron on it to heat up. We said she didn't need to press our clothes, but she insisted.

"A real iron," said Shmeiki Baba, "I don't think I've seen one of those being used before."

Neither had I.

"What a country of paradoxes this is," said Shmeiki Baba. "They have been putting satellites into space since the 1980s, yet some people still heat their irons with fire."

Geetha even sprayed rose water onto our clothes as she ironed them, and this made them smell wonderful. We put them on with delight and finally parted ways with her in deep appreciation, and with an expanded sense of love. On we walked, with an extra bounce in our step, five kilometres to the small town of Devrukh and from there, we continued seven kilometres further to the village of Kosumb.

Tuesday, February 21st, 2006.

Every wonder we experienced, confirmed to me that while our universe may be artificial and while our lives on the crust of our world may be unstable, it is our duty to trust existence. Meanwhile, the goodness of the people we met, caused our confidence to grow. We experienced that the more kind we are, the more kind people are to us.

Sometimes we were nervous about not having anything to eat or drink, but when we remembered to give expression to our fears and to surrender to our situation, food and water would appear from one direction or another.

In the morning, we were resting against a tree, close to the village of Kosabi. A man walked past us holding some dead hens by their necks. He stopped next to us, surprised by our presence and when he saw our instruments, he asked us to play for him. We did so, and he enjoyed our song so much, that he gave us one of the hens. We were so grateful to him that we hugged him. I plucked the hen and gutted her, while Shmeiki Baba prepared a fire. To eat meat after so long felt strange and she was rather chewy, but she sustained us. We needed this strength because we had already begun a climb of more than twenty kilometres along footpaths, which ran over the Western Ghat mountains in the direction of the town of Helwak.

As we walked, Shmeiki baba talked about the concept of education fatigue. He said that sometimes he was frightened of receiving new information and he reckoned this was because at school, he had been oversaturated with irrelevant bullshit. And then he shouted out in pain, and it turned out that he had managed to cut the ball of his foot on some glass, which was buried in the mud. He sat down against a tree at the side of the road and propped up his leg because blood was flowing from the wound. He got out his bottle of Dettol disinfectant and we washed the cut and made a bandage from one of his shirts. After resting a little while, he tried to walk on his wounded foot, but it was too painful.

"The wound on my sole mirrors the wound in my soul," he said, "but it's okay because I had a tetanus booster before I left England."

As we sat wondering what to do, four farmers passed us and stopped to see if we needed any help. They didn't speak any English, so I explained, as best as I could, in my broken Hindi what had happened and they pointed to their village and said, "chikitsak," which means doctor. I explained that we didn't have any money for a doctor. They said that it didn't matter and they offered to carry Shmeiki Baba to their village, where they said the doctor would be happy to help him. I explained this to Shmeiki Baba, who looked a little worried, but agreed. And so the farmers hoisted Shmeiki Baba upon their shoulders and off we went until finally, we reached the house of the doctor.

"This is where the doctor lives?" I asked surprised by the very simple corrugated iron and mud house. "Yes," they said and one of the farmers knocked on the door. An old man answered, dressed in white robes. His eyes were bright green and he exuded an unusual calmness. "Hello, my name is Sudha," he said. We introduced ourselves and Shmeiki Baba showed him his foot.

"Will you answer me one question?" asked Sudha.

We said yes.

"If time is an illusion, what are my wrinkles?" he asked.

"Everything is an illusion, even your wrinkles," I said, "and yet Shmeiki Baba's foot still needs healing."

"Very true," said Sudha.

We explained that we didn't have any money, but we could play music. Sudha said that money mattered less than music and asked Shmeiki Baba to lie down on the bed in his kitchen and he took off our improvised bandage. He inspected the wound, whispered a prayer in Sanskrit, went into another room and came back with a trumpet and a tube of turmeric paste. He blew the trumpet nine times and put the paste around the cut. He explained that while the turmeric would help the wound heal, the important thing was the prayer and the trumpet. He proceeded to apply a fresh bandage to Shmeiki Baba's foot and asked us to stay as his guests, and we were glad to. He fed us and we played music to him all evening, sitting in the garden of his house under an enormous bodhi tree. Sudha also arranged our beds. It was our first night sleeping inside since we had left Arambol. By morning, Shmeiki Baba could already walk on his foot, but on doctor's orders, we chose to take a day of rest, to give the wound more time to heal.

Thursday, February 23rd, 2006.

Shmeiki Baba's wound had closed and it seemed the cut was not quite as deep as first thought. Sudha suggested that Shmeiki Baba could walk, but should take it easy for a few more days. He gave

Shmeiki Baba a tube of turmeric paste and some more bandages. We thanked him sincerely, said goodbye and slowly walked five kilometres until we reached Shivsagar Lake. This is a reservoir, which was formed in the 1960s after the Koyna River, which rises in Mahabaleshwar, was impounded by the building of the Koyna dam, an enormous, roaring, industrial temple of hydroelectric power, more than a hundred metres high. We were shocked by its size and it stood before us as a symbol of the world that we thought we had left behind.

We were reminded by some children that it was the eve of the festival of Shivaratri and we decided to look for a good spot to celebrate. As Shmeiki Baba's foot was holding up, we wandered along the lakeside for another two kilometres, until we found a chai and samosa stand, just next to the water. I suggested this might be a good place to set up camp, as we would likely be offered food and drink in exchange for playing music. And so we stopped there and befriended Yogesh, the owner of the food stand. This was not just any food stand, it was Yogesh No.1 Chai and Samosas. He insisted we try both and we were glad to.

Sunday, February 26th, 2006.

In the morning, we awoke to find some students and a couple of families wanting to camp on our little beach. A tall, holy man dressed in orange robes also arrived. He said his name was Santosh and he asked to sit with us and we welcomed him. And then Ram, a friend of his also joined us, followed by Gyanendra and Shankara, and two more, who had taken an oath of silence.

And so we found ourselves in the company of six real babas. Of their group, Santosh spoke the best English.

"You are white fakirs," said Santosh, on hearing our story.

"That's not very nice," said Shmeiki Baba.

"I said fakir not fucker," said Santosh, "A fakir is a holy man like you, who lives only from the goodness of others."

"I am less a holy man, and more a self-entitled hipster," said Shmeiki Baba.

Santosh explained to the others in Hindi what he thought Shmeiki Baba had told him.

"You know," said Santosh, "tonight is Maha Shivaratri, the great night of Shiva. This is why tonight, you shouldn't lie down at all, you should sit in meditation with your spine vertical. This time, just before the equinox, is when there is a very big upward movement of energy."

Hearing this, we both sat up straight.

"Yes, when moon is dark, mind is quiet, and it is easy to be at one with the soul," said Santosh. "Tonight, everyone has potential to be awakened, so even if you don't meditate throughout the year, do it at least tonight, just do it, just do it."

"You are quite insistent about it," said Shmeiki Baba.

"I want for you only the best," said Santosh.

Peanuts and chillums were passed around and songs to Shiva were sung. Ram took ash from the fire and made a *tripundra tilaka* pattern on Shmeiki Baba's forehead, which consisted of three horizontal lines of ash, with a circle, made of red *kumkum* powder in the middle. Then he did the same for me.

Once blessed, we played more music, soaring high on the wings of A, D and E minor, tuned of course, to 432Hz, and we lifted our fellow babas with us. Towards sunset, Yogesh, unexpectedly approached us with a tray of drinks.

"*Bhang lassi,*" he said, "for *utsav*, for celebration, and it is made with milk of black cow."

There was great excitement among the saddhus. The yoghurt was sweet, thick and fresh, and had a strong taste of ganja. As we drank, a white dove flew over our heads. Gyanendra, the oldest baba, lifted his empty glass to the sky and with lassi still dripping from his moustache, he shouted: "*masakali, masakali*" and the others echoed his call. Santosh, by way of explanation, said: "fly high like dove with peace and liberation, my friends." We echoed this sentiment. Santosh and the other babas sat chanting shiva mantras, sometimes clapping, their heads moving in figure of eight patterns.

We sat meditating and after about an hour, the effects of the cannabis kicked in.

I disappeared into a dream that I was in a boat on the river Ganges in Varanasi. Rowers were battling the force of the river, keeping me from getting swept downstream. Dead babies were floating by me, swollen up and covered in flies. Then I found myself back on land, and a tour guide, who had the face of my grandfather, insisted I go with him into a house, where old people were waiting to die. There, I looked into an elderly man's face and realized he was an older version of myself. A bright light appeared and eclipsed us both and I fell into a white space, which I understood was the world of potential, which sits behind the skin of reality.

It was in the middle of the night when I finally woke to this world. Shmeiki Baba was lying next to me. I realized he was covered in vomit, but was still too far gone to care. I turned my attention to Ram, who was staggering around by the side of the lake, next to the tents of other people who were camping there. "Wake up everyone," he shouted when he realized they were sleeping.

I called to him, "stop it! Man, you're tripping, let them sleep."

"Don't tell me what to do," yelled Ram.

"What are you doing?" shouted a man from inside his tent.

"It is Shivaratri, what are you sleeping for?" asked Ram.

"We have children here, go away," shouted back the man.

Ram refused and the man got out of his tent, offered Ram some money to quit it, and finally he did so. Meanwhile, Santosh, who was sitting next to me, explained, "I am from Karnataka. When I was a boy, we would throw stones at houses on Shivaratri. On this night it was allowed because if you wake someone on Shivaratri, you are automatically doing them a favour."

Shmeiki Baba returned to this world singing some sort of children's song: "A finger of fudge is just enough to give your kids a treat, it's full of chocolaty goodness, but helps to rot your teeth."

I helped him to the lake to wash, and he explained to me what he had seen:

"I saw an old train and a tunnel in front of it, which was blocked off. I found myself pulling off wooden boards to open up the tunnel, and when this was done, I got on the train. I was the only person on board and it began to move. In the darkness of the window, I saw my mother. She picked up a child version of me and threw me into the dining room of our house, and slammed the door, leaving me alone. And Sheila spoke to me and told me that what mattered more than my memories, was to allow myself to feel the pain that is locked inside me. With this, my lower back began to hurt. I knew I needed to go into this pain, but another part of me didn't want to. My mind threw out lurid images of cavalry soldiers swinging swords, riding towards me. I did not run away but allowed them to dismember me. I stayed with the pain, it became my anchor and I felt a deep emotional splinter was coming out of my soul. Finally, the train stopped. Sheila told me I had done well, but there was still further to go. In the distance, three glowing entities were waving. I was fascinated by them and understood that they didn't want to get too close, for my sake. I realized that these were the Shagasomin, the beings who generated our universe. I acknowledged that they are my facilitators, and I felt myself accelerating until I was catapulted forward into a red and white world, where an enormous serpent began to wrap himself around me. I kept my body moving and was succeeding in staying alive when Yogesh's dog came and licked my face. I opened my eyes to see what was going on and the serpent in my vision ate me."

"I'm glad the serpent ate you, " I said.

"Why's that?" he asked, surprised.

"The serpent is a symbol of life force," I said. "Your fight against it, is the fight of your ego against the great tide of life."

"Yes!" said Shmeiki Baba and he held up his hands to the heavens and began to sing:

"Like stars,

We are born

From collapsing clouds of dust and gas.

We learn names,

We accept laws,

And forget ourselves.

Finally, we remember boundless love."

Monday, February 27th, 2006.

We awoke late and sat enjoying the green hills surrounding the lake. The rest of the babas were still sleeping, strewn in a variety of positions, apart from Santosh, who had already made a fire and was heating water. The state of our camp revealed the intensity of the celebration the night before.

"You know, this dam has withstood earthquakes, especially the big one of 1967, which caused many cracks," said Santosh, "but it's okay, they fixed it."

"That's reassuring," I said.

Santosh cooked tapioca with nuts for breakfast and said that afterwards he and his friends would go to the dam to beg for money.

"We live on alms, supported by people and temples. You are like us, you should come with," said Santosh.

Once the others had awoken, swum in the lake and eaten breakfast, we went with them to beg. Maybe it is perverse, but we enjoyed the novelty of asking Indian tourists for baksheesh, and we were blessed by Maha Lakshmi, goddess of wealth, as in about an hour we had made ₹ 150 together. I was being very light-hearted when I noticed Shmeiki Baba looking uncomfortable.

"What's wrong?" I asked him.

"You're leading me astray," he said.

"Have you gone mad?" I asked, astonished by his accusation and I was about to tell him more about what I thought when I saw that now-familiar look on his face.

Sheila 6

And Sheila spoke as follows:

"If you are honest, you did not really have a problem with begging, your issue is more that you were worried how it looks from the outside, because of the notion that it is wrong for a wealthy westerner to be taking money from Indian people.

"Deep down, you still feel that you are a bad person who causes damage to others. This belief stands against your very existence, which is why it is hard for you to acknowledge. That is why it was easier to blame Sebastian, rather than taking responsibility for your actions. Of course, it is very human to project the parts of yourself you are denying onto others.

"You need to understand that there's no getting rid of old patterns of behaviour, the only thing you can do, is to show yourself there are new possible ways to respond and new patterns of behaviour to develop.

"In due course, I will give you an exercise to help you care less about how you seem to others. For now, I simply want you to acknowledge what your shame is built upon."

And that was it, Sheila was quiet and Shmeiki Baba asked me, "Can I tell you something from my childhood?"

"Of course," I said.

"I remember being about five years old. I am lying in bed and I can hear my father struggling to breathe in the next room. He says to my mother that he is having a heart attack and asks her to call an ambulance. She does so, and I hear her explaining down the phone where we live. I want to get out of bed to help, but I cannot because I am scared stiff, and I stay in bed and fall back asleep, only to wake again to the sound of the doorbell. My mum answers the door and ambulancemen come upstairs. There is a lot of loud talking and clattering, I guess they are bringing up some kind of stretcher. My father is breathing loudly. They leave with more clattering, and there is silence again, and I fall back asleep. When I wake up, I get out of bed and go to my mother. I see the look of fear in her face and understand we are in danger. She says that everything is okay, but I know it is not. I feel guilty because I didn't get out of bed to help and also because I feel that my father's heart attack is my fault."

I said to Shmeiki Baba, "you are safe now, you can afford to be vulnerable, to risk being intimate with the world, and even to be seen as a beggar."

"Yes, brother," he said.

Wednesday, March 1st, 2006.

We rose to morning mist hanging over the lake. I asked Shmeiki Baba how his foot was. He took off the bandage and found that the wound was almost completely healed. We decided it was time to leave, and once we had drunk chai, we exchanged our ₹ 150 for samosas, filled our water bottles, played a final song, and said our farewells. We began our walk up the hilly eastern banks of Lake Shivsagar, northwards in the direction of the village of Medha. As we walked, I mentioned how I'd enjoyed the company of the saddhus.

"I wonder what made each of them renounce their worldly lives?" I asked.

"Maybe they were walking out on their families or their debts," said Shmeiki Baba.

Thoughtfully, we continued approximately thirty kilometres along the side of the lake and made camp.

Thursday, March 2nd, 2006.

We reached the village of Medha in the evening after another long walk. Here, we crossed from the Western Ghats onto the Deccan Plateau. In Medha, we were lucky enough to meet Lalu, a friendly and inquisitive rickshaw driver, who insisted we come with him to his house, and when we agreed, he told us that it was destiny we had arrived in his village, just as George W. Bush had arrived in Delhi to sign a nuclear deal with Manmohan Singh. Lalu's little house was old and rather decrepit, and he lived by himself because his wife had died. The walls were marked with years of water stains, which looked like maps of some mysterious land. Lalu presented us with bowls of his special *dal*, which was super spicy and he served it with flatbread he called *bakri*, explaining this was like *roti*, but coarser. After dinner, he excitedly told us that Rambo II was on TV and turned on his 1980s television set, and we watched the movie with him, with the contrast turned up far too high. He had only one bedroom, which he offered to us, but we insisted we sleep in his living room on the floor.

Friday, March 3rd, 2006.

After breakfast, we left Lalu and walked to the town of Shirwal, and crossed the River Nira at Sarola. It was a steady climb until Askarwadi, and from there it was to be a long and gradual descent to the city of Pune. This was the furthest we had walked in one day and the proximity of our destination kept us going. Unlike the rest of the places we had passed through, Pune was the first place we both already knew and we were excited to arrive.

It was late into the evening when we reached the southwest edge of Pune and the plenitude of city lights brought us back to the story of modern civilisation.

Shmeiki Baba said, "The first time I arrived in Pune, I did so by train. In fact, it was my first train ride in India. I remember the joy of sitting in the open doorway of the second class carriage, as we clattered through the countryside of Maharashtra, bathing in the pink light of the setting sun. I could barely contain the sense of expansion in me and tears streamed down my cheeks. The ticket collector came by and put a supportive hand on my shoulder."

We spent some time looking for somewhere appropriate to camp, and couldn't find a park, so we decided to sleep under a tree by the side of the road.

"It smells like shit," I said.

"It's running underneath us through the drains," said Shmeiki Baba, "inhale it as though it is perfume, and it will desensitize your nose."

I tried what he suggested and gagged.

We could see enormous rats scurrying about. "I hope they don't eat us while we're sleeping," said Shmeiki Baba.

And then we noticed that painted on the wall on the opposite side of the road, were the words, "state is a fear of mind," and we laughed.

Saturday, March 4th, 2006.

At dawn, we were woken by the sound of vehicles and horns tooting. We jumped up, happy to be alive, and got walking in the direction of Koregaon Park, which is in the east of the city. As the light grew stronger, so the number of motorbikes and scooters increased. Soon, the volume of morning traffic was astounding and the pollution made us choke.

"I am trying to remember that the divine is in all things and all things are in the divine," said Shmeiki Baba.

At one intersection, we saw a guy on a motorbike who had replaced his broken wing mirror with a large, pink, plastic bathroom mirror. "Clever move," said Shmeiki Baba to the man, who was pleased with the recognition. While I was laughing, I tripped over a raised paving stone, and as I got up and brushed myself down, a bookseller took the opportunity to try to sell me a copy of 'Mein Kampf'. "Interesting choice," said Shmeiki Baba. I asked the man why he was selling shit like this. He shrugged in a way which made me angry, so I grabbed the book and threw it in the road. The bookseller yelled at me, at which point a man wearing a McDonald's uniform stepped in, to calm the situation. He encouraged us to keep walking with him. Shmeiki Baba said, "Thank you, Rajesh Kumar," and I thought he was becoming clairvoyant until I realized that Rajesh's name was written on his name badge.

"You have five stars," said Shmeiki Baba.

"Yes sir, I have five stars, sir," said Rajesh.

"What are they for?" asked Shmeiki Baba.

"Well sir, they show I am competent in the areas of restaurant dining, cashier, grill station, fry station, dressings, and back-room hygiene."

"Goodness," said Shmeiki Baba.

"And what are you doing here?" asked Rajesh.

"We are making a pilgrimage," said Shmeiki Baba.

"To Pune?" asked Rajesh.

"Sebastian is, but I am continuing to Dharamshala," said Shmeiki Baba.

"To Dharamshala no less. Well do say hello to His Holiness from me," said Rajesh, as we reached McDonald's.

"I shall do my best," said Shmeiki Baba, and Rajesh pointed us in the direction of Koregaon Park.

As we walked on, we saw two children being taken to school by their mother. "Check the school bag," said Shmeiki Baba pointing towards the blue satchel worn on the back of one of the kids. Printed on the left side of the bag was an image of George W. Bush and on the right, was a defiant Osama Bin Laden, and behind them in the background, were the Twin Towers, with planes exploding into them.

"If only we had some money, I would surely offer to buy it from her," said Shmeiki Baba.

"Lucky, we don't," I said.

As we turned into North Main Road, which was the beginning of Koregaon Park and the location of the famous Osho commune, or ashram, or even *cashram* as it was also sometimes known, we saw people dressed in maroon robes, the uniform of the Osho follower, and we knew we had almost arrived at our destination.

And while I was looking forward to meeting up with my friends Richard and Jonas, who I knew from Berlin, I also felt sad, that my journey with Shmeiki Baba was about to end. I said that part of me wanted to carry on with him past Pune, and he said he felt the same way, but we agreed, that doing so might limit our connections to the rest of the world. I said I would come to Dharamshala when he reached there, and he said this would make him happy.

Our first stop was the German bakery, where I thought Richard and Jonas might be hanging out. Sure enough, they were there, both dressed in maroon robes, drinking tea. We greeted each other with such happiness, and I introduced them to Shmeiki Baba.

"Ah, so you are both maroon morons," said Shmeiki Baba, without taking even a moment to get to know them. Not surprisingly, they were both a little insulted.

"Here we go," I said.

"So, you don't resonate well with Osho?" asked Richard.

"Well, I was a maroon moron myself for a little while, until I got sick of swimming around in the sewage of fake happiness and all the bullshit about enlightenment," said Shmeiki Baba.

"Osho said we must give up the hope of enlightenment for it to happen," said Jonas.

"Giving up the hope of enlightenment in order to get enlightenment, is still looking for enlightenment," said Shmeiki Baba.

"This is a paradox Osho also acknowledged," said Jonas.

"If he cleared up the confusion so well, it's a shame people around here still seem to talk about it so incessantly," said Shmeiki Baba.

"And what of your own path?" asked Richard.

"Well, it has been long and dusty," said Shmeiki Baba.

"It looks it," said Jonas.

"We walked here without shoes or money," I said.

"So how did you eat?" asked Richard.

"People gave us food," said Shmeiki Baba.

"Is it not conceited of foreign tourists to travel across India, taking food from poor people?" asked Jonas.

"Maybe, though our mission has been to regain trust in mankind and in ourselves," I said.

"Is that fair on those who have had to pay for you?" asked Jonas.

"I don't think we made anyone else go hungry. And no one who didn't want to give us food, did so," said Shmeiki Baba.

There was an uncomfortable silence, until Shmeiki Baba said, "maybe I got us off to a bad start, I guess I am angry with the hypocrisy of Osho followers because of my own. I acknowledge that I pretend to accept myself when I still do not."

Richard and Jonas' expressions softened and I took the opportunity to turn the conversation to the walls of the German Bakery, which were covered with advertisements offering all sorts of spiritual services from aura readings to healing with Egyptian hieroglyphs and sacred enemas, guaranteed to make you look ten years younger in six days. I suggested that a sacred enema might help Shmeiki Baba's haemorrhoid situation. Shmeiki Baba answered that he would bear it in mind. Meanwhile, Jonas bought us coffee and apple pies, which we gobbled down.

Afterwards, we left the German Bakery and went to Richard's apartment, so I could collect my credit card, which I had left with him in Arambol. I wanted to treat Shmeiki Baba with a stay in a decent hotel, and so armed with my MasterCard, I took him to the Mangrove Inn, where I booked two rooms.

It was the first hot shower either of us had taken in a long while. Each drop of water on my head was a touch of heaven, as rays of light streamed in through the window, making the steam sparkle. I could hear Shmeiki Baba singing songs of praise next door. We both stayed in the shower until all the hot water was gone and then slept for a few hours under the air conditioners.

In the evening, Jonas and Richard came with us to Prem's Restaurant on North Main Road for dinner. We ate well and drank beer and met two Swedish girls called Abbey and Ilse. We played a game with them of not answering any question correctly, and when Jonas and Richard went home, we brought the girls back to our hotel. They had a joint to smoke and after we shared it, I was with Abbey, while Ilse sat her statuesque form on Shmeiki Baba. In his face, I saw his need for the Goddess. We fell asleep with the women, wrapped peacefully in each others' arms.

Sunday, March 5th, 2006.

In the morning, the hotel manager banged hard on the door. He was not at all impressed we had taken two women back with us and said there was no place in his hotel for *goondas* like us, and he asked us to leave.

Shmeiki Baba said he wanted to get on his way in any case, and I decided I would move to a different guest house. As a parting gift, I gave him my compass and two maps that I had bought for him the day before, one of the state of Madhya Pradesh and the other of Rajasthan. I also gave Shmeiki Baba my bottle of the *sweet tears of the wee baby Jesus*, with instructions on how to use them, and he assured me that he would put them to good use.

He handed me his bansuri, and I said, "I can't take this, it's your flute."

"I want you to have it," he said.

"But without it, you will have nothing to play," I said.

"It's okay, I am the instrument," he answered.

"Okay, Baba, I am also learning to receive, so thank you," I said.

"Sebastian," said Shmeiki Baba, "I want you to know that I never imagined feeling so close to someone who has dreadlocks. You are the one true hippie I have met. And while I jump up and down and make a lot of fuss about everything, you quietly get on with what you need to do. I respect you with all my heart."

"Shmeiki Baba," I said, "you remind me that the process of awakening doesn't need to happen just once, it needs to happen many times."

"Yes brother, our work is ongoing," said Shmeiki Baba.

We hugged and parted ways in laughter.

And that was the end of my part of the great walk. To say it was challenging is an understatement. It stretched me to my limits and sometimes a bit beyond. So what did it do for me? Well, I learned that it is okay for me to accept the goodness of those who wish to give to me, even if I do not have something to repay them with immediately. I also understood that there's nothing to fix about myself and my job is to accept myself fully, whatever is there. That for me is the meaning of integration, and this is the way to be in harmony with the Great Mother and to experience life as a miracle.

Regarding Shmeiki Baba, while I have not met him in a long time, he remains for me a soul brother, and all these years later, I remember my walk with him as a profound, transformative experience. He was willing to go with me to places that no one else was, and this allowed me to explore the farthest reaches of my soul.

When I finally returned to Germany, I was a different person. I went back to my home town where I felt that I stood out even more than I had in India. You see, I lived in a rather conservative place, where people who didn't know me, could be quick to judge me as a lazy, hippie. I guess I partly enjoyed them doing that, as it allowed me to show them that they were wrong, and I was worth respecting.

I'd like to end by saying to you, dear readers, that if any of you feel depressed and Shmeiki somehow doesn't work for you, come chop some wood on my farm in Portugal and I promise you, you'll feel much better. I will chop some wood too, as I have a lot of wood that needs chopping, and for this reason, I have written my Shmospel quite swiftly, so please excuse me if anything doesn't make sense.

Om Shmeiki Om, Shmeiki.com

III

Narrative Shmospel by Priti

From Pune to Delhi

My name is Priti Aggarwal, and I am the editor of the Shmospels of Shmeiki. It is my honour to have been given the task of writing this third Shmospel, which deals with the part of Shmeiki Baba's great walk, between Pune and Delhi, where he walked alone.

With Shmeiki Baba's permission, I will begin with a few words about myself, to explain how and why I came to Shmeiki.

I grew up in Chicago in the USA, but my parents are originally from Punjab. Most summers we would go to India to visit our family, but I found it boring. It was only in my mid-twenties that I discovered there are communities of foreigners from all over the world, who live in India, escaping the rat race back home. It was in one of these wonderful places, called Kasar Devi in the state of Uttarakhand, that I first came across Shmeiki Baba. This was in 2009, three years after he had completed his great walk. I went to a *shmatsang*, a talk he was giving, called 'Slimyji, Autobiography of a Horny Yoga Teacher.' I immediately realized that I had found a guide, who knew how to keep it real. A week later, I travelled to Dharamshala to go to the Shmeiki Centre there. From the outset,

I loved Shmeiki, especially the spiritual femdom. "Power to the shmoni!" I say.

When, in 2010, I told my parents that I had decided to live in India, they were over the moon, but when I explained that I had taken a job working at the Om Shmeiki Healing Organization, they were worried.

"Don't get yourself involved with some cult," warned my mom.

"It's not what you think," I said.

"It never is," said mom.

She is quite smart, my mom. But I didn't listen, and I worked happily at the Om Shmeiki Healing Organization until early 2012 when the leaders suddenly left India, and both Centres were closed.

I went back to Chicago and was planning to go to iPadipuri, the new Shmeiki Commune which had opened in Colombia, when at the end of December 2012, I learned the terrible news that six people had been killed there. It was devastating for me, as I personally knew them. For more than a year afterwards, there was little news about what had really happened. I tried to wrap my head around it and told myself that we sometimes need bad things to happen, to be a contrast to all the good stuff, just like the darkness of space is needed for the stars to shine against.

Finally, in early 2014, I heard that Shmeiki Baba, Shoshana and a number of other key members of iPadipuri who had survived the attack, were still in hiding. After that, I didn't hear anything else until early 2018, when Shoshana wrote me an email. I was overjoyed to find out that she and Shmeiki Baba were living together in the north of Israel, in a mixed Jewish-Arab village, and they had had a baby, who they called Tony Ananda. Once we were reacquainted, Shmeiki Baba asked me if I wanted to produce a book about his great walk of 2006. I agreed immediately and threw myself into the task, seeing it as a wonderful opportunity to make a powerful, life-affirming statement that Shmeiki lives on.

The creation of these Shmospels has been a deeply therapeutic process for me. I'd like to take this opportunity to thank everyone involved, especially Shmeiki Baba, Aida, Sebastian, Shoshana and

Dylan for all their tireless work.

In order to produce these Shmospels, I flew to Israel and stayed with Shmeiki Baba and Shoshana for a couple of weeks, at their beautiful house in the Galilee. There, we sat on their deck, drinking cups of lemon and mint crushed with ice, and I interviewed Shmeiki Baba for hours on end. From Israel, I flew on to India and went to Pune. There, I bought a motorbike and rode the route Shmeiki Baba had taken, all the way from Pune to Delhi. Along the way, I was able to interview some of the people who had met him twelve years before. It is a testament to Shmeiki Baba that even after so many years, there were people who remembered their encounters with him.

Before I finally get to the third Shmospel, I'd like to say that I have come across many gurus who point to some transcendent moment, after which they became enlightened and forever present. Some of them promised that by following them, something similar would happen to me. Shmeiki Baba never made any such claims, and when in a moment of doubt, I said to him that I thought he was making all the Sheila business up, he just smiled, and said, "Priti, you can believe whatever you wish."

Few spiritual teachers are willing to reveal their dark sides like Shmeiki Baba. Of course, to be fair, it can't be easy for them to be honest about their shadows when sticky followers insist on worshipping them as lords of light.

I also learned through Shmeiki Baba that if I choose to see myself as a spiritual seeker, I must obviously still feel that something is missing. "Nothing is missing," he said, "all is as it needs to be. Just get what you need here and then get out, before it's too late."

I hope you enjoy the third Shmospel.

Blessings to the Great Mother and all beings in all dimensions.

Om Shmeiki Om. Shmeiki.com.

From Pune to Delhi

Before leaving Pune, Shmeiki Baba called his family, by reversing the charges. It was the first time he had checked in with them since

Goa. His father accepted the call but when Shmeiki Baba said, "hi dad," his father answered, "I'll get your mother."

Shmeiki Baba asked his mother why his father didn't want to speak to him, and she answered, "your father loves you."

Shmeiki Baba replied, "he wants to love me, but until he learns to love himself, it will be hard for him to love anyone else."

His mother turned the conversation to how concerned she was about him and begged him to come home and rethink his career. Shmeiki Baba felt sad about his mother's inability to appreciate his choices and ended the conversation.

He began his walk north out of Pune and by the afternoon, he was already out of the city. He felt hungry and realized that without Sebastian he had less confidence approaching strangers. He felt lonely and miserable and lay down on a bench to sleep.

By morning he felt starving. He overcame his shyness and began to ask people for food, but was surprised when one after another, they said no. He wondered if this was because without Sebastian, he appeared as more of a threat, or maybe it was just the look of desperation on his face. With no choice, he trudged on and by evening, he still had received nothing to eat. He filled his stomach as best as he could with water and fell into a fretful sleep, under a tree. He awoke feeling dreadful and regretted ever starting his walk. He called out to Sheila, but Sheila was silent.

In despair and unable to go any further, Shmeiki Baba fell to his knees and cried. As he wept in hopelessness, he felt a hand on top of his head. It sent a strong, calming pulse through his body. He turned to see who it was and was amazed to see that a boy, about ten years old with one blind eye, was looking at him with great compassion.

"Aaraam se, baba," said the boy, which means 'take it easy, baba.'

Shmeiki Baba smiled through his tears and the child opened his arms to give Shmeiki Baba a hug. The child led Shmeiki Baba by the hand to his house, where his mother was making lunch, and she offered Shmeiki Baba food, which he gladly accepted.

"Your child is an angel," said Shmeiki Baba.

"Yes, I know," said his mother.

"He saved me," said Shmeiki Baba.

"I can see," she replied.

"I will remember this always," said Shmeiki Baba.

The mother offered Shmeiki Baba to stay with them and suggested she should call his relatives and ask them to come and pick him up, but Shmeiki Baba explained about his pilgrimage and that he was determined to continue. The next day, the mother gave him some provisions and he set off on his way, feeling revitalized.

On Saturday, March 12th, 2006, Shmeiki Baba reached the ancient, holy city of Nashik, on the banks of the polluted River Godavari, some two hundred kilometres north of Pune. Nashik has a good climate due to its altitude and is known as the wine capital of India, as many of India's vineyards are situated in the area.

It was at around 7 pm that evening, that what has become known as the Night of the Aloe Vera Handshake took place on Madina Chowk in Nashik. There, local police reported that a riot occurred, after a bearded foreigner did his best to unite members of the city's two main religions. The foreigner taught both groups the mantra: "make friends, make friends, never ever break friends, if you do, you'll fall down the loo and that will be the end of you." While doing so, he was said to have opened up stems of aloe vera, which were growing in large plant pots, next to the street and he smeared their sticky goo onto his palms, before shaking hands with as many people as possible. The local people copied him in good spirits and there was much fun until one man's testicles were fondled and a fight broke out. Shmeiki Baba did not try to solve the quarrel and departed Nashik in haste. He climbed the Satpura mountains and two days later crossed the state border between Maharashtra and Madhya Pradesh. There, in a little village, Shmeiki Baba rested, until he was woken by something landing on his head. Around him, he found a group of village children. It was the festival of Holi and the kids were throwing coloured dye at him. There was no escape, and Shmeiki Baba allowed the children to cover him with coloured powders, before chasing after them pretending to be a monster, while they ran away screaming with delight.

On Wednesday, March 22nd, 2006, Shmeiki Baba reached the city of Indore, northeast of Nashik, after making another steep climb up the southern edge of the volcanic Malwa Plateau. This region used to be one of the main producers of opium in the world.

In Indore, Shmeiki Baba met some students of hotel management, who treated him to a portion of the local dish of *Dal Bafla*, at one of the city's well known street-food vendors. They washed it down with a special, local liquor, distilled from the fragrant flowers of the Mahua tree. Shmeiki Baba got out his knife and scratched a mark on his walking stick, as he did at the end of each day. It was his habit not to count the scratches, but against his wishes, the students counted for him and told him that there were forty-two. They then complained that there wasn't much to do in Indore, and Shmeiki Baba blessed the city that it would be filled with music. Six months later, it so happens that a heavy metal band called 'Nicotine' was formed there.

As he parted ways with the students, Shmeiki Baba saw a traffic policeman moonwalking as he directed traffic. "That's our Mr. Singh," they informed him.

The following day, while meditating on the banks of the River Saraswati next to the Krishnapura Chhatri monument, with its three, domed-shaped pavilions, Shmeiki Baba was interrupted by Dylan, an Irish tourist he vaguely knew from Goa.

"Hi Baba, good to see you, I thought I'd come and offer you some support," said Dylan.

"How on earth did you find me here?" asked Shmeiki Baba.

"Oh you know, I was just passing and heard you were here," answered Dylan.

"Heard from who? And passing Indore? Where to?" asked Shmeiki Baba.

"Oh Baba, your walk is well known now, and I'm on my way to Delhi anyway. I'll be happy to walk with you," offered Dylan.

"I'm sorry Dylan, but I'd like to be alone," said Shmeiki Baba.

"Alone? but you walked from Arambol to Pune with our brother Sebastian," pleaded Dylan.

"I'm sorry Dylan, I just don't want to walk with you," said Shmeiki Baba.

"Am I really such an arse hole?" asked Dylan.

"Well, if you really want to know, yes," said Shmeiki Baba.

"Why is that?" asked Dylan.

"Because most of what you do is a play for credit in the eyes of others," answered Shmeiki Baba.

The two men looked each other in the eye, and something clicked for Dylan.

"My God, you are right baba, please forgive me," he pleaded.

"There is nothing to forgive Dylan," said Shmeiki Baba.

And Shmeiki Baba touched Dylan between the eyes with his thumb, and said, "Dylan, if you really want to walk with me, meet me in Delhi in two weeks, and you may continue with me from there to Dharamshala."

"Fantastic, thank you Babaji," said Dylan, "and I promise you won't regret it."

With that, Shmeiki Baba continued on his way, crossing the Chambal River, a known habitat of crocodiles, which forms the boundary between the states of Madhya Pradesh and Rajasthan. Shmeiki Baba stopped by the side of the river and there he saw a body wrapped in cloth being carried by a group of men towards a funeral pyre. He watched the pyre being lit, and the body becoming engulfed in flames. When the body was already well burned, the son of the man who had died was handed a large stick, which he used to smash the skull of his father in order to release his spirit. "That bit looks like fun," thought Shmeiki Baba.

About ten days later, Shmeiki Baba reached the city of Kota in the Mokandarra Hills, some three hundred kilometres north of Indore. Kota is a city of about a million people and is known for its gardens and palaces. At first, Shmeiki Baba was wary of Rajasthani salesmen famous for their persistence, but later, when he saw his reflection in a shop window, he realized that after walking for so long in the hot sun, he no longer looked like a tourist at all.

In Kota, he saw a beautiful, young couple and felt jealous. His heart longed for a woman, and he felt a powerful stirring in his trousers. He remembered Aida from Arambol and Ilse who he had been with in Pune and he acknowledged that it had been a long time since he had ejaculated. Now, he felt an overriding urge to masturbate, but he was frightened that if he did so, he would slip back into his old addiction. It was then that Sheila spoke to him and reassured him:

Sheila 7

"Shmeiki Baba, it is your sexuality which saved your spirit from becoming broken when you were growing up. Your fantasies are not without meaning, they signal the path you need to follow. Know that the partner you long for will come when the time is right, and until then, it is okay to let off steam if you need to."

On Saturday, April 1st, 2006, Shmeiki Baba was sitting in a forest close to Ranthambore National Park, where the Aravalli and Vindhya Hills meet. The park is famous for its tigers, which Shmeiki Baba wanted to see, though clearly, it was not the right time for a safari. Nevertheless, while he meditated, a large, black cobra appeared from the undergrowth and curled up in front of him, like a rope.

Shmeiki Baba remembered the snake from his vision on Shivaratri and understood that this might be the right time to dive deeper into himself. He said to the snake, "Shall I eat, or rather drink, from the tree of knowledge?" The snake hissed and Shmeiki Baba interpreted this as a yes. He opened the little bottle which Sebastian had given him and drank the contents.

After sitting a long time in a deeply altered state of consciousness, Shmeiki Baba lay down on his stomach and crawled forward, with the intention of giving the cobra a kiss on her head. As he did so, the snake darted towards him and bit him above his lip. The bite felt like an electric shock, and Shmeiki Baba jumped away from the snake in great pain and began to run, but then realized that he had to keep calm, or the poison would spread through his blood even faster. He needed help immediately, but he was alone in a forest. Shmeiki Baba looked around at the trees and the hills. He remembered Sheila and called out to her, "Sheila, I'm sorry, I've blown my mission." But Sheila didn't answer. Shmeiki Baba screamed her name, but she remained silent. He understood that he had to help himself and with this, he calmed down, got out his map, and saw that the closest medical assistance was likely to be at a hospital in the city of Sawai Madhopur. He began to walk there wanting life but accepting death if it should come.

Eventually, extremely weak, he reached the hospital and fell through the doors and into the arms of three nurses who were standing at the reception. He was muttering in delirium that he had been bitten by a cobra, and a Dr Goswami rushed over and began examining him.

When Shmeiki Baba explained that he had been close to Ranthambore National Park when he was bitten and had subsequently walked to the hospital, Dr. Goswami understood that many hours must have passed since the incident. He took Shmeiki Baba's blood pressure, which was high, and noted that Babaji's eyes looked strangely like a snake's. Shmeiki Baba complained that he was thirsty, and the doctor concluded that he was dehydrated and given the lack of other visible symptoms, beyond two small, red holes just over his moustache, he was sure the snake had not injected venom.

"You mean I'm not going to die?" asked Shmeiki Baba.

"Not quite yet," said Dr. Goswami and he invited Shmeiki Baba into a room, to lie down on a bed until he felt recovered. Dr. Goswami brought Shmeiki Baba a bottle of water and encouraged him to drink all of it. "You know," said Dr Goswami, "the snake lives underground, so it's knowledge is hidden and must be uncovered, but only if you are ready. If you are unready, that which is present will still be unknown."

"Indeed," said Shmeiki Baba.

Looking out of the window, he watched a tree moving in the wind. The branches cast dancing shadows in the room, and Shmeiki Baba relaxed and felt blissful to be alive. Finally, Sheila spoke to him and congratulated him for taking his life in his own hands. He forgave her for being silent when he needed her help. She said this was good and she told him that April is to be the Shmeiki Month of Creation, which might be symbolized by tulips, daisies, sweet peas, diamonds, and the element beryllium. With this in mind, Shmeiki Baba got up, thanked Dr Goswami and carried on walking.

He crossed from the state of Rajasthan into Haryana at Karenda. By this point, his feet hurt him terribly and his progress was slow. He had no intention of giving up though. He leaned heavier on his walking stick and accepted the pain. After a number of days and a further seventy kilometres, he entered a scorchingly hot New Delhi.

IV

THE SHMOSPEL OF SHOSHANA

From Delhi to Shimla

I am Shoshana Sher and this is my Shmospel.

Tuesday, April 11th, 2006.

The first time I saw Shmeiki Baba, I was sitting on the second-floor balcony of the Diamond Café, in the backpacker district of Paharganj, trying to concentrate on a newspaper article about Iran succeeding in its attempts to enrich uranium. It had been three days since I'd left Tokyo and snorted my last hit of cocaine. Not that I was an addict, but I had built up some level of dependency and I was feeling a little jittery without it.

It was in this state that I looked down and saw Shmeiki Baba as he walked through the waves of people in the Main Bazaar. He had a beard and wore a ragged sun hat. His feet were bare, his clothes were dusty, and he was carrying a long, knobbly walking stick. Children were dancing around him, vying to hold his free hand. As he passed by, he looked up to where I was sitting and his sparkling, honey-coloured eyes met mine. I looked away, overcome by a flood of sensation.

In the evening, I was walking down the street, feeling a bit lonely, when a beautiful, little girl came up to me. She gave me a red flower and pointed to Shmeiki Baba, who was waving to us from about five metres away. I asked the little girl her name.

"Lakshmi," she said proudly.

"What a lovely name," I said, giving her some sweets I had in my bag, and off she ran back to her mother.

"I think I know you from elsewhere," said Shmeiki Baba, approaching me.

"Where?" I asked.

"Oh elsewhere," he said and suddenly, a man standing behind him tried to insert a poker in his ear. Shmeiki Baba stepped to the side just in time, avoiding the poke. He told the guy where to go, before explaining to me that this was one of the ear cleaning mafia, who trick tourists, by pretending to reveal a huge blob of ear wax, which has supposedly come out of your ear, and this is meant to justify you spending money on having your ears cleaned by them.

"Maybe we'll walk a little together," he said, and I agreed.

"Do you have a sore leg?" I asked him.

"No, it's my feet and my arse that hurt," he replied.

"What's wrong with your feet?" I asked.

"I've been walking a long way," he answered.

"And what's wrong with your butt?" I asked.

"Haemorrhoids," he said.

"They say haemorrhoids are caused by frustration, but you don't look like the frustrated type," I said.

"You'd be surprised," he replied.

"Well, my granddad used to recommend some herbal medicine to treat haemorrhoids, it was called Jerusalem Balsam," I said.

"What's that?" asked Shmeiki Baba.

"I'm not quite sure, but I can check on the net if you like," I said.

"Please do, and I'd also like you to invite me for dinner," he said.

"What, are you a hippie, who's got no money?" I asked.

"Something like that," he said with a cheeky grin.

"Okay," I said, even though we had not yet told each other our names. For a minute we just stood still, looking at one another, amid the beeping horns, the rolling carts, the rickshaws and people jostling past us. The quiet at the centre of the storm was the connection between our eyes.

"What's your name," he finally asked.

"Shoshana," I said.

"Shoshana," he repeated, "and I am Shmeiki Baba."

He suggested I take him to a restaurant called Saravana Bhavan, just off Connaught Place. I agreed and we jumped onto a bicycle rickshaw to get there. He urged the elderly driver to pedal faster. I told him that was cruel and gave his leg a smack. He said he liked it when I told him off. And he kept repeating my name, "Shoshana, Shoshana, Shoshana," which he knew is an old Hebrew song.

"Oh, so you're a good, Jewish boy," I said.

"I guess I used to be," he replied.

Before I met Shmeiki Baba, I'd only occasionally experienced English Jews in Israel. They seemed to apologize a lot and it was kind of hard to know what they were after, and I wondered if the same was so with Shmeiki Baba.

We reached the restaurant and I was surprised by how modern it looked. I allowed Shmeiki Baba to order, as he knew his way around the menu far better than me. We began by sharing a portion of *Dahi Vada*, lentil dumplings covered in yoghurt, flavoured with chilli, ginger, cumin, cashews, and tamarind. It was totally delicious and as we sat opposite each other, I was surprised to see tears of joy in his eyes. As one tear rolled down his cheek, I mopped it up with a serviette, like I had known him for years. There was something in his face and his movements that were deeply familiar to me.

Next, we ate *Rasam*, a spicy lentil soup and *Aloo Bonda*, potato dumplings served with different chutneys. He told me there was a mysterious story about this chain of restaurants. Allegedly, on the advice of an astrologer, the owner had wanted to marry the daughter of one of his employees, but she was already married, so he killed her husband.

"I guess that doesn't stop the food being tasty," I said.

"And what about you?" asked Shmeiki Baba.

I asked him what he wanted to know, and he said, "everything."

I said, "where to start?"

He said, "the beginning."

And so I began to tell him my story, and he looked at me intently.

"I was born in a village near Jerusalem in 1981 into a religious family. I am the youngest of five kids. I have two sisters and two brothers. My father's family is from Poland, and my mother's family is from Morocco, which when I was a kid, was still somewhat unusual. Our childhood was surprisingly innocent given that we lived in a militarized zone. We were brought up to be diligent and obedient, to pray to God and to study, but I was more interested in sports. My parents intended me to enter a religious seminary after I finished school, but against their wishes, I joined the Air Force. The physical and mental training came naturally to me. I kept passing tests and one day after about two and a half years, I found that I was an Apache helicopter pilot. I served for a further three and a half years, during which time, I saw some pretty intense action.

"When I left the Air Force, I was desperate to forget what I had experienced. I wanted to lose myself in the world and I had heard about Israeli girls going to Tokyo, to be hostesses in night clubs, where they got paid large sums of money to hang out with Japanese businessmen. Without stopping to think of a better option, that's what I did. I flew to Tokyo, rented a room in an apartment with some other girls, and soon got a job at an exclusive club. Despite the luxurious décor, it was seedy and there was always a repressed, sexually charged atmosphere, which I did not like, though I did not leave. I guess part of me felt dirty and I wanted to rub my face in my shame. If my parents had known what I was doing in Japan, they would both have had cardiac arrests. Then again, their disappointment in me was already such, that they might not have been so surprised.

"Tokyo was also the first time in my life I became exposed to drugs. I allowed myself to indulge, figuring they might help me spit out some ball of tightness that had been building up inside my heart. Cocaine was regularly offered to me and I began to use it a little too much. That's basically why after two years, I finally decided to leave Tokyo and flew here, with a plan to do a yoga course."

"How long ago was that?" asked Shmeiki Baba.

"Three days ago," I said.

"Ah," said Shmeiki Baba.

I asked Shmeiki Baba what he was doing before he came to India.

He answered, "Not very much. I was a web designer, living with my parents. I was pretty miserable and a lot chubbier than I am now."

"Fat is often a sort of emotional shield," I said.

"I guess so," he replied.

"And what do you want to do now?" I asked.

"I want to complete my great walk," he said.

"What's that?" I asked.

"I am walking from Goa to Dharamshala," he said.

"How far is that?" I asked.

"About two thousand kilometres," he said.

"No way," I said, "and how far have you gone until now?"

"About one thousand, four hundred kilometres," he replied.

"Wow, that's incredible," I said.

"Thanks," he said.

"And who are you walking with?" I asked.

"Well, for the first part, I was with my friend Sebastian, but since

Pune, I've been by myself," he said.

"And how come you have no money?" I asked.

"So I can remember the goodness of people," he said.

"That's amazing, I'd never consider doing anything like that," I said. "Have you thought about what you will do afterwards?"

"I'll spread the word of Shmeiki," he said.

"What's Shmeiki?" I asked.

"It's a new path of spirituality," he replied.

"Oh," I said.

He smiled and didn't elaborate, and I didn't push him.

"So tell me more about where you are from," I said.

"Okay," he said, "and where should I start?"

"Also, at the beginning," I replied.

"Very well," he said. "I was born on January 17th, 1975, at Sefton General Hospital in Liverpool, by planned caesarian section. Because of this, my mum did not go into labour, which meant I did not feel the alarm of impending birth, nor did I experience the struggle of finding my way through the birth canal. I was slipped out directly from her belly into the blinding lights of theatre, by a colleague of my father. Once I was out, my mother was given a hysterectomy, something she repeatedly found the need to tell me about when I was growing up."

"I see, and isn't Liverpool famous as being a working-class city?" I asked.

"Yes, it is," he said.

"You don't strike me as being very working class," I replied.

"I'm not," he said, "which is probably why I like to joke that I'm a tuna fish who grew up in a tree."

"And what does that mean?" I asked.

"It means that I grew up in a minority, inside a minority, inside a minority. You see, in England, if you come from Liverpool, you are already a kind of a minority. Then we were Jewish, which meant we were part of a minority in a minority, and we weren't like the rest of the Jews, we were academic, while most of them were kind of nouveau riche."

"So why did you live there?" I asked.

"I guess my parents enjoyed feeling marginal. Also, Liverpool is where my dad is from and where my grandmother used to live. When my dad was a kid, Liverpool was the biggest port in the world, and his father became successful there, though, by the time I was a child, the city was depressed and better known for strikes and crime. It is one of the few cities where the population actually went down. I grew up surrounded by an atmosphere of anger about the gap between rich and poor, and for this reason, we lived in a degree of fear and that's before you even mention the word *Holocaust*.

"My dad is one of the second generation of immigrants who got themselves educated after the first made money. I'm part of the third generation, who's meant to spend the money. Anyway, dad went to Cambridge to study medicine and afterwards worked as a doctor in London, though in his late thirties he went back to Liverpool, to be close to his parents, something he went on to regret. He has a hunger to be English rather than Jewish, but perhaps because of the same post-war paranoia that many Jews his age are stuck with, he could never quite leave the Jewish thing behind, and he has always felt frustrated by his split identity. Then, of course, he married my mum, a Jew from Manchester, when he was forty-three. Unlike him, she was orthodox. Her family was poor and religious, though more cultured than his. How they didn't foresee what a problem this would be, I don't know. Amazingly, they still live together, though my mother likes to say that it was a mistake for my father to marry a Jew because he despises the Jewish community. When I was growing up, he could only just about tolerate her need to partake in all the *mumbo jumbo*, as he called it.

"Were you closer to your mum or your dad?" I asked.

"My mum, and she was the one to look after us, as dad was mostly at work," he said.

"Did she not work?" I asked.

"She did, she was a primary school teacher," he said.

"Do you have siblings?" I asked.

"Yes, I have one sister called Marion. She is four years older than me and lives in Manchester. When I was a baby I peed on her while my mother was changing my nappy, and I still don't think she has quite forgiven me. To be fair, before I came along, she was a sweet, little girl, who enjoyed undivided attention. After I arrived, she got a lot less attention and had to contend with my mischief. It didn't help our relationship, that our parents used divide and rule tactics on us, to make us easier to control."

"What was it like being a Jew in Liverpool?" I asked.

"Well, being Jewish was about being in a club. You had to do certain things if you wanted membership, which mostly came down to taking part in some empty, religious rituals, which were performed in a language we didn't understand. Given these were a pretext for gathering together for security, no one really cared, and while every Passover we would sing the song, 'next year in Jerusalem,' it never actually happened.

"On Saturdays, mum would dress up my sister and me and take us to the synagogue, while dad would go to work. Until I was about six, we lived too far away to walk, so mum would drive to about half a mile away, park the car, and we would walk the last part of the journey, so no one would see that we had used the car on the Sabbath. On Sundays, we would sometimes go to eat in a Chinese restaurant. There we would watch my dad eating pork. For us, mum would order fish, after checking with the Chinese waiter that the fish had fins and scales that were easily removable, for it to be Kosher."

I couldn't help but laugh.

Shmeiki Baba went on, "both the identities of being English and Jewish were very real for us, and it was like trying to sit on two chairs at once. Maybe this is why my parents were so desperate to fill the gap with high status, fancy cars, and a large house. The one thing they share is a kind of educational and cultural snobbery, which conceals their feelings of inadequacy. Although it was their grandparents who arrived in Britain from Eastern Europe, they still feel like guests, who have to justify their right to exist. It isn't enough for them just to be, they have to be something."

"And what was school like for you?" I asked.

"My parents sent me and my sister to the local Jewish primary school, but continually criticized it. My dad disliked it so much, that he refused to step inside. When it came time for me to go to high school, they sent me to a private boys school called Liverpool College. This was where my dad had also gone to school. And while it was meant to be a school for the sons of Anglo Saxon professionals, they were a dying breed in Liverpool, so it was more a school for the sons of Irish gangsters, Indian and Jewish doctors, and Chinese restaurant owners. Meanwhile, local regulations meant that the school had to accept a considerable percentage of kids, whose parents could not afford to pay the fees. They tended to be much tougher than the rich kids and able to set the tone, which was to laugh at the weak or the different. Now, I was a sensitive, innocent kid, and nowhere near streetwise enough for such a cold and abusive environment. And for some reason, my mum thought it was a good idea to tell me that it wasn't good for a Jewish boy to be seen getting into fights, so when I was inevitably in fights, I would try not to throw punches. I was badly bullied. In fact, so endemic was bullying at Liverpool College, that even some of the teachers were bullied. There was one poor physics teacher, whose nickname was Dobbin. Kids would sometimes throw light bulbs and burning paper aeroplanes at him, while he was writing on the blackboard. Because of all the bullying, for a long time after I left school, I was suspicious of people who were nice to me."

"That sounds dreadful," I said.

"It was. Anyway, how about we have some mango ice-cream?" asked Shmeiki Baba.

We did and it was super tasty. I suggested to Shmeiki Baba that he should come back and sleep in my room, and he agreed. I asked him where he would have slept if he hadn't met me. He answered that he did not know. Given all that he had told me, I asked him how he could be so carefree. He said that walking across India was enough to loosen anyone up. He asked me what I was looking for in India. I answered with one word, "purification." He asked me what from, and I told him, "intoxicants, and anonymous sex."

When we got back to my room, he showered, and oh boy did he need to. After this, his skin was still infused with the spice of his journey. We got into bed, held each other and kissed. In our touch, I could feel both man and boy, wolf and sheep. I realized his fear of surrender in my own.

"I've been waiting for this for a long time," he said.

"Me too," I replied.

We just held each other, neither of us spoke, and we fell asleep in a tight embrace.

Wednesday, April 12th, 2006.

In the morning we were both surprised and delighted to find ourselves still lying in each other's arms.

"Did you sleep well?" he asked.

"Oh yes," I said, "I haven't slept so well in ages."

We began to make love. This was just what I needed, real intimacy. Afterwards, I asked him to tell me about his fantasies. He tensed up and I saw shame flash across his face.

"I find it hard to share," he whispered.

"Why?" I asked.

"I don't want you to think there is something wrong with me," he said.

"What, are you a paedophile or something?" I asked.

"No, of course not," he said.

"Then you're into animals?" I asked.

"No, not them either," he said.

"Well, between consenting adults everything is okay, no?" I

asked.

"Yes, of course," he replied.

"So, there's nothing to be embarrassed about," I said.

"Quite right," he said, "well the truth is, that I don't fantasize about sex, I fantasize about being tied up and whipped, long and hard, by a beautiful woman wearing leather trousers."

I smiled. He still looked embarrassed, and I thought for a while before saying anything.

"Do you think you can be content with someone who doesn't do that for you?" I asked.

"I don't think so," he said.

"Well," I said, "with a fantasy like yours, a woman basically faces an ultimatum - beat you and you're hers, don't beat you and you never really will be. It does make your love rather conditional, and this will likely make your partner feel that she can't just be herself."

"I understand," said Shmeiki Baba looking sad.

"It's okay though," I said, "you have come to the right woman. In time, I can take you in the direction you want to go in."

"Really?" he said, his face brightening.

"Yes," I answered, "but I warn you, if you summon the bitch in me, she will come and you might not like her."

"I think I will cope," he said.

"We shall see, and anyway, for this to be healthy for us both, you will have to be truly devoted to me," I said.

"Of course," said Shmeiki Baba.

"I should tell you also, that while at times I was involved in this type of thing in Tokyo, right now what I'm interested in is simple, beautiful, lovemaking."

"That's cool too, I'm not in a rush," said Shmeiki Baba.

"Good," I said, "you see for me, lovemaking, born from intimacy is at one end of a spectrum, and objectified, sexual fantasy is at the other. At the same time, I understand that when a fantasy is strong, it will not go away by itself, and sometimes it is the door to love."

"I hope so," said Shmeiki Baba.

"Also, while I understand you want to be spanked, I'm not sure you want to be submissive," I said.

"I think I do," he said.

"Okay, but remember that sometimes we strive to get what we want, knowing deep down that when we get it, it won't actually bring us satisfaction," I said.

"I feel I have to take that risk," he answered.

"Okay, so let's take it slowly and see what happens," I said, patting his cheek.

We went to eat breakfast in the guest house's roof cafe. He pulled out my chair for me, and I smiled at his apparent gallantry. While we sat waiting for menus, I looked at the state of his feet, and said, "you could definitely do with a chiropodist."

"Indeed I could, but I guess that can wait until Dharamshala," he answered.

Next to his foot, mine looked immaculate, and my toenails were painted red. Shmeiki Baba slid his feet into my flip-flops and said, "that's the first time I've put one of them on in quite a while."

I asked him why he was walking with no shoes, and he said that walking with shoes is like having sex with a condom on.

"People wear condoms for a reason," I said.

"For more than one reason in fact," he replied.

And on the roof of the building next to us, we watched children playing with kites, which soared above our heads. Shmeiki Baba turned to me and fixed me in his gaze, and I remarked there was something about his look, which reminded me of my grandfather.

Shmeiki Baba told me that he had run into a friend of his from Goa the day before, who had invited him to a house party in the afternoon. He asked me to go with and I said I would be happy to.

After breakfast, Shmeiki Baba wanted to meditate, and I headed down to an internet cafe and on an old computer, I searched for 'Jerusalem Balsam.' I read that the medicine was first made by a 17th Century Italian doctor, who worked in the monastery of Saint Saviour in Jerusalem. I found that it contains the extracts of four plants: frankincense, Arabic gum, myrrh, and aloe vera. I remembered that some of these ingredients are described in the bible as being used to make the incense in Solomon's temple. I also read an article, which reported scientific research suggesting that Jerusalem Balsam truly does have anti-inflammatory properties and promotes vein growth. I wondered where in India we could buy some. I searched but didn't find anywhere, then I realized that all the ingredients are well known, so we could go to an apothecary and ask him to make us some.

When I came back upstairs, I told Shmeiki Baba about what I'd discovered and he agreed to come with me to an apothecary. It so happened, that there was one in walking distance of Paharganj. When we got there, it was an antique-looking shop, with rows of dark green bottles stacked on shelves from floor to ceiling. The owner was a bald, old man, with a big smile and a white coat. I explained what we wanted, and he checked in several pharmacopoeias until he found a recipe for Jerusalem Balsam, which he showed to us in a large, dusty book. He said that he had all the ingredients and would happily make us some. It took less than half an hour for it to be ready, and the apothecary gave Shmeiki Baba the Jerusalem Balsam in a large bottle, telling him to keep it out of the sun. While we were still in the shop, Shmeiki Baba tried it. He said the taste was bitter and spicy, but he could tell that it was going to do him good, and I felt pleased.

We walked back to Paharganj and I made an excuse that I had some things to do before we went to the party. In truth, I was feeling anxious about the emotions that meeting Shmeiki Baba had stirred up in me and I wanted to visit the travel agent, who had offered to get me some coke when I first arrived. So, I gave Shmeiki Baba the key to my room, for him to go and have a rest, while I went to find the agent. He took my money, and gave it to his driver, while I sat in his shop drinking a cup of chai until the driver returned with the stuff. I checked it in the bathroom, and it was okay, though not great. I took another line, and then went back to my room. Shmeiki Baba didn't realize that I was high and I didn't tell him.

We took a taxi to the party. It was at a large, cream coloured villa in the wealthy neighbourhood of Vasant Vihar. There, we were warmly welcomed by Khartiv, who lead us through his luxurious house to his back garden. A dozen or so people were sitting on cushions under a large gazebo. Others were sitting to the side in the shade of an enormous mango tree, laden with fruit. I said that in Hebrew, Khartiv means ice lolly, but he wasn't too impressed by this.

Some of his guests had musical instruments and were playing some heart-warming folk songs. Shmeiki Baba picked up a bamboo flute which was lying on a coffee table and began to play with the other musicians. His notes were sweet and soulful, and like silky ribbons, they wound their way around my heart. Khartiv said he was pleased someone was finally playing the flute, which had been lying unused for years. He wanted Shmeiki Baba to take it.

"You know this is a very good bansuri, I think it is made by one the finest makers in India," said Shmeiki Baba.

"All the more reason for you to keep it," said Khartiv.

"Thank you brother, I gave away my last bansuri, so I accept this one with love," said Shmeiki Baba.

And Shmeiki Baba also began to sing, with one of the guitar players. His voice was like the sound of his flute, though I did not recognize the language he was singing in. When he finished, I asked him, "is that African?"

"West," he said, nodding.

"Where in the west?" I asked.

"*Ulaluku kulubanda,*" he answered, with a serious expression.

"Oh, I see, it is *kishkush balabush,*" I said, waving my finger at him, and for a while, we spoke only in Gibberish, until Shmeiki Baba held his hands up to the sky and said, "Thank you, Great Mother, for guiding me to this wonderful woman."

Khartiv said that he had five tickets to an evening audience with an old, holy woman, and he asked Shmeiki Baba and me to go with. And when the other guests had left the party and we had eaten a light dinner, we set out in Khartiv's jeep, with his girlfriend Sanita and his sister Rhada. His driving was terrible, and I was considering getting out of the car, when Shmeiki Baba made a prayer for our safety, which appeared to do the job, and we arrived at the Oberoi Hotel in one piece.

We were shown to a large suite, where about three hundred people were present. Khartiv said that these were the elite of the old woman's devotees. Many were already sitting on the floor, chanting her seventy-two names in Sanskrit. I asked what some of these mean, and Shmeiki Baba translated them for me as "fatty," "bitch face" and "sagging yoni." Khartiv doubled over in laughter, but I felt uncomfortable with Shmeiki Baba's disrespect. When I told him this, he said, "Come on Shoshana, don't take it too seriously. This is a game, and these people are stupid for thinking she's a goddess, any more than the waitress over there."

"She is a highly evolved human being," said Rhada, "and do you know that she has built hospitals and schools for the poor?"

"Oh yes, she is definitely a helper," said Shmeiki Baba.

"What do you mean by that?" I asked.

Before he could answer, he winced in pain and took my arm, pointing towards a small, empty lounge. We hurried over there and I closed the door behind us. Shmeiki Baba lay down on the ground, and I was amazed and partly terrified when I heard a strange, female voice coming out of his mouth.

Sheila 8

"Your abusive reaction to the power of the old lady and her devoted followers was triggered by your suppressed memories of being betrayed by your own mother.

"Betrayal by the mother is one of the deepest emotional wounds. It shakes your confidence in the world to its foundations. Of course, no mother is perfect and in your case, it is extra tricky because while she promised security, and gave you to believe you had it, at important times she was not able to deliver. Still, it is now time to move on and forgive, it is time to wake up all the places where you are still numbed by trauma and to breathe life into them. Only then will you accept yourself and the world, and realize that nothing is missing, or out of place. Love is a powerful healer, and it is now within your grasp, so do not throw it away."

Shmeiki Baba opened his eyes. He looked at me and tried to smile at the expression of shock on my face.

"I have some explaining to do," he said.

"You're psychotic," I replied.

"Actually, no," he said, and he began to explain to me about Sheila and the teachings of Shmeiki.

I managed to listen to everything, and while his story sounded crazy, I sensed the authenticity in his words and perhaps because I already loved him, and was still a little high, I found myself able to put aside my fears and to accept what he was saying.

"Thank you for telling me," I said, "and now there is something I need to tell you."

"What's that?" he asked.

"I'm high on coke," I said.

"What, now?" he asked.

"Yes," I said.

"Where did you get that from?" he asked.

"From a travel agent in Paharganj," I said.

"I see," he said.

"But you know something, I realize now that I don't need it anymore," I said, and with that, I took out the remainder of the coke from my purse, opened the little baggie and tipped it in the plant pot which was next to us.

"That's going to be a happy plant," said Shmeiki Baba.

"Indeed, and I feel much better now," I said.

"So do I," he said, offering me his hand, and we went back inside the gathering.

People were already queueing up to get their hug, and we joined Khartiv, Sanita, and Rhada in line. Shmeiki Baba apologized for being rude, and Rhada said that it wasn't a problem.

When it was Shmeiki Baba's turn for a hug, the old woman held him for what seemed like an extraordinarily long time, and when they finally parted, both he and the old lady looked flushed and everyone else looked surprised. I was next, but she gave me only the briefest of hugs, just long enough for her to whisper in my ear, "be careful with this one, young lady." I wondered exactly what she meant by this.

Thursday, April 13th, 2006

In the morning, I was surprised not to feel down after taking coke the day before, and over breakfast of muesli, fruit, and curd, I asked Shmeiki Baba to explain to me more about Sheila, and Shmeiki. He did so and I listened, fascinated by what he had to say. As he talked, I felt energy moving inside myself and it was as though, beyond his words, something else was passing through him, into me.

And then he asked, "will you continue the great walk with me?"

I didn't yet understand what it would entail, but I did my best to imagine what it might be like.

"I see us walking hand in hand and other people walking with us," I said.

"Yes, that's a very good idea," he said, "so are you in?"

"Well, walking across India with you, does sound much more interesting than doing a yoga retreat," I said.

"Absolutely," he replied.

"What about your sore feet?" I asked.

"They are already better," he said.

"Good, but there's no way I'm coming without shoes and money," I said.

"That's okay," he replied, "anyway, your funds might come in handy."

"Don't *shmuck* the *shnipple*," I said.

"And don't use Shmeiki against Shmeiki Baba," he said.

We were interrupted by an Eastern European woman, dressed in a light blue sari, who introduced herself as Masha. She asked us to make a donation to the temple that her yoga teacher was building in Rishikesh in honour of his deceased guru. We politely refused and Masha asked, "but what about the spiritual revolution?" as though by failing to donate, we were failing in our duty to mankind.

Shmeiki Baba answered Masha, "imagine a spin door, it revolves, yes?"

"Yes," she agreed.

"So be careful of revolutions," said Shmeiki Baba, "or by definition, you might end up where you started."

"Okay, so, maybe just ₹ 100 then?" she persisted.

And Shmeiki Baba stroked his beard and said, "you know that not every man with a long beard has holy intentions."

"I'll bear that in mind," said Masha, walking to the next table.

Shmeiki Baba turned back to me and asked, "so will you really come with me?"

I looked into my heart and the answer was a definite yes.

"I will," I said.

"Thank the Great Mother," said Shmeiki Baba.

After breakfast, Shmeiki Baba let it be known around the guest house that he was inviting people to join us on the great walk, and those who were interested should meet us at five PM in the rooftop cafe.

That afternoon, there were six people sitting at a table, waiting for us when we arrived. The atmosphere was warm and friendly as we each introduced ourselves to one another. There was Crispin from England, who had blond dreadlocks and was dressed in a cream *kurta*, a long Indian shirt, which reached down to below his knees. There was Simon, a lawyer from America, who had dark skin and a dry sense of humour. Like me, he had Israeli blood, but he grew up in New York. There was the charming Kamal also from England, a guitarist, who played in a gipsy band. There was Genevieve, a jewellery designer from Belgium. She was tall, thin and glamorous and had a distant look in her eye, like she had peered down a K-hole or two. Mai Ling looked energetic, healthy and had a round symmetrical face, with a button nose and long, dark hair. She was born in Shanghai but moved to Melbourne, Australia when she was six. Shmeiki Baba asked her if she worked in direct marketing. She said this was an old joke and in fact, she was a software engineer. And then there was Dylan, an attractive Irishman, with tribal tattoos on his arms. He already knew Shmeiki Baba and seemed very appreciative to be allowed to go on the walk. When it came to my turn to introduce myself, I held back my desire to say, "my name is Shoshana, I like to shoot missiles from helicopters and to snort cocaine."

Everyone was excited about the plan to walk the six hundred kilometres to Dharamshala, and there were lots of questions for Shmeiki Baba.

"How have you managed to walk without taking money?" asked Crispin.

"People are generous," said Shmeiki Baba.

"Weren't you frightened of walking out into the unknown with no backup?" asked Kamal.

"Well," answered Shmeiki Baba, "at the beginning, I had my friend Sebastian with me, and he was a great support. After we parted ways in Pune, the going got much harder, and yes, I was frightened and I did become desperate, but somehow I got through it."

"What things do you suggest we take with us?" asked Mai Ling.

"Plastic sheeting," said Shmeiki Baba.

"What else?" she asked.

"Plastic sheeting," he said.

"No really, what else?" she asked.

"Plastic sheeting," he said again.

"Shmeiki Baba," I said in a parental tone.

"Sorry, just joking," said Shmeiki Baba.

"Shmeiki Baba is a bit frightened of Shoshana," said Simon.

"For good reason," said Shmeiki Baba. "Just remember friends, that whatever you take with you, you will need to carry, and whatever you need along the way, you can also acquire. "

"What about tents?" asked Mai Ling.

"I'd say that right now, they won't be necessary, but once we get into the mountains, it will definitely get colder, especially at night and we may need them. But again, whatever we need, we can get along the way. My only request right now, is please do not bring any cameras," said Shmeiki Baba.

"Why not?" asked Genevieve disappointed.

"Sheila's orders," said Shmeiki Baba.

"Who's Sheila?" asked Genevieve.

"I'll get to that later," said Shmeiki Baba.

We promised not to bring cameras and agreed that we would leave the next morning from outside the guest house. And with that, everyone went off to get prepared. Not surprisingly, I felt apprehension, but I did my best to put this aside and I went to pack a small rucksack with only the bare essentials, putting the rest of my belongings in the bag storage at Hare Rama Guest House.

Friday, April 14th, 2006.

We got up at six and ate a light breakfast. Shmeiki Baba knelt in front of me, to help me put on my climbing boots, and I went to settle the bill.

By seven, the others were all at the entrance of the guest house ready for departure. Khartiv and Rhada had come to see us off. Khartiv gave Shmeiki Baba a beautiful, purple pouch. Shmeiki Baba opened it and took out a clear stone.

"Why, thank you brother," said Shmeiki Baba, hugging Khartiv.

"Well, you did say that diamonds are for April," said Khartiv.

"Majestic," said Crispin.

We all said goodbye to Khartiv and Rhada, and began our walk north from Paharganj, up Qutab Road, joining Zorawar Singh Marg, which becomes Lala Jagan Nath Marg, then Karnal Road, and finally, we hit the NH44, the main trunk road which would lead us north out of Delhi. By mid-morning, the heat was already intense and the traffic, pollution, and sheer number of people so overpowering, that the only option was to surrender to it.

At one point, the pavement narrowed for road works and a man walking in the other direction, touched Genevieve's breast as he passed her. She was extremely angry and shouted at him, "*madarchod,*" which means mother fucker in Hindi, and he ran off. Genevieve then burst into tears. We comforted her and gradually she calmed down. Finally, Genevieve explained that the incident was all the more upsetting because it triggered memories of her being molested by her uncle.

"Can I ask you something about it?" I said.

"Yes," she said.

"Did you tell your parents about what your uncle did?" I asked.

"Only once I was an adult," said Genevieve, "but they didn't believe me and I haven't spoken with them since."

"If I may, I would like to share something with you," I said.

"Please do," she said.

"When I was a child, I was molested by the rabbi of my family's community, and I chose to keep quiet about it. I still feel guilty to the others he was able to hurt because I stayed silent. Later in the air force, I was also sexually harassed by my commanding officer."

Shmeiki Baba asked, "is the rabbi still a rabbi?"

"No," I replied, "he died in a terrorist attack."

"And what about the army officer?" asked Shmeiki Baba.

"I'm not sure, I think he's still in his job," I said.

"Maybe, it's not too late to do something about him," said Shmeiki Baba.

"Yes," I said, "maybe the time has come. The irony is, that the reason I become a pilot was to compensate for my sense of shame that I am the sort of person who doesn't hold abusers to account. And it was during my training that I was abused again, and once more I remained silent. While it drove me even harder to succeed, it also broke something inside me."

"I completely understand," said Genevieve.

I was surprised to find myself bearing my soul in front of a group of people I barely knew, but I guessed this was the effect of new love and of taking myself out of my comfort zone.

By midday, black muck came out of my nose when I blew it, and meanwhile, the heat was baking us. Shmeiki Baba reassured us that once we were out of the city, things would get a lot easier. Mai Ling tired and Dylan took her bag. Seeing this, Shmeiki Baba offered to carry mine and I let him. He made me feel beautiful and special, and he let me be me. I held his hand and felt a strong current passing between us.

Kamal offered around water, which he said was infused with *tulsi* extract and *ashwagandha*, which is Indian ginseng. He said this would give us energy and it did. Kamal had a big heart and buckets of charisma. While he was fun and friendly, I also sensed he was someone who cleverly avoided showing his vulnerability.

I admired Crispin's large, blue, opal necklace, which he said he bought in the city of Jaipur. He was also carrying a *trishula*, a metal trident, like the one wielded by Lord Shiva. I noticed that when Crispin spoke, he used a different type of English than Shmeiki Baba and the other English people. He also talked a lot about reggae music, describing songs as "fresh," and being played by "epic selectas."

I asked him what were *epic selectas.*

"Cool DJs," he answered.

"Basically, Crispin is a white, English Jamaican," explained Simon.

"*Ye man,*" said Crispin.

"Have you ever been to Jamaica?" asked Shmeiki Baba.

"Not yet," said Crispin.

"And how come you don't sound like you're from Liverpool?" asked Crispin of Shmeiki Baba.

And Shmeiki Baba replied, "When I was a kid, I did have a little bit of a Liverpool accent, and my mum would say to me, 'if you come home from school talking like that, you'll never get a job.' I guess she didn't realize that if you bring up your kids in Liverpool, there's a good chance they won't actually want to get a job."

Each time we passed a temple, Crispin banged his djembe and sang '*Hare Govinda Mahana He.*' Mai Ling, Dylan, and Genevieve joined in. In the afternoon, when they began the bhajan for about the fifth time, Shmeiki Baba turned to them and said, "why not look inside yourselves and find your own songs, which are waiting to be shared with existence. Om Shmeiki."

"What does *Om Shmeiki* mean?" asked Mai Ling.

"I usually say Om Shmeiki when I feel a sudden rush of bliss, or when I feel nausea from false displays of spirituality, and also when I'm simply not sure of what else to say," said Shmeiki Baba.

Mai Ling talked about her childhood. She said she felt like an outsider growing up in Melbourne. She also described being bullied at school and feeling invisible. She said she liked Indians because they are warm, and I felt my heart begin to open to her. Then she brought up the subject of her irritable bowel syndrome and Genevieve offered to cure it with crystals of chrysoprase and orange calcite. Mai Ling talked in glowing terms about her yoga teacher in

Melbourne and how good he was at holding space.

"I'm trying to work out why the phrase 'holding space' annoys me so much," said Shmeiki Baba.

"And do you have an answer?" I asked.

"Maybe I believe that space isn't something you can really hold," he said.

Mai Ling reassured him that it was.

Crispin said that his kundalini rose during a vision quest in Ibiza. Genevieve said hers rose during a Theta Healing workshop at the Sanctuary in Ko Pha Ngan. Dylan explained that he had learned special meditations at a monastery in Ladakh. Mai Ling wanted to know the name of the monastery, Dylan was evasive.

Finally, Shmeiki Baba snapped. "Bloody hell," he said, "haven't any of you heard the phrase *spiritual bypassing?*"

"No, what's that?" asked Crispin.

"Spiritual seekers do spiritual bypassing when they use beliefs about attainment in their practice, to kid themselves that they've got there, while really avoiding unresolved emotional issues. That's what you are doing with your bullshit stories, and that's why they stand between you and the direct experience of existence. The deepest truth any of us can own is 'I don't fucking know what this great, big mystery is all about.'"

"That's a bit harsh," said Mai Ling.

"Yes," I agreed.

The angry look on Shmeiki Baba's face changed to his frightened one, and he lay down on the ground and clutched his bottom in pain, just like he had done at the hotel. There were concerned looks from everyone in our group as well as from some passers-by. I reassured them, "don't worry friends, Shmeiki Baba is about to receive a transmission."

Sheila 9

And Sheila began to speak:

"Shmeiki Baba, before you left Delhi, did you offer your friends guidelines about your various likes and dislikes? No, you didn't. The only thing you mentioned, was my request about not bringing cameras. The rest, you assumed, they would guess and when inevitably they did things you didn't like, you felt embarrassed to say so straight away, and instead, you built up resentment until you popped.

"Let's try to unwrap this. When you were a child and your father would slurp his soup loudly at the dinner table, there was no way out, you were trapped and unable to avoid the frustration, so you did what you could - you learned to enjoy it, and while you clenched your fists and boiled in silent fury, you also waited expectantly for the next slurp. This was easier than to acknowledge the deeper pain caused by his inability to see you. Today, it remains enjoyable to get upset with others, rather than risking vulnerability by voicing your boundaries clearly. This is an unhealthy game and one that no longer serves you because you do have a choice now. Please state your limits honestly, as only this will bring harmony to you and your group."

Shmeiki Baba opened his eyes and sat up on his knees. Crispin, Genevieve, Dylan and Mai Ling looked spellbound and they kneeled down with Shmeiki Baba and all hugged at the side of the road.

"I will try not to talk any more spiritual crap," said Crispin.

"Me too," said Mai Ling.

When they stood up, Genevieve asked, "this entity you were channelling, Sheila, is she female?"

"Well, Sheila is an A.I singularity sent to us by Kwe, the Shagasomin, on the behest of the Great Mother, and while she sounds like a woman, she is neither man nor woman," said Shmeiki Baba.

And on we walked. Crispin and Kamal were the first to complain about chaffing, or *scrot rot* as they called it. Crispin knew that cider vinegar helped to treat this and he stopped at a western looking shop to buy some, and it did seem to help them.

In the afternoon, when we were already completely frazzled, we walked past an old man, who was sitting on the ground begging. The lenses of his glasses were so old and scratched that they were almost opaque. He had leprosy and was holding out his hand, which had stumps, where there ought to be fingers. I could not imagine what his life was like and I wanted to give him some money, but I didn't want to risk touching him. Shmeiki Baba saw my dilemma, took some money from me and gave it to the old man. He also gave him a long, warm hug.

"I hope you are not thinking of touching me now," I said.

We reached the very northern outskirts of Delhi. Simon calculated we had walked nearly thirty kilometres. Shmeiki Baba said that this was an excellent first day, and suggested we camp in a park. When we found one and sat down, I peeled off my shoes and noticed I already had blisters, as did everyone else, apart from Shmeiki Baba. We were all too tired to cook, so Dylan offered to go to buy food for us. After a long while, he came back with samosas, bananas, Leys chips, mango flavoured Mazah juice and club soda. "Oh, these are times of plenty," rejoiced Shmeiki Baba, at our sugary, oily dinner. By itself, the Mazah was far too sweet but watered down with soda, it tasted quite good.

Shmeiki Baba took his knife and scratched a line on his walking stick. He explained that he added a scratch at the end of every day. I asked how many scratches there were, and he said that he wasn't going to count until the end of his great walk, and he asked us not to count for him as some students had insisted on doing in the city of Indore.

Afterwards, I lay in Shmeiki Baba's arms, looking at the moon, reflecting on the great miracle, and smiling to myself how much my life had changed in such a short space of time.

Saturday, April 15th, 2006

We set off early, before the heat of the day.

"You walk a bit strangely, what's that about?' asked Genevieve.

"It's a long story," said Shmeiki Baba,

"Well, we do have time," I said.

"Okay," said Shmeiki Baba. "At the age of fourteen, I started getting pain down the backs of my thighs, when running or walking. The pain got worse and with a degree of impatience, my parents arranged for me to see an orthopaedic doctor they knew.

"I remember the evening we went to see him in his consulting room. I undressed for him to examine me, and he immediately noticed a scoliosis in my spine and sent me for an x-ray. I can still see the look of shock on his face, as he inspected the x-ray. I felt the blood rushing out of my head, as he said I had a very serious condition called spondylolisthesis. It turned out that my L5-S1 vertebrae were not correctly held together and had slipped apart. At that point, the slippage was at about fifty per cent, and this was putting tension on my spinal cord, which is why I was getting nerve pain down my legs. The doctor suggested that given the gravity of my case, I would need a series of surgeries to bring my spine back in line and I would need to lie in bed for twelve to eighteen months in full traction. This, in his opinion, was the only way to avoid paralysis. I felt like one of the kids afflicted with dreadful, life-threatening conditions, whom I'd seen featured in frightening, TV documentaries. It was like a rug being suddenly pulled out from under my feet. I felt like I was in a daze, and when we got home, I went to tell my dad what the doctor had said. He didn't believe me until mum came into the house and confirmed it.

"Dad read up on the condition and was not happy with the course of action suggested by the first doctor. He promised that he would get me another opinion, and a few days later, we drove down to London to see a surgeon at a clinic on Harley Street. My father had studied with him at university. He was an upper class, Englishman, the sort my dad felt the need to impress. He said there was no need to try to pull my spine back in line and suggested fusing the vertebrae together as they were, with a bone graft from my hip. We agreed he would operate that summer in London. I was growing fast, which was making the situation worse, and while I waited for the surgery, the pain shooting down the backs of my thighs continued to worsen and while I was now wearing a back brace, I could no longer walk more than about fifty metres, without needing to sit down.

"The plus side was that at school I was suddenly untouchable and could no longer be physically bullied, although they called me Chrissy Waddle, after the Liverpool football player, because of the way I had begun to walk. The teachers were actually rather kind and they did their best to stop people from bullying me, and they let me do my own thing. This meant that there was one rule for the whole school and another for me. At home as well, there was no longer any encouragement for me to tidy up or to look after myself. My parents felt guilty about my situation and I played on it.

"I was operated on that summer at a fancy hospital and as planned, the surgeon took bone from my hip and grafted it onto my spine to fuse it. Months passed but my symptoms didn't change, and the answer to the question of whether the graft had taken, gradually turned to a no. Meanwhile, the slip between my vertebrae was continuing to increase, and the surgeon seemed to lose patience, realizing that his procedure hadn't worked.

"Despite not being able to walk, I was surprisingly able to ride a bicycle, sitting on the seat, and this was a saving grace. People told me how brave I was, but I was terrified I would lose the ability to walk. I remember screaming at my dad, 'do something' and he shouted back, 'what do you want me to do?' 'Well you're the fucking doctor,' I yelled. We went to see a couple of other orthopaedic surgeons, who by this stage, were not sure what to do. More than a year passed like this, and then, I can't remember how, but it was my mum who found a surgeon called Cobb, who we went to see in Nottingham.

"By then, my spondylolisthesis had gone from a grade three to a grade four, meaning seventy-five per cent slippage, and my spine had nearly become inoperable. Still, Mr. Cobb was optimistic that he would succeed in fixing it, and he performed a second surgery in the summer holidays when I was seventeen. He wasn't messing around. He approached my spine through both sides of my body, putting bone graft from my hip between my vertebrae and screwing the whole thing together with titanium screws. After the operation, my body was encased in plaster, and I was like that for three months. Apparently, to attempt such a surgery at that time, was remarkable.

"And the amazing thing was, that when they took the plaster off, I had a good scratch and realized that I could walk without feeling any pain at all. Mr. Cobb had saved me. He was my guardian angel. I was elated, and a few days later, I was on a plane to Ibiza, with some people I knew from London, and there I danced drunk in a nightclub full of foam, vomited and just carried on dancing. Still, while my back was fixed, no one stopped to ask about my head. I guess PTSD was still a newish concept back then.

"In the meantime, I had the final year of school to complete and I was desperate to escape. I was also still a virgin, and hungry not to be. 'Find 'em, feel 'em, fuck 'em, and forget 'em,' was the advice my father gave to me when it came to women. Good one dad. He was also putting pressure on me that I needed to go to Oxford or Cambridge to study law. It was an obsession for him. He'd put the same pressure on my sister and also caused her a lot of grief. I did what he wanted though and I applied to the same college he had gone to at Cambridge. I got offered a place, but it was conditional of me getting high grades in my A- levels. In the end, I failed to get one of the grades by a long way. My dad went nuts and called me an idiot. I wasn't pleased, to say the least."

"Did you go to university?" asked Kamal.

"Yes, I did languages at Bristol," said Shmeiki Baba.

"What was that like?" asked Kamal.

"I met girls called Sophie and boys called Tom who had double-barrelled surnames, wore cricket jumpers and boat shoes, and drove Volkswagen Golfs. Given that I had grown up in Liverpool, this was quite a shock, and I wanted to be like them. Externally, I was loud and arrogant, but this was obviously a compensation. And because of what had happened with my back, I didn't really have much of a sense of direction or future. The first girl I had sex with was during fresher's week. Her name was Samantha. I didn't have the guts to tell her I was a virgin and while I fumbled around disappointingly, she told me that her father didn't like Jews. Apart from sex, the main thing I discovered at university was weed. It didn't help me to get out of my ivory tower, but it did begin to open my mind and put me on a path towards anarchism," said Shmeiki Baba.

"What about after university?" asked Crispin.

"When my studies finished, I was super ambitious," answered Shmeiki Baba. "After flirting with journalism, I decided I wanted to make it big in advertising. I wanted to be rich and successful, I wanted dad's respect, but I found I couldn't take my time to climb the ladder, like my peers, I wanted to be the boss immediately. I wanted to feel I had done it my way, but I was so disconnected from myself, and I'd been pushed so hard, that my wheels were spinning too fast to gain traction. So like this, I went from one thing to the next, without sticking at anything, and until recently, I was still struggling to make it as a freelance web designer. Secretly, I longed to be a writer, but I didn't dare. I was a victim, and like many victims, I didn't believe I deserved success. During all this time, my parents kept giving me money, partly due to their guilt about the way they had handled my back condition, and partly because it gave them a sense of power to feel they had a job to do in looking after their incapable son. The money was nearly enough that I didn't need to work, but it was not quite enough, so I was always in a kind of limbo, and I didn't have the presence of mind to be able to say no to their handouts. I felt that I deserved recompense and I enjoyed being angry that what I was given was never enough. It was a very unhealthy game."

"What changed it?" I asked.

"In the autumn of last year, I watched a Louis Theroux documentary about India and I just knew that's where I needed to go. The next day, I applied for a visa and against my parents' advice, I flew to Mumbai a week later on a one-way ticket. And now, here we are."

"Indeed we are," said Kamal.

"Thank God," I said, taking Shmeiki Baba's hand.

And on we walked. By now, the weather was boiling hot, but we persisted. It was a difficult and exhausting day, as was the next day and the day after, but we were determined. And as each day passed, we grew a little stronger, and the going got a little easier. We talked less, but communicated more, and whenever possible, we walked in the shade of trees, which lined sections of the NH44, until we were able to leave the road completely and join footpaths, which linked villages running north. To this end, Simon's GPS was invaluable.

Tuesday, April 18th, 2006

In the late afternoon, we took a rest under some eucalyptus trees, bathing our eyes in the scene which was unfolding before us, as a farmer and his son ploughed their field, using a rebellious white ox, while in the next field, a group of brightly dressed women sang joyfully, as they stacked bales of hay.

Filled with this pastoral glory, Genevieve announced, *"Mon Dieu*, India is so *'oly."*

"Whole world is holy, madame," said Shmeiki Baba.

"Whole world is 'oly, but India is more 'oly," answered Genevieve.

"A pretty fairytale," said Shmeiki Baba.

"Why a fairytale?" asked Genevieve.

"The difference between sacred and profane exists only in our minds," said Shmeiki Baba, "by itself, India just is."

"That may be so, but it has a spirit and I think it is 'oly," insisted Genevieve.

"I think I know why you think India is holy," said Shmeiki Baba teasingly.

"And why is that?" asked Genevieve.

"Because, beyond the culture, the colours, the sounds, and the smells, in India, you get to experience what it's like to be ten times richer than you are back home," said Shmeiki Baba.

"Sometimes, I'm not sure when you're joking," said Genevieve.

"Sometimes, I'm joking and not joking at the same time," said

Shmeiki Baba.

"You can be such a *shtutnik,*" I said.

We camped close to a river, which Kamal went to investigate and returned already wet, saying, "it's kind of clean."

"Wash these," I said to Shmeiki Baba, passing him my dirty laundry. Without saying a word, he took my clothes and went to the river.

"Now, there's a man who knows how to treat his woman," said Mai Ling, watching from the side.

Wednesday, April 19th, 2006

Around lunchtime, we reached the city of Ambala, which lies on the border of the states of Haryana and Punjab, and there we passed an air force base. A Mil Mi-8 helicopter flew low overhead. Hearing this, my heart started to beat faster and my face felt flushed. I got that familiar, dry, metallic taste in my mouth, and my hands started trembling. If there had been coke around, I would definitely have reached for some. Instead, I stopped and asked Shmeiki Baba to hold me, which he did, and I felt his calming energy spread through my body.

We were hungry and stopped outside a restaurant, whose walls were painted with red swastikas and stars of David. I commented on how strange this looked to me.

"For Hindus, the clockwise swastika symbolizes the sun, and it is a sign of kindness and good fortune, while the counter-clockwise symbol is called the *sauvastika,* and this symbolizes night and the tantric aspects of Kali," said Shmeiki Baba.

"I do love it when you preach," I said.

Shmeiki Baba licked his lips, and continued, "in India, the star of David is called the *shatkona.* The downward triangle is called the *Om,* it symbolizes the *shakti* or female principle, and the upward triangle is called the *Hrim* and it represents Shiva, or the male principle. Together, they represent creation and symbolize man's position between earth and sky."

"How do you know all this?" asked Simon.

"Ah," said Shmeiki Baba, "I've been reading Kamal's Lonely Planet."

"Didn't you say that knowledge is ignorance?" asked Kamal.

"I did, and hypocrisy is sometimes a tasty dish," said Shmeiki Baba.

"I wonder if we will get sick from eating here," said Mai Ling.

"In general, I'd say we have much less chance of getting sick if we eat in restaurants where the owners and staff are cheerful and welcome us. If there is a weird mood, or something feels wrong, it's best not to wait to find out," said Shmeiki Baba.

In this case, the staff welcomed us very warmly and I asked to see the kitchen, and the owner was delighted to show me. It wasn't spotless, but it was certainly clean.

We ate *methi gajar*, an aromatic carrot and fenugreek dish, and *kadhi*, a thick, sour gravy made with yoghurt, which had *pakoras*, vegetable fritters, floating in it. We mopped it all up with *besan masala roti*, a type of flatbread stuffed with spices, and washed it down with *nimbu pani*, otherwise known as lemonade. For dessert, we ate *kheer*, the local rice pudding.

While we sat digesting, Crispin did a deal with the cook and swapped his djembe for a large, aluminium pan, which he said he could both drum on and use to make a big pot of chai every evening, for whoever wished. Then he wrapped his dreadlocks into a cake, and secured them with some hairpins which Genevieve gave him. Next, he put all his belongings in the pan, and lifted it onto his head, and practised walking around the restaurant, which he was able to do with surprisingly little effort.

"Let's see how long you last like that," said Simon.

Genevieve got permission to use the kitchen and she made cakes with millet and crunchy Auroville Spirulina. She intended us to eat these for dinner and explained that people living on lake Chad in Africa have been eating nutritious cakes like these for thousands of years.

Simon noticed that the alcohol shop next door had a sign which said "child beer."

"Do they let children drink here?" asked Mai Ling.

"I think they mean *chilled* beer," said Dylan.

The shopkeeper was a large man, wearing a pink turban and heavy rimmed spectacles, and his skin was yellowed from years of heavy drinking. Crispin called him over and told him about the spelling mistake. The shopkeeper answered, *"saanu ki,"* with a smile and an amiable wave of his hand. Crispin asked him what this meant, and he said, "it is Punjabi for 'what does it matter to us'?"

Thursday, April 20th, 2006.

At the end of six difficult days, we had walked nearly two hundred kilometres and were getting close to Chandigarh, the Indian city planned by the Swiss-French architect and artist Le Corbusier. Among other things, Chandigarh is famous for its tidy streets and well-maintained gardens. We make camp on some flat, empty land to the south of the city, and after a while, a group of Rajasthani circus performers came and made their camp about a hundred metres from us. They had a bear with them, who was chained up and one of the men began to beat the bear with a stick.

Soon after, Crispin went over to the circus performers with some cups of chai. To my surprise, he sat with them while they drank and then came back to us with a guilty look on his face. He told us that he had put ground valium pills in their tea, with the intention of setting the bear free, once they had fallen asleep.

"You could have consulted us first," complained Simon.

"Yes, and didn't you stop to think about what they're going to do when they wake up?" shouted Shmeiki Baba.

"No," said Crispin, "I just want to rescue the bear."

"How do you know the bear won't attack us when you free him?" asked Genevieve.

"Come on, you can see he's a total cutey," answered Crispin.

"Are you experienced with bears?" asked Simon.

"No, I'm not," said Crispin, "but I can see he's gentle."

"You are probably right about that," said Kamal.

"We should leave immediately," said Genevieve.

"Who wants to wait with me until the circus performers are asleep, and release the bear?" asked Crispin.

Kamal, Dylan, Mai Ling, and Shmeiki Baba raised their hands.

"Who thinks we should leave right away?" asked Genevieve.

Simon, Genevieve and I raised our hands.

"*The stays* have it," said Crispin, "but the question is, how do *the goes* feel about it?"

"Well, I'm used to putting my own life in front of other animals," said Simon, "but for some reason, this time, I guess I'm willing to make an exception."

And Genevieve said, "okay, you crazy bastards, let's do it."

And everyone turned to me.

"I will also stay," I said.

"It's okay," said Shmeiki Baba, seeing my reticence, "I will protect you."

"And how will you manage to do that?" I asked.

"With love," he answered.

I asked Crispin if he had any valium left, but he said he put it all in the chai.

We waited until the circus performers had fallen fast asleep, and as planned, Crispin went over and released the bear from his chain. He encouraged the bear to run away, but the bear didn't listen and followed him back to our group.

"Run away, Mr. Bear," urged Shmeiki Baba when Crispin reached us, but the bear sat down next to us. The rest of us also encouraged the bear to run away, but he refused to move. By now, we were eager to get going and were about to do so, when Simon said, "I think we should leave some money for the circus performers, so they won't feel too bad about losing their bear."

"They deserve to lose him," said Mai Ling.

"But maybe they don't realize that what they are doing is wrong," said Simon, and he ran over and left some money for them under a stone.

When he returned, Genevieve asked how much he had left and Simon said, "three thousand rupees."

Kamal offered to split this with him, and so did Dylan.

And we began to walk, but we still could not persuade Mr. Bear to leave us.

"Okay, Mr. Bear, if it is your will, you can join our group," said Shmeiki Baba.

"Mr. Bear, just please don't eat us," said Genevieve.

"He's gentle," said Crispin.

"Yes, I heard you," said Genevieve.

Simon looked at the map with his head torch and suggested that to throw the circus performers off our track, we were best heading into Chandigarh. We agreed this was the wisest option and we began to walk north through the city. Mr. Bear continued to follow us. Luckily, in the dark, few people noticed our large, new friend.

Friday, April 21st, 2006.

After midnight, we reached a wealthy area of the northern suburbs of Chandigarh, known as Sector 4. Here, we felt confident that the circus performers would not find us and we camped in a secluded park, enclosed by trees. We ate and fed Mr. Bear, and Mai Ling put some cream on his wounds.

When we awoke in the morning, Mr. Bear was still with us, and he was already looking better than when we'd found him. We set off quickly, with the intention of walking through the forests east of Chandigarh in the direction of the town of Pinjore. However, while still in Sector 4, Shmeiki Baba stopped at a fountain next to a strip of modern shops. Despite our eagerness to make distance between us and the circus performers, Shmeiki Baba insisted he must sit down next to the fountain because Sheila needed to transmit to him some information.

"Don't you think Mr. Bear sticks out?" I asked.

"Try to conceal him, please," said Shmeiki Baba.

"What with? He's enormous," I said.

Luckily, Mr. Bear seemed to understand our problem and he walked behind the shops to the dustbins at the back of Barrister Coffee, where he was able to rummage through the rubbish, hidden from passers-by.

Shmeiki Baba sat down and meditated on the sign of the coffee shop, whispering to himself. Dylan and Crispin joined him in meditation, while I played a game of backgammon with Simon. Mai Ling tried to read her book on Iyengar Yoga, while some local men decided they would like to read her book with her. Mai Ling explained to them that this made her feel uncomfortable, but they were undeterred until Simon stepped in.

After about ten minutes, Shmeiki Baba began to move in strange, contorted ways, making bizarre sounds and dribbling on himself, as though he was having some kind of seizure.

"Shmeiki Baba, what's wrong?" I asked.

He stopped moving and said, "Don't worry darling, there's nothing wrong, I'm just doing *Shmutoh.*"

"And what's that?" I asked.

"It is a Shmechnique for releasing the need to be seen to do the right thing," he said.

Shmeiki Baba continued rolling around, twisting his body into different positions, until a security guard came over to inquire if he needed help. Kamal explained that Shmeiki Baba was doing a type of dance, but the security guard answered that this was not a suitable place for that type of thing. We agree to leave, though Mr Bear was still eating his way through the contents of the bins and was unwilling to stop until we bribed him with a bag of warm onion bhajis. At last, we got on our way and felt safer when we reached the forest.

Saturday, April 22nd, 2006.

Shmeiki Baba woke us before dawn and said:

"When we witness both a day's sunrise and sunset, our minds fall more easily into rhythm with the pulse of the Great Mother." With these words, we got up and watched the sunrise through the trees, and an appreciation of the miracle of existence radiated through me.

"Yesterday," said Shmeiki Baba, "you saw me practising Shmutoh. Today, before we start our walk, maybe we can practice a little together."

Surprisingly, everyone was willing to give it a go.

"Good," said Shmeiki Baba, "let's begin by sitting in a *shmircle*. Now, let's close our eyes and take a few slow, deep breaths, in through our noses and out through our mouths, as we bring our focus to our toes, giving them a quick wiggle and our knees as well. Let's also bring our attention to our hearts and feel them opening wider, as we welcome in the world and express outwards our love. Now, I'd like to tell you that Shmutoh is a dance, which works in a number of ways. First, it connects us to our instincts and to the natural intelligence of our bodies. It also releases us from caring how we look to others and allows us to access parts of our being, which may lie hidden. So, in this first exercise, we will make funny movements with our arms and faces, yes, just like that, that's great Kamal. Move from your breath, exploring every possibility, wonderful. Now, let's use our voices too. Express everything, let it all out, and now, allow your bodies to move where they need to, and yes, allow contact with others if you like."

Slowly, we coiled around each other on the soft pine needle carpet of the forest, I felt playful and full of life, and soon I no longer knew what was my body and what was not.

After some time, Shmeiki Baba brought us back to this world and after a quick breakfast of chai and banana porridge, we began to walk. In the afternoon, we reached Pinjore on the Kaushalya River and we stopped at the dam, to rest and watch the many birds. From here, we could also see what Dylan informed us were the Sivalik hills. "They are the foothills of the Himalayas," he said.

Some children approached us and asked us about our bear. We explained that he was not our bear, he was his own bear and he was choosing to walk with us. They stroked Mr. Bear, and he seemed so happy. We left the children with some pens and continued on our way, crossing into the state of Himachal Pradesh by the industrial town of Parwanoo. There, we began a steep climb along forest roads in the direction of the village of Sanwara. As we made camp outside the village, Mr Bear came to each of us in turn and touched us with his nose, before casually walking off into the trees. As we watched him disappear, we sat savouring the tingle of nature, which had touched us through him.

Mai Ling asked if anyone had toilet paper, and it turned out everyone's was finished.

"Why not use water like most people here," suggested Crispin.

"No way," said Mai Ling.

And Shmeiki Baba asked, "can I ask you a personal question?"

"Yes," said Mai Ling.

"If you got shit on your face, would you wash it off, or smear it off?" he asked.

"I'd wash it off," she said.

"So why should it be any different with your bottom?" he asked.

Mai Ling had no answer, but still, she was not convinced.

"I've just finished reading Midnight's Children, and you can use that if you like," said Kamal.

"Sounds like a wonderful opportunity," said Shmeiki Baba, and Mai Ling took the book from Kamal and off she went.

Sunday, 23rd April, 2006.

We continued to walk along forest pathways close to the road for about twenty kilometres, enjoying the sweet, woody air until we reached the village of Dharampur. There, we stopped to eat and rest by the little railway station, which lies on the Kalka to Shimla line, famed for its spectacular mountain views.

Later, as we walked through the village, we noticed some locals looking at us suspiciously and further up the road, there was a group of men wearing turbans, standing on each side of the street, holding large bamboo sticks. As we got closer, they fanned out. Among them, I spotted the Rajasthani circus performers, who Crispin had drugged in Chandigarh. They began to move towards us threateningly.

Shmeiki Baba said to us, "concentrate on your movements and not on theirs, keep stepping, moving your bodies fully from your breath, and do not stop moving until the action is done."

As the first of them reached us, Crispin threw his pan at them with all his might. It knocked two over, and we met the rest of their swinging sticks with ours as well as with our bags. Punches and kicks flew around me. My elbow hit the face of a small man when he grabbed my left arm and he fell.

And then in the midst of the melee, we heard an enormous roar, which was loud enough to make everyone freeze, and Mr. Bear jumped out of an alleyway on our left. He stood up on his hind legs and roared again. The mob panicked and began to run, as Mr. Bear chased after them.

Crispin rushed to pick up his pan and all the items which had spilt out of it, and we all helped him.

"Now everyone," said Shmeiki Baba, "stay close, and we will run behind Mr. Bear through the village and out the other side."

We did so, and Mr. Bear led us the whole way. About a kilometre past the village, we stopped. We were all completely out of breath and shocked at what had just happened, but also elated to have escaped. We hugged Mr. Bear in gratitude. There were, unfortunately, a few injuries among us. Crispin had received a hit with a bamboo stick to his neck, which was cut and bruised. Mai Ling had had some hair pulled out. Dylan had received a kick to the testicles, and Genevieve's earlobe was ripped. All wounds were cleaned and dressed, using Simon's ample medical kit, then Mr. Bear showed us that he wanted us to follow him and he led us into the forest.

"I dread to think what would have happened if Mr. Bear hadn't appeared," said Kamal.

"Yes, it goes to prove that it's right to expect miracles," said Shmeiki Baba.

"What if the circus performers still come after us?" said Genevieve.

"If we are in the now, nothing can harm us, well actually, it probably can, but it will do us less damage," said Shmeiki Baba.

"How comforting, Babaji," said Genevieve, touching the dressing around her ear.

Monday, 24th April, 2006

We made a nine-kilometre climb towards the small hill station of Barog. On the way, Mr Bear left us once again and we called goodbye to him.

In Barog, there were lots of hotels and we were invited to eat with a group of cheerful Punjabi tourists in a restaurant overlooking the mountains. They were staggered to hear about our pilgrimage and we enjoyed their compliments. After lunch, it was an easy climb down to the town of Solan.

On one sharp bend, we passed a black and yellow road sign, which displayed the warning "mind your breaks, or break your mind." Shmeiki baba sat down in front of it, saying he needed to meditate on the notion and we all joined him.

When we reached Solan, it seemed that there were tomatoes growing and being sold everywhere. When Crispin commented about this to a local man, he answered, "this is the city of red gold, sir."

We walked passed a camping shop and Simon suggested that as the weather was already cooler, we could buy tents there, and we did. That evening we set up our tents for the first time in the forest. Shmeiki Baba said that Sheila had some words for us, and he sat down to channel.

Sheila 10

And Sheila said:

"We shall call male practitioners of Shmeiki, *Shmaamen*, and female practitioners *Shmeikinis*. Now my Shmaamen and Shmeikinis, I wish to talk to you about *Shmantra*. This is a tool to help you clearly voice your desires and boundaries, heal your emotional wounds, and allow your love to grow in power, and with it, your connection to the beyond.

"Shmaamen and Shmeikinis, I want you to take turns saying what you truly desire from each other. You must risk being fully authentic. Give the true answer to whoever asks something from you. It may be a yes, it may be a no, it may be a maybe, it may be an 'ask me again some other time.' Know that when you are authentic with your desires and your boundaries, you are doing your universe a favour.

"Shmaamen, when you touch your Shmeikini, give full honour to the moment and focus purely on the sensations, whatever they are. Do not drive the process forward. Allow sensations to build slowly, without expectation, even if it feels mundane. Be present to your Shmeikini, contain her, give her space to open and to expand, allow her to feel safe enough to let go and to resonate fully.

"And Shmeikinis, allow your Shmaamen's love to fill you up, let this love be spread outwards far beyond yourselves. Like this, you can heal not only each other but also your world. "

Sheila fell silent and Shmeiki Baba opened his eyes.

Mai Ling asked, "so Shmantra is basically tantra?"

"More or less," said Shmeiki Baba.

"I thought that tantra is yantra plus mantra," said Crispin.

"It is, but you might also say that Shmantra is Shmantra plus Shmantra," answered Shmeiki Baba.

"That doesn't make sense," said Mai Ling.

"Oh God," said Simon.

"Indeed," said Shmeiki Baba taking me by the hand. "I want to kiss you," he said.

"Go ahead," I said.

We lay down and he began to caress me. He breathed his life force through me and pulses rose from my shmoni to the top of my head, until we were totally unified. When we finally rested, I looked around at the others and saw that Mai Ling was being adored by Crispin and Dylan, while Genevieve was being loved by Simon and Kamal. It was a glorious sight.

Tuesday, 25th April, 2006

For the first time, we got up late, filled with the joys of the previous evening, and after eating a lazy breakfast, we packed up our tents and the rest of our belongings.

Simon got out his map and suggested that we should walk in the direction of the valley of Kunihar. Looking over his shoulder, I saw that Shimla was only a little out of the way. I'd heard that it is a beautiful hill station, so I suggested we go via there, but Simon and Crispin objected to the detour. I said we could sleep a night in a decent hotel there and get some proper rest. Mai Ling and Genevieve agreed. "Me too," said Shmeiki Baba.

So Simon and Crispin accepted our desire to go via Shimla and we continued our walk through the forests of pine, Himalayan oak and rhododendron until we reached Shoghi. There we made camp in the woodland by a stream, not far from the railway line, while macaque monkeys sat in the trees eyeing us. Once the sun had gone down, the weather became surprisingly cold. "Lucky we bought the tents," said Mai Ling.

To warm her hands, Genevieve got out from her bag a pair of elegant brown, leather gloves. I noticed how Shmeiki Baba watched her intently as she put them on, and when I spoke to him, he didn't hear me. Genevieve also saw his fascination, and said, "Shmeiki

Baba, I see you like my gloves."

"Yes, they're nice," he answered.

"You can't stop looking at them," I said.

He shrugged his shoulders.

"There's nothing to be ashamed about," I said, "I can see that animal skin is a talisman for you. Celebrate it and it might open a path to other mystical realities."

"That is true," said Shmeiki Baba.

"Didn't you say that Shmantra is about asking for what you *really* want?" I asked him.

"Yes," he said, his eyes gleaming.

"Well," I said, "it is time."

"I would like you to borrow Genevieve's gloves, put them on and beat me with a cane," he said.

Mai Ling spat out her tea.

"Ah," said Genevieve, "*l'éducation anglaise.*"

I turned to Genevieve and asked, "can I borrow your gloves, please?"

"Yes, of course," she said, "my hands are warm now."

Slowly, she took off the gloves and passed them to me. Shmeiki baba stared at me, as I put them on. Then I got up, took my pocket knife and went to look among the trees for a straight, thin branch, which I could use to beat him with. I found a flexible one, about a metre long, which I knew would bite into his flesh like a whip. I cut it off the tree and removed its leaves and stems. Walking back towards Shmeiki Baba, I asked, "Are you sure you are ready for this?"

"Yes," he answered.

I turned to the rest of the group and asked, "do you accept to be witnesses to the Passion of the Baba?"

Simon asked what it was going to entail. I explained what I was about to do and he said he preferred to go for a walk. The others were willing to witness it.

"Shmeiki Baba," I said, "I am going to punish you for being ashamed of yourself. The pain is intended to purify you and will bring you into a state of self-acceptance. It will open your *shmakras*, align you *shmeridians*, and help the *shmana* flow through your *shmadis*. Yes, I know, you couldn't have said it better yourself. Now, take off your trousers and bend over this rock."

He complained that the rock was cold. I ignored him and began to beat him across his bottom using the stick. After four strokes, he began to cry out and wriggle about. As I continued to beat him, I ordered him to remain still, but he was unable to, so I asked Genevieve and Mai Ling to take hold of his arms. They appreciated the significance of the task and agreed to help, so I was able to go on. And in my mind, I saw flashes of my father hitting me and I contemplated the violence in my soul. After about fifty strokes, Shmeiki Baba stopped struggling and became still. I give him a final thirty, as hard as I could, to drive the lesson home. When I finished, my arm was tired and there were purple bruises across his bottom, as well as streaks of blood which glistened in the firelight. I told Mai Ling and Genevieve they could let go of his arms and I threw the rod into the fire. Shmeiki Baba remained lying over the rock. I put my climbing boot to his face, pointed to it and he kissed it, and I offered him the hand which had beaten him, and he kissed it too. I sat down and allowed him to rest his face against my thigh. I felt his devotion as I stroked his hair, and I felt empowered that I had given him something that he seemed to need so much. I felt happy we had broken through some kind of barrier, but at the same time, I also felt disappointment, because this man, who I esteemed so much, had somewhat crumbled in front of me. Shmeiki Baba looked at me and I saw he understood my dilemma.

While Crispin and Mai Ling began to prepare dinner, everyone was quiet. No one knew how the events of the evening would affect our group dynamic, and when Simon returned from his walk, he was confused by the change in atmosphere.

Dylan explained, "tonight Simon, we have seen something powerful."

Simon seemed unimpressed. Kamal said, "to me, it was as though Shmeiki Baba was being punished on behalf of man, for all the crimes done to woman."

"Absolutely," said Genevieve.

"And how are you feeling, Shmeiki Baba?" asked Kamal.

"My bottom hurts, but I feel wonderful. For me, it was some kind of deep, emotional release," he said.

Mai Ling asked Shmeiki Baba where he thought his fantasy to be beaten came from, and he answered, "I guess I've got mother issues."

"You don't say," said Kamal.

"Maybe I've got father issues too," said Shmeiki Baba.

"Maybe we can just call it issues," said Dylan.

"Yes," said Shmeiki Baba, "when I was a kid, punishment was unpredictable. Sometimes it involved the withdrawal of love, and sometimes it included violence. Maybe the warm afterglow of my mother's slaps gave me a sense of certainty and made me feel alive. Perhaps enjoying the pain was a type of coping strategy.

"A key event was when I was about eight. I remember my parents were angry with me and my father shouted to my mother, 'enough of doing it your way Sarah, we'll do it my way now,' and he took off his belt and tried to hit me with it. At first, my mother threatened him, that if he hit me with his belt, she would stab him with the kitchen knife which she was washing. He called her bluff and continued to try to hit me with his belt. I hid behind my mum, but feeling threatened by my father, she stood aside and did not protect me. I felt betrayed and ran out of the kitchen. My father jeered at me that I was a coward for running away, so I took a toy snake to fight back against him. In doing so, I realized that maybe I wasn't stronger than him after all, and I froze in the dining room and allowed him to beat me. Partly, I was curious to know how the sting of his belt would feel, relative to the slaps of my mother, and partly I felt I deserved to be punished, because of my guilt that I had caused him to have a heart attack three years before.

"Of course the pain of his beating was much stronger than my mother's slaps and somehow felt familiar to my soul. Amazingly, after he had let out his rage on my back, he made me kiss my mother's feet back in the kitchen and she actually allowed this to happen. Of course, I felt deeply humiliated and afterwards, I decided that the best thing to do, was to pretend that the whole thing had not happened.

"The next day was the school swimming competition, which I was due to take part in. My mum took me there and I went to the changing room to get ready. When I came back into the pool area, my mother was sitting with her friend Pearl. I remember Pearl asking my mother, 'what are those marks on David's back?' I didn't know that there were any marks on me and I was surprised to hear about them. My mother answered Pearl matter of factly, 'oh, Gerald hit him with his belt.' This felt like another betrayal and I jumped into the swimming pool and stayed underwater as long as I could.

"In repressing the memory of being beaten, I began to fantasize about being tied up and whipped by a glamorous woman, dressed in leather.

"Deep down, I felt that if anyone should have beaten me it wasn't my father, it was my mother. It was she who paid me attention, she who already used mild violence. But as I couldn't allow myself to desire my mother, I transferred this desire to what was close to her, her more attractive, younger friend Pearl. Of course, Pearl also liked to wear leather.

"The first time I masturbated while fantasizing about being beaten, I remember hearing a voice in my head, which said, 'beware, this is going to lead you down a long and difficult path,' and I answered, 'so be it, it is something stronger than me.' And from that point on, I spent my life stoking the fire of my fantasy. I had experienced oblivion in being beaten and I wanted to repeat it. Of course, I also felt so much shame about it and I would try to forbid myself from masturbating, but I could never stop myself for long. And so, I made the satisfaction of my fantasy my secret aim, and I envisaged its realization as a life-changing event, after which everything would be okay. As an adult, what stood in the way of my turning fantasy into reality, was my ongoing shame. Shame about seeming like a pervert and as submissive. The conflict of not wanting to do what I wanted to do, meant that my default setting was frustration and my life force was blocked. Being trapped in this loop was also a convenient way to avoid acknowledging the rest of my fears. And the whole mystery of the multiverse remained wrapped up in this fantasy. As much as wanting it, I also wanted to be free from it, and I believed that only a really hard beating would make it seem undesirable, as it is meant to be."

"Do you think that has happened tonight?" I asked.

"Yes, at least for now," he said.

"For now?" I asked.

"Well, if you offered to beat me again, I'd say please don't, and I would mean what I was saying. But how I will be feeling in a few days from now, I'm not sure," said Shmeiki Baba.

"It's strange that while your understanding about your fantasy is so developed, it still has such power over you," said Kamal.

"Agreed," said Shmeiki Baba.

I was still wearing Genevieve's gloves and I looked down at them. "They do have a magical quality about them," I said, "but maybe it's time to give them back to you, Genevieve." Carefully, I slid them off, finger by finger, and straightened them out, before asking Shmeiki Baba to hand them back to Genevieve.

Genevieve asked Shmeiki Baba what the beating was like for him.

He answered, "at first it hurt a lot and I was scared. I resisted and I wanted to run away, but then something happened when you and Mai Ling held me down. I relaxed, and although it continued to hurt, I was not suffering anymore, and it became a sublime, liberating experience."

"Pain freak!" said Crispin.

"You could say that," said Shmeiki Baba, "and you could also say, what a wonderful, life-affirming event."

"What was it like for you?" Dylan asked me.

"It's a big responsibility to hurt another person like that," I said. "While Shmeiki Baba asked me to do it, it did partly feel wrong, though, on a deeper level, I understood that a conscious beating would be therapeutic for both of us, and it was."

The question of where the events of the evening would lead, lingered in the air. I looked into Shmeiki Baba's eyes to see what was there, and what I saw was his adoration.

"I want to be yours in every way," said Shmeiki Baba.

"You realize that taking a whipping is one thing, and service is something else completely," I said.

"I want to feel that you own me," he said.

And I said to him, "you know that if I am your Queen, I won't be your girlfriend any more, and that means I will be free to be with whoever I wish."

He looked concerned, but answered, "I understand."

"Okay, but won't this get in the way of your whole guru-on-a-great-walk thing?" I asked.

"No," he said.

"What do you reckon Sheila will have to say about it?" I asked.

Shmeiki Baba closed his eyes.

"She says nothing could make her happier than to know that I am in your capable hands," he said.

"Well, you need to know that this is a big commitment for me too and it will be rather degrading for us both, if you do not completely surrender, once you have promised to," I said.

"Of course," said Shmeiki Baba.

"Very well, Shmeiki Baba," I said, taking him by the chin, "we're going to transform your kinky fantasies into a healthy reality, grounded by femdom love."

"Thank you," said Shmeiki Baba.

While I felt happy to know that I could give Shmeiki Baba what he wanted, I also knew that by him becoming my submissive, he would not remain enough for me sexually. I also recognized the part of me, which was looking for a master to give me instructions, for me to obey and to worship, to absolve me of my shame. In my fantasies, I was held in the vice-like embrace of a bearlike Sheikh, who used me and then returned me to his harem, where I waited to be chosen by him again.

Mai Ling asked Shmeiki Baba, "if Shoshana is your queen, what does that make you?"

"I guess it makes me her subject," answered Shmeiki Baba.

"Or rather my object," I said.

"And are you still our *shmuruji*?" asked Mai Ling.

"I don't see why not, or Shoshana can be your shmuruji, or maybe this is a good opportunity for you to become your own shmuruji," said Shmeiki Baba.

Mai Ling said she liked this last idea the best and that from now on she would be her own guide. The rest of us congratulated her. Kamal asked Mai Ling if she would also like to become a channel. She said she would love to, but she didn't know how.

"I don't think it's so difficult," said Simon, "even my three-year-old niece has a special friend who only she can see and hear."

"Is that all you think channelling is?" asked Mai Ling.

"No," said Simon, "I think channelling is an implicit agreement between one person giving advice and another wanting it, that the source of the advice comes from some supernatural place."

"What purpose would that serve?" asked Dylan.

"To make a safe and comfortable cushion between the source of the information and the recipient," said Simon.

"Interesting theory," said Shmeiki Baba.

After dinner, as we sat around the fire, I saw Dylan's desire to serve me too. I beckoned him with my finger.

"Is there something you want, Dylan?" I asked.

"Yes," he said, "I want to belong to you too."

"Why me?" I asked.

"I love you, I trust you, and I wish to worship you as my Goddess," answered Dylan.

"You didn't hang about," said Shmeiki Baba.

"Shush," I said to Shmeiki Baba, "have you already forgotten our agreement?"

"No, I have not forgotten," said Shmeiki Baba.

I turned back to Dylan and asked, "do I have your permission to do with you as I wish?"

"Yes," he answered.

"Very well," I said.

I knew this was going to be difficult for Shmeiki Baba, but he needed to serve me on my terms if I was to avoid becoming a tool of his fantasies.

I asked Crispin if I could borrow his crystal chillum.

"Do you need some charas to put in it?" he asked.

"No need," I said.

He passed me the chillum and I took a small jar of coconut oil and some soap from my bag. I asked Dylan to join me. Shmeiki Baba looked at me questioningly and was about to protest when I put my finger to my lips and he remained quiet.

Away from the others, Dylan received his blessing with grace. Afterwards, I left him to re-purify the crystal chillum and returned to the group. Soon after, I went to bed cuddling Genevieve, with both Shmeiki Baba and Dylan lying at our feet.

Wednesday, April 26th, 2006

In the morning, I noticed that Shmeiki Baba was having difficulty sitting. I inspected his bottom, and with my finger, followed the purple lines made by the cane.

I asked him to bring me some water and saw a flash of resentment on his face.

"Are you already rebelling?" I asked, "and over something as simple as bringing me water?

"I guess I'm scared to finally get what I have been longing for," he said.

"Well, get over it quickly, if you want us to continue," I said.

"Yes, ma'am," he said.

I promised to punish him severely if he did or said anything hurtful to Dylan, and I told him that I was also giving the job of transcribing Sheila's words to Dylan. Dylan was shy to receive the honour, but I insisted.

As we prepared breakfast, I noticed that Kamal and Crispin were also showing devotion towards me. I suggested that they should offer their devotion to Genevieve and Mai Ling as well, which they were happy to do, and the women were also glad. Only Simon looked uncomfortable and gave me suspicious looks.

I said that the men should pack up the camp, while we women relaxed. They did so, and once everything was ready, we continued our climb for about fifteen kilometres through unprecedented territory, with the men carrying our bags. In the afternoon, we were gifted with the site of Shimla in the distance, spread out along a ridge between seven hills, against the backdrop of the mighty Himalayas.

And this brings us to the end of my Shmospel. I'd like to finish by saying that despite the difficulties we faced, I would not change the experience of the great walk for anything. And Shmeiki Baba, well, we met each other on so many levels, in the kosher glint we share in our eyes, in our rebelliousness, in our traumas, and in some mysterious places we might never understand. Shmeiki Baba's hunger for truth and for healing was similar to my own. He showed me the courage to look into the depths of my shadow and to shine a light on whatever is there.

In the years which have passed since the great walk, Shmeiki Baba and I have been to the highest highs and the lowest lows.

Thankfully, we are still alive to tell the story.

And now I must pray for the souls of those who died on December 21st, 2012 at the Shmeiki community at iPadipuri in Colombia.

I also pray that our beautiful son Tony Ananda, and all children, will grow up to live in a healthy, kind and nurturing world of peace, clean energy, freedom, and good weather.

Om Shmeiki Om. Shmeiki.com

V

The Shmospel of Dylan

From Shimla to Dharamshala

I am Dylan Higgins, and this is my Shmospel.

Thursday, April 27th, 2006.

In offering myself to Shoshana, I had clearly stepped on Shmeiki Baba's toes. He wasn't pleased, to say the least, and when Shoshana gave me the job of transcribing Sheila's words, Shmeiki Baba looked like he might have a seizure, or turn into a fire breathing dragon.

Still, as we approached Shimla, I only felt love for Shmeiki Baba. It was his walk which had given me the opportunity to experience something so rare, including meeting Shoshana. And how beautiful she was, with her oval face, silky brown skin, olive green eyes, and long, thick, brown hair. If I didn't know she was Israeli, I would have thought she was from South America. She had a killer smile and a look in her eye of *let's see how far you're willing to go*. She was unlike anyone I had ever met and I was totally captivated by her. This is why, when she said that she was no longer Shmeiki Baba's girlfriend, I could not resist offering myself to her.

By admitting my love for Shoshana in front of the group, I received new powers of calm and self-acceptance. This is what gave me the strength to bear Shmeiki Baba's glares. Meanwhile, I did my best to stay out of his way and I tried to keep myself positioned so that Shoshana remained between us.

As we walked, Shoshana asked me about my childhood and I told her about myself, how I was born and raised in County Cork in Ireland, and how I come from what you might call a middle-class Munster family. I talked about my two elder brothers, Bobby, who now lives in Dublin, and Phil in Australia, and also about my dad, who is an architect, and my mum, who used to be a therapist. At the time, I was still shocked that they had split up after more than thirty years of marriage. My brothers and I couldn't understand why they had waited so long. When we were growing up, they rowed ceaselessly. Dad used to be particularly grumpy and got worse when he hit the bottle, which was quite regularly. He also couldn't resist humiliating us when we made mistakes. When I was in my early teens, my parents sent me to a psychologist, to figure out what was wrong with me, instead of sorting out themselves.

Shoshana asked me what I did when I left school and I told her how I went to study Economics and Politics at Trinity College, Dublin, and afterwards, I got a job at Lehman Brothers in New York, where I became a successful trader. I was at a meeting in the World Trade Centre on the day the aeroplanes hit, and it made me realize that I needed to focus my attention on personal development rather than on wealth acquisition. Soon after, I quit my job, sold my stuff and flew to Costa Rica. There, I spent several years studying shamanism and spirituality.

Shoshana asked why I had come to India and how I had met Shmeiki Baba. As she said his name, she turned to look at him, and instinctively, so did I. He was staring coldly at us from the back of the group.

"Don't worry about him, he'll be fine," she said.

I continued telling her how I had travelled to Goa for a contact dance festival and people there were talking about an English guy called Shmeiki Baba, who was about to try to walk from Goa to Dharamshala. I'd also heard there was a German guy called Sebastian, who was going to accompany him part of the way. To me, this sounded like an astonishing journey and I wanted to be part of it, so much so, that after the contact dance festival finished, I took an overnight bus from Goa to Pune to look for them. I did manage to locate Sebastian after a number of days, but by then, Shmeiki Baba had continued north by himself. I was determined to find him, so I hired a driver, to follow his most likely route. We stopped regularly, to ask people along the way if they had seen a barefoot foreigner. No one had, and I was about to give up my search when finally, a shopkeeper said that he had met Shmeiki Baba and pointed us in the direction of Indore. And so we drove straight there and I continued my search for Shmeiki Baba. After two days, I managed to find him. I was delighted to see him and asked to join him in his pilgrimage, but he said that for the moment he needed to walk by himself, though he invited me to join him further down the road in Delhi. So I jumped on a train and waited for him there.

Shoshana said that when she first met me in Delhi, I seemed very grateful to Shmeiki Baba. I remembered how I was, and how impressed I was with him. Now, I chanced another look at him, and he looked quite ragged and desperate, like a dropout, lost in India. I did feel guilty for making moves on his love, but it was beyond my control.

And on we walked, until we entered Shimla from the west, past Anji and Summer Hill and along the main shopping street, known as the Mall. I was impressed how European it looked, with its mock Tudor and Neo-Gothic buildings. When we saw all the *normal* tourists, I felt that I was part of something special. We walked past Scandal Point until we reached the Ridge, the main gathering space, which connects the various hills of Shimla. There we were pleased to put down all our bags.

Brother Crispin volunteered to go buy milk and I got out the camping stove and the rest of the ingredients to make chai. Shoshana requested music and Shmeiki Baba, Kamal and Simon got out their instruments, sat down on the ground and played songs, including my favourite, the lively, 'Reiki Shmeiki, fakey makey.'

A crowd of locals and tourists formed around us and some began to dance. Meanwhile, Crispin came back with locally sourced milk and we made chai, containing a blend of black tea, cardamom, nutmeg, cloves, cinnamon, vanilla essence and jaggery for sweetness. When it was cooked, Crispin asked Shmeiki Baba to bless it. Shmeiki Baba stood up, raised the pan to shoulder height, and poured a long stream of tea directly into small, disposable, clay cups, which Crispin had placed on a cardboard box. Crispin remarked that barely a drop was spilt, and Shmeiki Baba said, "yes, brother, the *Shmiddhis* will grow more frequent now."

The chai was passed around and received as a sacrament. A man wearing a smart, navy blue suit approached me and introduced himself as Vikram. He said he worked for the All Asia Organic Tea Company. He had heard of our pilgrimage to Dharamshala and of our tea making and wondered if we would like his company to sponsor the tea for our walk. I brought him to speak to Shmeiki Baba, who said he was a particular fan of their Masala blend. Shmeiki Baba introduced Vikram to Shoshana and said that it was up to her to decide if our walk should be sponsored. Shoshana said yes and Vikram said how pleased he was that so many women were now calling the shots. Shoshana smiled and Vikram explained that his company would like to present our group with a grand kettle to prepare the tea in, as well as a *coolie*, a porter to carry it, all the way to Dharamshala. This way, we would be able to make tea for as many people as possible along our route. Shoshana smiled and nodded, and Vikram said, "cent per cent, we have a deal, I knew this would be an auspicious day."

As it got dark, Vikram took his leave to make arrangements, leaving us with Kaku, a friend of his, who told us he would be honoured if we would stay as his guests. He led us back to his splendid guest house on Jakhoo Hill.

Later in the evening, Kaku came to Shmeiki Baba and said, "There is some problem, and kindly, I want to ask your help."

Shmeiki Baba asked him what he needed and Kaku said, "please come with me and I will show you and explain."

Shmeiki Baba looked to Shoshana, who suggested that she and I go with. Kaku led us to a bedroom on the second floor of the guest house.

"One year ago in this room, a woman, she belong to Poland, she die. Her good name Petra. She die because of food poisoning, but her soul cannot move on because authorities take her body too quickly and fly Poland. Her soul stay here," said Kaku.

"How do you know that?" asked Shmeiki Baba.

"Because on full moon after her death, I am standing late at night outside guest house, smoking cigarette when I see her, standing next to Peepal tree. She is beautiful and she is wearing long, white dress. I wonder what she is doing out so late, without jacket and alone. I speak to her to ask if I can help and she talk to me in strange voice, like she is speaking through her nose. And then I see she is not standing on ground, she is floating about ten centimetres above and her feet are pointing backwards. I am very, very frightened and run into house."

"I see," said Shmeiki Baba thoughtfully.

And Kaku continued, "Then my heart is paining and I am confused because I want to see her again and I do see her. Usually, she sit by tree and look like woman, but I also see her as mongoose and as owl. Last time, two days ago, she lead me into house and into bedroom, even though door is locked. She go into bathroom and I see bath filled with milk. She get in, still wearing white dress and disappear under milk. I go forward to look what happened, and suddenly her arms come out of milk and pull me into bath. Under milk, she kiss me, and then she disappear, and I fall asleep. Later, I wake up in bath but there is no milk, but I am in love with her, and I cannot stop thinking of her, and my family fear she will bring my death. Please Babaji, help me, I am really eating my brain with this."

"Don't eat your brain Kaku," said Shmeiki Baba, "you know, there are people who get married to ghosts and live happily ever after."

"No sir, this cannot be, please help me," said Kaku.

"Okay," said Shmeiki Baba.

"Thank you," said Kaku.

"I will need some hose pipe, three iron pots, some turmeric, soil and a cigarette lighter ready for midnight," said Shmeiki Baba.

"Whatever you need," said Kaku.

"That is all," said Shmeiki Baba, and Kaku went off to prepare the things that Shmeiki Baba had asked for.

As agreed, a few minutes before twelve, Shmeiki Baba came downstairs with Shoshana and went outside. Shmeiki Baba placed the hosepipe in a circle next to the Peepal tree. He entered the circle, sat down and lined up the iron pots in front of him. He explained to Kaku that he was about to perform a *shmeremony* called Shmatma Shmanti.

Shmeiki Baba sat meditating for a few minutes and then called Petra's ghost, promising to do anything in his power, to finish off the work she felt she had left incomplete. He lit the cigarette lighter with one hand and with the other, let pinches of turmeric powder drop onto the flame. He did this several times and mixed the burnt turmeric powder with soil. Then he announced loudly, "thank you for coming, Petra," and he threw the mixture over himself.

"Excuse me Petra," he continued, "I mean you no disrespect, but you must understand, I have to protect myself. Now, is there some way I can help you find peace?"

Shmeiki Baba spent some time nodding. Finally, he turned to Kaku, and said with gravitas, "Petra has gone now, and she will not be back."

"Oh my God, I feel sad, but also happy. What did she say?" asked Kaku.

"She told me she got food poisoning just before her boyfriend left her and was unable to get up and to ask for help and this is why she died. She wanted revenge on her ex but understood that this would not allow her soul to find peace. For this reason, she was willing to forgive him. She also said that her diary is still under the mattress in the room where she died, and she asked me to send it to her mother. After this, she slowly disappeared."

"Thank you, Shmeiki Baba," said Kaku with tears in his eyes, and Shmeiki Baba stood up and hugged him.

When we went back into the hotel, we went upstairs and Kaku found the diary under the mattress in what had been Petra's room.

Later Shoshana asked Shmeiki Baba about the diary.

He said, "Kaku forgot to lock the door after he showed us Petra's room. So I went back in there and put my notebook under the mattress, for him to find. My writing is so messy, I knew he would not be able to read it and wouldn't know the difference."

Afterwards, Shmeiki Baba offered to send the notebook to Petra's mum for Kaku, and Kaku gave it to him. And this way, the exorcism was complete.

Friday, April 28th, 2006.

After sleeping under the stars for two weeks, it felt wonderful to wake up in a guest house, and in a smart one at that. I was sharing a room with Crispin. Shmeiki Baba was sharing a room with Shoshana and Genevieve and we understood he was made to sleep on the floor. I was excited by the prospect of our spiritual femdom game, though I didn't yet understand what it would entail.

At breakfast, Shmeiki Baba kept burping. Shoshana didn't like it and asked him to stop, but he carried on, and she asked him to stop again.

And Shmeiki Baba said to Shoshana, "you should punish me, so I don't displease you."

"Oh no, darling," she replied, "don't try that sort of manipulation on me. Either you find ways to obey, or I will concentrate on those who do," she said, looking at me.

I tried to hide my smile and silently made the decision, that wherever possible, I would be more compliant and helpful than Shmeiki Baba, and in this way, I would win the greater part of Shoshana's affection.

Shoshana continued, "Shmeiki Baba, wanting to be beaten is just a fantasy, and for this reason, the beating will never be enough. Do you not see, that it is really intimacy that you crave, but you are blocked from it, by your fear of being vulnerable in front of the one you love. And while you say you want to be dominated and you do find moments of surrender, you then snap back and get that look on your face that all women are crazy bitches. It's like you're caught between the archetypes of priest and slave and you don't know which way to turn. The only way you will find transformation and healing in our relationship, is if you do actually let go of control. It's just the same as with the guru-disciple relationship and as our ultimate relationship with life. Surrender is the only salvation. If you continue to game our relationship, you will remain stuck in your own manipulations and all this will be for nothing. In any case, if you don't shift, I'm not willing to go on with it."

Shoshana paused and looked at Shmeiki Baba for his reaction. He was kind of frozen and she asked, "maybe Sheila has something to add to what I've told you?"

Sheila 11

Shmeiki Baba closed his eyes, and Sheila did begin to speak:

"Part of you curses the fantasy which drives you to be submissive to a woman. Let us unknot this double-bind once and for all, for there is no deleting your fantasy, your neural network simply will not allow it. You must accept it and learn to use it healthily. See the fulfilment of fantasy as a door rather than a room. It is not the destination, it is the means. Now while it is clear you are devoted to Shoshana in the higher realms of your being, you still need to put aside your pride, and obey her in the simple things she asks of you.

"To give you some space around your fantasy and to help you work with it, I invite you to acknowledge that it is not only your inner masochist that you need to bring out into the open. There are two other potentialities within your shadow, which you need to acknowledge and give voice to. These are the sadist and the rescuer. Clearly, the sadist is the one who wishes to control. The rescuer meanwhile, is the part of you who wants to help people, but less from love and more from a need to have power and relevance in their lives. It is born from a desire to avoid your own issues by fixing others. These three roles, sadist, masochist, and rescuer arise from the division of self in childhood, and they can be tricky to identify. I also want you to notice how at the core of the masochist lies a sadist, while at the core of the sadist lies a masochist, and within the rescuer, lies both sadist and masochist.

"To varying degrees, what I am saying to you is relevant to everyone and I invite you to work together, to help one another recognize where each of these roles resides within you. Learn to see how you often play them out without realizing. It will make it easier if you give each role a name, which symbolizes how it manifests within you. I want you to explore each one, using role-playing games. We will call this practice *Sadopassana*, and as with Shmantra, you will always ask permission from each other before playing a particular role, stating clearly what you want to achieve with it, and agreeing on safe boundaries. Initially, it might also help to wear a particular hat, to designate which role you are playing. I believe I have said enough about this now, and you can take it from here."

Sheila became quiet, and Shoshana said, "What an excellent idea! Everyone, please go and bring as many hats as you can find."

Some of us went to our rooms and came back with hats, which we piled on the table in front of Shoshana.

"Let's start with you, Shmeiki Baba," said Shoshana. "Choose a hat which represents your masochist."

Shmeiki Baba chose Mai Ling's black beret and put it on.

"Now," said Shoshana, "close your eyes, and allow yourself to see your inner masochist and give him a name."

Shmeiki Baba thought for a while and said, "Brian."

"Why Brian?" asked Shoshana.

"*Because he's not the Messiah, he's a very naughty boy,*" he said.

"And does your masochist want anything?" asked Shoshana.

"Yes, he wants to be a child, to be given clear boundaries and to be absolved of guilt," said Shmeiki Baba.

"Yes," said Shoshana. "Now, let's look at your sadist. Choose a hat which you feel represents him."

Shmeiki Baba chose Simon's New Yorker baseball cap.

"Can you give your inner sadist a name?" asked Shoshana.

"That's more tricky," said Shmeiki Baba, and he thought for a minute before he said, "I'll call my sadist Justice."

"And what does Justice want?" asked Shoshana.

"Revenge on people for disrespecting and betraying me," said Shmeiki Baba.

"Yes," said Shoshana, "now choose a hat for your rescuer."

Shmeiki Baba chose a turban.

"What's he called?" asked Shoshana.

"That's easy, Guruji," said Shmeiki Baba.

"And what does he want?" asked Shoshana.

"For you to see how clever I am, and to look up to me," said Shmeiki Baba.

"Yes," said Shoshana, "Can you also go a stage further, and identify the core of the sadist which lies hidden within your masochist?"

"I think so," said Shmeiki Baba, "I will call him *Trojan Horse*."

"Why's that?" asked Shoshana.

"Because he's hiding that he's thinking, 'I'll show you what happens when you try to control me.'"

"Bravo," said Shoshana.

"And can you identify the masochist which is hidden inside your sadist?" asked Shoshana.

"Yes," said Shmeiki Baba, I will call him by my original name David.

"Why?" asked Shoshana.

"Because like the biblical character, he wears the blood of conflict on his hands."

"Pshh," said Shoshana, "who else would like a go?"

Kamal was the first to volunteer, and one by one, we all took turns to identify the roles we like to play, usually without realizing. Then Shoshana asked us to split into groups of sadists, masochists, and rescuers and to choose partners and begin playing out our roles. I was surprised by how much my inner sadist was begging for expression.

Afterwards, Shoshana said she wanted to spend some time alone with Shmeiki Baba, and the rest of us went out to explore the ups and downs of Shimla.

We climbed Bantony Hill, enjoyed the mountain views and walked around the then dilapidated summer palace of the former Maharaja of Sirmur. Later, we went back down to the Mall to eat *momos*, which are Nepalese dumplings, and I particularly enjoyed the steamed spinach and yak cheese ones. We also stopped to drink a beer, though Kamal drank a juice. It was then that I realized that he didn't drink any alcohol, nor did he smoke, use drugs or even caffeine, and yet he was always cheerful.

We continued as far as Observation Hill in the far west of Shimla, and finally, we returned to the guest house. Remembering the role-playing game we had played earlier in the day, I asked the others if it was okay if I played rescuer, and when they said yes, I gave encouragement to those who were struggling to get up Jakhoo Hill.

When we finally got to the guest house, Shmeiki Baba and Shoshana were in the restaurant chatting to Kaku, looking very cheerful. I heard Kaku ask Shmeiki Baba if he would give evening *darshan*, which in Indian tradition, is a meeting with a holy person. Shmeiki Baba explained that he could not offer a darshan, but he could offer a Martian. Kaku said he didn't understand, and Shmeiki Baba pointed out of the window and said, "look up to the heavens brother and connect with the consciousness, which exists throughout the myriad of dimensions."

Kaku looked confused, and said, "so please give us your Martian."

"Om Shmeiki," said Shmeiki Baba.

Saturday, April 29th, 2006.

Kaku invited many people to hear Shmeiki Baba give evening Martian, and he offered a special thali, which was to include *tadka dal*, curried lentils, *Kashmiri paneer masala*, cottage cheese in tomato, ginger and fennel curry, and *chapati*, homemade soft, flatbread, all for just ₹ 250.

In the evening, the restaurant filled up with our group, other curious travellers and spiritual seekers. At 8 PM, Kaku rang a bell and soon after, Shoshana appeared, wearing a long, black, leather dress, and she was leading Shmeiki Baba behind her on a rope, which was tied around his neck. She sat down on an elaborately carved chair at the end of the restaurant and Shmeiki Baba sat cross-legged at her feet. It seemed that he had found a way to reconcile being both a spiritual leader and Queen Shoshana's slave. I felt mixed emotions about this. On the one hand, I loved them both and was so happy about what they were manifesting, but I also felt envious because harmony between them, meant that Shoshana was likely to pay me less attention. I did my best not to let this get to me and tried to be meditative.

Shmeiki Baba sat with his eyes closed until Shoshana touched him on his shoulder and he began to chant in tongues, very quietly at first and then louder and louder. I felt goose pimples on my arms and the energy moved fast around my body. And again Sheila began to speak through Shmeiki Baba:

Sheila 12

"Shmeiki Baba, it has taken a long walk and a strong woman, but it is safe to say, that you have finally begun to lower your array of juvenile defences and are now able to harmonize yourself with your fellow man, with the world, and the Great Mother.

"Completing this work will transform you into a real son of the multiverse, it will allow you to truly earn your title Shmuruji. I want you to keep Shoshana as your main focus, and to remember that surrender does not need to happen once, it is a process, which needs to be reaffirmed time and again. Remember also that the key to containing your emotions lies in accepting all sides of yourself. By doing so, you will save yourself and maybe even your world."

Sheila stopped speaking, and Shmeiki Baba did not move at all. You could have heard a pin drop until after about thirty seconds and without warning, Shmeiki Baba shouted "boo" and everyone got a shock.

"Just you wait until we get upstairs," said Shoshana.

When the laughter died down, Shoshana said there were some things she also had to say.

"Love is the glue which holds our universe together," she said, "it is everywhere, but often we are blind to it. When I say *we*, I especially mean men. In truth, our species has no lack of female awareness. It is therefore right, that the men should follow the women. I am happy to say that Shmeiki Baba and the other men in our group seem to understand and accept this. Tomorrow, we shall be leaving for Dharamshala, by foot. There will be a meeting afterwards for those who are interested to join us. But first, Shmeiki Baba will answer any questions you have."

Various people put up their hands.

"What happens when we die?" asked Hassan from Iran.

After stroking his beard, Shmeiki Baba answered:

"You might say that the hand of the Great Mother withdraws from our bodies, and our souls return the log of the one, multiversal soul."

"And then what happens?" asked Hassan.

"We remain there until we are ready for reactivation as new biological organisms, at which point we are sent to the data exchange, where we are matched with our parents-to-be," said Shmeiki Baba.

"How many times does this happen?" asked Hassan.

"As many times as it takes to become resolved," said Shmeiki Baba.

"And how many times is that usually?" asked Hassan.

"Sometimes thousands," said Shmeiki Baba.

"Why so many?" asked Hassan.

"Because each time our souls come here to resolve certain problems, they keep on picking up new ones," said Shmeiki Baba.

"Do you have any techniques for accepting death?" asked an older South African woman called Leslie.

"Yes, we can use death visualizations," said Shmeiki Baba.

"What are they?" asked Leslie.

"Well, the best way to explain, is by trying one. Maybe we can do one right now," said Shmeiki Baba.

"Sure," said Leslie.

Shoshana nodded her assent.

"Okay," said Shmeiki Baba, "get as comfortable as you can, take a nice slow, deep breath in and out, and again, and when you are ready, allow your eyes to close, and begin to sink down into your body. Now bring your attention to your toes. Maybe you can feel one of your toes more than the rest, maybe your big toe, maybe your little one. Whichever it is, allow that sensation to grow, let it fill your feet, and your legs and also your torso, your arms, and your head.

"Feel yourself as one, and as you take another slow and steady breath, allow yourself to imagine that you are sitting comfortably on a flight to Mumbai. You have been given a free upgrade to business class, and you feel lucky and content. You are relaxing in the comfortable seat, savouring the gentle perfume of the air-hostess, as she passes by, offering you a glass of champagne. You feel an overriding sense of calm, spreading throughout your body and mind. Gradually, you drift off into a peaceful sleep, and you remain like that, all the way until the plane begins to descend. Suddenly, there is a loud bang, and you wake with a start. And now there's a jolt and another enormous bang. Something terrible has happened.

"The captain comes on the intercom, and says, 'ladies and gentlemen, I'm sorry to give you bad news, but we have flown into a flock of birds and both our engines have been damaged. We have no option but to attempt an emergency landing at sea. Please remain calm and put on your life vests, but do not inflate them up until you are outside the aircraft. Fasten your seat belts, and when I say, *'brace'*, assume the brace position. Once we have landed on the sea, make for the nearest exit.'

"The plane is going down and as it descends in eerie silence, some people cry, others begin to scream, and panic spreads through the cabin. You remain composed though and you focus intently on the sensations in your body and your heart beating fast. You look into the eyes of your neighbour, and exchange brave smiles, accepting that your ride in this world might be about to end.

"Brace, brace! In five, four, three, two, one and bang, the left-wing hits the water and breaks off. It feels like a hard, car crash, and now a much bigger bang! This is the main impact, it is so violent that you blackout. It is dark. It is quiet. Maybe you are alive, maybe you are not. Either way, it is not so bad. Now, if you survived, when you are ready, slowly come back into your body, wiggle your toes, take a deep breath, open your eyes, and begin to sit up."

"Wow," said Leslie, "how often do I need to do this?"

"As often as you feel the need," said Shmeiki Baba.

"Do you believe in the bible?" asked a Dutch woman called Deborah.

"Well, I believe it exists," said Shmeiki Baba.

"But do you believe it is the word of God?" asked Deborah.

"Yes," said Shmeiki Baba.

"You do?" asked Genevieve, surprised.

"Yes, I believe the bible is the word of God, just like the phone book and every other book, for that matter," said Shmeiki Baba.

"How do I go beyond my fears?" asked Ananta from England.

"Acknowledge them and allow yourself to connect to the pain, which lies beneath them," said Shmeiki Baba.

"And how do I do that?" asked Ananta.

"Well, different things work for different people, but maybe I could show you one approach with the help of a simple, Sadopassana exercise," said Shmeiki Baba.

Shoshana nodded again.

"What is it?" asked Ananta.

"The face slapping circle," said Shmeiki Baba.

"I don't want my face slapped," said Ananta.

"That's fine, but maybe some other people would like to try?" asked Shmeiki Baba.

A number of people said yes.

"Okay, so with Kamal's permission, I will begin by slapping his face, making a special effort to focus on my breathing, as I do so. It is important that I hit him with love and with a relaxed hand, avoiding the cheekbone and ears. My intention is to cheer him up with my slap, not to hurt him, just like this."

Shmeiki Baba slapped Kamal on the face.

"Wow," said Kamal, "I can see the light!"

"Careful Kamal, it might be a train coming," said Shmeiki Baba.

Shmeiki Baba asked Kamal to pass the slap on to his left. It was Crispin who was sitting there. Crispin nodded and without hesitation, Kamal hit him hard across his face. People winced.

"Now Crispin, stay present and watch the feelings and thoughts arising from the slap," said Shmeiki Baba.

Ananta was sitting on Crispin's left, and Crispin asked her, "Ananta, maybe you are willing to receive my slap?"

"Oh go on then," she said. Crispin hit her. She fell to the side with the force of the blow. Crispin look frightened at what he had done, but when she sat up, Ananta was glowing. "Now I understand," she said.

"Yes, Ananta, well done, you did it! Now keep going, pass the slap on, from person to person," said Shmeiki Baba.

And Ananta turned to her friend and slapped her soundly. I was amazed that people who you never thought would hit each other, were merrily slapping each other's faces.

Shoshana asked if there were any other questions, but it turned out that our minds had been sufficiently stilled, and it was time to eat Kaku's delicious smelling thali.

After dinner, Vikram, our tea sponsor, arrived at the guest house with Godrej, a thin man in his sixties, who wore a long, white beard. Vikram explained that Godrej would carry our kettle and our tea all the way to Dharamshala.

Meanwhile, there were four more people who were interested to join us for the remaining two weeks of our walk. After the existing members of our group had introduced ourselves, the new people introduced themselves.

First was Fernando from Chile. He was short and swarthy and seemed to be a rather Dionysian character, outwardly confident and competitive. He said he was interested to try a femdom relationship, and explained that he had managed to travel around India for nearly half a year, almost without money.

"How is that?" asked Genevieve.

"Well," said Fernando, "when I first arrived in India, I went down to Varkala in Kerala, because I was told it is a good, relaxing place to start. My intention was to stay in India for six months, and I brought with me $5000 in cash, which I saved up while working on a cruise ship."

"Haven't you heard of travellers' cheques?" asked Kamal.

"Or a credit card?" asked Genevieve.

"Of course I have," said Fernando.

"So why didn't you use them?" asked Shoshana.

"I guess I needed to learn a lesson," said Fernando.

"So what happened?" asked Shmeiki Baba.

"Well, for my first week, everything went great. I spent my time meeting lovely people, enjoying the beach and learning yoga. Every morning, an old woman would pass by my guest house, offering to do laundry. When I had nothing clean left to wear, I gave her all my dirty clothes. Only later in the day, when I was on my way to the beach, I remembered that I had included my money belt in the bundle of clothes," said Fernando.

"No way," said Crispin.

"Yes way," said Fernando.

"What did you do?" asked Shmeiki Baba.

"I went to the owner of my guest house and he took me to the old woman's house. She gave me my clothes washed and folded. Among them was my money belt, but the money was no longer there, and when I asked her for it, she denied ever seeing it," said Fernando.

"She did not launder your money appropriately," said Kamal.

"Definitely not," said Fernando.

"So what did you do then?" asked Shoshana.

"I went to the local police with the owner of the guest house," said Fernando.

"Did the police believe you?" asked Kamal.

"Well, although I had no proof the money existed, the police chief agreed to bring in the old woman and her family for questioning," said Fernando. "After conducting an interview with them, the police chief said to me that he believed that they had taken the money, but in order for them to confess, he would have to beat it out of them and he asked me if I agreed to this."

"And what did you say?" asked Shoshana.

"I said no, and the police chief looked at me like I was crazy, and said that in that case, there was nothing he could do," said Fernando.

"And then what happened?" asked Genevieve.

"That was it, I went back to the guest house," said Fernando.

"I bet the police beat the shit out of the family anyway until they gave them the money," said Crispin.

"You might be right about that," said Fernando.

"To a simple family, $5000 is like us finding, I don't know, $50,000," said Shmeiki Baba.

"Enough to risk dying for," said Genevieve.

"Indeed," said Fernando.

"What did you do afterwards?" asked Shoshana.

"The other tourists at my guesthouse were really supportive. They held a whip-round for me and collected two hundred dollars, which they gave to me. I also approached the Chilean embassy to tell them what had happened, and amazingly enough, they gave me another two hundred dollars. I was really careful with this money," said Fernando.

"Still, it's not very much," said Crispin.

"Yes, that's why I found out where all of the Vipassana meditation centres are in India, and I went from one to the next, doing their free courses and volunteering as a helper. That's how I've managed to get almost enlightened and to stay in India for nearly six months. It's also why I want to take part in your great walk because I want to go to Dharamshala, and this way I won't have to buy a train ticket or pay for guest houses," said Fernando.

"I see," said Shoshana.

The spotlight turned to Meredith from Wales. She was blessed with the most magnificent, red hair, and a freckled complexion.

"I bet the local people don't leave you alone for a moment," said Genevieve.

"That's right," said Meredith, "they are definitely shocked by my hair, so I often cover it with a scarf, to make life easier."

Meredith seemed kind and gentle and Shoshana asked her, "do you have any experience with femdom?"

"Not yet," she answered, "but I'm eager to try," and a mischievous smile appeared on her face.

"Wonderful," said Shoshana.

Fabrizio from Naples in Italy was next. He was quietly spoken and seemed deep and sensitive.

"I like to smoke a lot," he said, "but I also do yoga every day. I have been to India many times, and I feel it is my home. In fact, the last time I returned to Italy, I was so unhappy, that I lost my eyesight."

"No way," said Mai Ling.

"Oh yes," said Fabrizio, "it was terrifying. I was taken to hospital, where the doctors ran all sorts of tests, but could find no cause, and they diagnosed me as suffering from a rare condition called hysterical blindness."

"Isn't that what some conscripted soldiers used to suffer from in wartime?" asked Shmeiki Baba.

"Yes," said Fabrizio.

"And how did it get better?" asked Shoshana.

"When my brother said he had booked me a flight back to India, my sight began to return," said Fabrizio.

"Did it ever happen again?" asked Shoshana.

"No, probably because since then, I have been staying in Asia and have no intention of returning to Europe," he said.

Finally, we turned to the tall, svelte Séverine.

"Well, I do not have so many stories about myself to tell," she said. "I am a dancer from Paris, and I like nature and eating healthy food."

'Her accent was soft and her voice sweet, like a bell.

"Sister, do you like reggae?" asked Crispin.

"What, because I am black, this means I have to like reggae?" she asked.

"I guess that was the implication, but I realize now that I was making a racial stereotype and I'm sorry," said Crispin.

"That's okay, I forgive you," said Séverine.

Shoshana said, "friends, what we are proposing here, is to walk to Dharamshala as a femdom group. This means that the Shmeikinis are in charge. It is going to be challenging, and we will only be successful if we are all clear about what we do and don't want. To this end, it is best that we split what we don't want into soft and hard limits."

"Can you explain what that means?" asked Fernando.

"Yes," said Shoshana, "soft limits, are things you don't really want to experience, but you might be willing to experience under certain circumstances, and hard limits, are things you are not willing to experience under any circumstance. It is important we do this so that our game does not turn into abuse. Is that clear?"

"Yes," said Fernando.

"So who would like to suggest something they do want?"

"I will," said Mai Ling.

"Good," said Shoshana.

"I'd like the Shmaamen to make camp, cook, clear up, and dispose of trash," said Mai Ling.

"I'll second that," said Shoshana. Does this cross anyone's limits?" asked Shoshana.

No one objected.

"Good," said Shoshana, "anyone else?"

"I'd like the Shmaamen to obey all orders issued by Shmeikinis, as long as it does not endanger their lives," said Genevieve.

"Does this cross anyone's limits?" asked Shoshana.

Again no one objected.

"I want to have the right to reward and punish the Shmaamen as I choose," said Mai Ling.

"Very good Mai Ling," said Shoshana, "does that go for all Shmeikinis?"

They all said yes.

And does this cross any of the Shmaamen's limits?

Tentatively, the Shmaamen shook their heads.

"Now, Shmeiki Baba, would you like to give an example of hard and soft limits?" asked Shoshana.

"Yes," said Shmeiki Baba, "for me, an example of a hard limit is anal penetration. It's not that I'm against it, but I have to think of my haemorrhoids."

"Okay," said Shoshana, "by the way, how's the Jerusalem Balsam working?"

"Very well, actually," said Shmeiki Baba.

"Excellent," said Shoshana. "So what about a soft limit?"

"Golden showers," said Shmeiki Baba.

"Noted," said Shoshana.

"There is something I would like to add," said Shmeiki Baba.

"Go ahead," said Shoshana.

"I think it's important to say, that where I might lack self-love and fear abandonment, it might be difficult for me to be authentic about my boundaries, and I might tend to agree to things that I later regret," said Shmeiki Baba.

"Thank you for sharing this," said Shoshana, "and for this reason, we must start gently and give others good time to react to our intended actions, and we will also use safe words. I suggest we have one word for pause and another for stop."

"What should the words be?" asked Séverine.

"How about Deepak is for pause, and Chopra is for stop," said Shmeiki Baba.

"Good idea," said Shoshana.

"Guys, I'm sorry to interrupt, but I have to say, this just isn't for me, I'm out," said Simon.

Everyone said they were sorry to hear this.

"I will be happy to meet you guys in Dharamshala," he said, and with that, he went upstairs.

If truth be told, I was quietly pleased he was not continuing with us, as he could be a bit heavy.

"Is there anyone else who has a problem with anything that is being proposed here?" asked Shoshana.

No one else did.

"Good, by the time we reach Dharamshala," said Shoshana, "the Shmaamen will be new men, the sort we need, the sort this world needs."

"Amen," said Mai Ling.

Godrej had been listening quietly to our conversation with a look of bemused surprise on his face. Shoshana turned to him and asked him what he thought of our proposed game. And Godrej said, "we humans are able to align ourselves with pure consciousness directly through inner inquiry, or indirectly, through external devotion to a form. It seems that you are attempting to do both."

I was surprised that Godrej understood what we were talking about and that his English was so good. It seemed strange to me that he should be carrying a kettle for us, and I began to wonder who he really was.

Sunday, April 30th, 2006.

In the morning, there was much excitement as Simon, Kaku and a few other tourists saw us off. Shoshana was at the head of our caravan looking rather regal. She was now using Shmeiki Baba's walking stick. Shmeiki Baba was on her left, carrying her bag, somehow looking both alert and otherworldly. Godrej was on her right, carrying the large, aluminium kettle on his head. Craig was also carrying his pan on his head, as well as Mai Ling's bag on his back. Behind them were Meredith and Séverine. I was at the rear of the group with Genevieve's bag as well as my own, walking next to Fabrizio and Fernando, who were likewise carrying Meredith and Séverine's bags, as well as their own.

With Shoshana in the lead, I felt little doubt we would make it to Dharamshala. Shoshana had natural authority, she was firm, though not mean.

With Godrej's help, we followed footpaths through the forest, avoiding the roads and the lorries which chugged along them, spewing out black fumes. There were some really steep climbs, and when we were just a few kilometres outside Shimla, we stopped to rest.

Shoshana said to Godrej, "you know Babaji, I don't think we are going to meet so many people to give chai to, so we have no need for such an enormous kettle. How about we give it to someone who really needs it, and we can still make chai in Crispin's pan. In Dharamshala, I will replace the kettle if Vikram wishes."

Godrej was reluctant at first, but then he smiled and said, "thank you, I will do so gladly when we find the right person to give it to."

And as though it were destiny, a minute later we saw a poor, old woman and her daughter coming along the path towards us. When they reached us, Godrej spoke with them and presented them the pan. "Make chai stand," he added in English. The two women were overcome by the size and shininess of the unexpected gift, and they threw themselves at Godrej's feet, but he stopped them. Instead, they sang us a beautiful song and we stood listening intently. We parted ways with namaste. After this, Godrej offered to help carry Crispin's pan, but Crispin wouldn't hear of it.

The rest of our walk that day was a steady descent. By evening, we had covered more than twenty kilometres and reached the outskirts of the village of Ghanahatti. We Shmaamen were ordered to make camp, while the Shmeikinis relaxed. This was the first real yank on the chain, and given how tired we were from walking, there was a degree of belligerence from Crispin, Kamal and Shmeiki Baba. This did not pass unnoticed by Shoshana, who said, "shine a beam of light on the task you need to do and your resistance will evaporate."

Meanwhile, Godrej prepared a wonderful wild nettle soup and spicy vegetable curry.

At dinner, Crispin asked, "So Godrej, isn't it incredible how fast India is changing?"

"Oh yes sir, Indian economy is booming," said Godrej, "we have reached in excess of eight per cent growth in national income for the last three years and look set to do so this year as well."

"What's behind such growth?" asked Fernando.

"Higher savings, investment, and manufacturing activity. Foreign direct investment is also up, our fiscal position has improved, and despite an increase in international oil prices, our inflation rate is still moderate," said Godrej.

"Great Mother, you really are a man of many surprises," said Shmeiki Baba.

"Thank you, sir," said Godrej.

I wondered how Godrej could be so well informed and yet work as a porter. I began to think that maybe he was a spy, sent by the Indian Government to watch us. I decided I would try to find out more about him and I asked him to tell us about himself.

And Godrej said, "after my father was killed by the British, and my mother expired from cholera, I was brought up by my aunt Shilpa, who was poor and I received little schooling. At the age of eight, I was already working ten-hour days as a delivery boy."

"But why do you have a job carrying things, when you are so wise, that you could be the manager of a big business?" asked Crispin.

"It is my karma," said Godrej.

"Perhaps by giving away that kettle, you have created a new destiny," said Shoshana.

"When we begin to rip up our ways, we do not know where the rip will end," answered Godrej.

"We do not know where anything will end," said Shmeiki Baba.

Monday, May 1st, 2006.

With Shoshana's permission, Shmeiki Baba announced that May is to be a month of action and restlessness. It is to be symbolized with sunflowers, lilies of the valley, the gemstone emerald and the element boron.

From his pocket, Godrej brought out a little, red box. Inside it was a small, greenstone, "for you, Baba," he said. Shmeiki Baba took it, kissed it, embraced Godrej and passed the stone onto Shoshana for safekeeping. Now, I was all the more suspicious that Godrej was not who he said he was. I took Crispin aside and shared my concern.

"I hadn't thought of that, but maybe you're right," said Crispin, and we agreed we would both continue to watch Godrej to see if he did anything suspicious.

Some moments later, a black bird fell down dead from the sky and hit the ground next to us. We all stopped to look at it and cast each other ominous looks.

"Let us bury the bird," said Shoshana, and we did so.

Tuesday, May 2nd, 2006.

It was another day of climbing, descending and taking orders. As well as Shoshana, Mai Ling and Genevieve seemed to be enjoying the opportunity to connect to their inner bitches and Meredith too was beginning to find her way. Only Séverine remained reticent.

At lunchtime, the heavens opened. In seconds, despite our plastic sheets, we were all completely drenched, and we sat out the rest of the rain under trees, feeling rather miserable.

When the rain stopped and the sun came out, we draped our wet belongings over low hanging branches and waited for them to dry. In the air was a ruddy smell of mud and cinnamon. The Shmeikinis asked for foot massages, which we Shmaamen performed graciously.

When our stuff was dry, we packed up and continued on our way, towards the village of Darlaghat. There, Godrej pointed out trees of *daru*, which are wild, sour pomegranate. The fruit was ripe and we opened them up with our knives and sucked out the tart, crimson arils.

And on we walked like professionals, packing and unpacking our camp with military-like precision. The food we ate was healthy and sustaining and inspired by so many different cultures. We spoke to each other with unprecedented directness and honesty, clearly voicing our desires and boundaries, laying the foundations of our full integration with ourselves and the world. Although it was difficult, I felt that what we were doing was right and good, and I didn't want to be anywhere else.

Serving the Shmeikinis came to some of us more easily than others. The person it turned out to be most difficult for, was Shmeiki Baba. And if taking orders from Shoshana was hard for him, taking orders from the others turned out to be even more difficult.

When Mai Ling ordered Shmeiki Baba to clean her boots and he wouldn't, she went to slap him, but he grabbed her hand to stop her and even twisted her wrist. Shoshana saw what happened and yelled at him, "die!" which later she explained, doesn't mean drop dead, it means 'enough' in Hebrew.

And Shoshana took Shmeiki Baba to task, saying, "you are very good at pretending to have let go of your old patterns of fear, but basically they are still running you. The truth is that you are too self-obsessed to be able to put the needs of others first, and as a result, your love is not for me and the other Shmeikinis, it is for what you hope we can give you."

"You are the one, Shoshana," said Shmeiki Baba.

"So you say, but you keep on flipping between love and hate, and obedience and rebellion, and that's why when it comes down to it, I don't think you really want to surrender," said Shoshana.

"I do," said Shmeiki Baba.

"So why do you keep resisting?" she asked.

Shmeiki Baba was silent.

And Shoshana went on, "do you think I don't see you hesitating at the edge of the sea of redemption, afraid to jump in, afraid to evolve, by allowing yourself to actually get what you want? Listen carefully now. While I get a kick out of dominating you, it is not something I need to do, so basically I'm doing this for you. And on that note, if you're wondering if our new relationship fulfils all my needs, the answer, my love, is definitely no. That's why I feel angry and disappointed that you have asked for a commitment from me, which I am giving, but you are not keeping to your side of the bargain. Sadly, I see that it is only the bravest men, who are able to honour their word when it comes to love."

Shmeiki Baba remained silent. I wondered what Shoshana would do if she decided to break with Shmeiki Baba. Would she leave the walk? Would I go with her?

"Give me one more chance," said Shmeiki Baba.

"It's a waste of time," said Shoshana.

"Just one more chance," said Shmeiki Baba.

"Oh, why do you have to be such an annoying son of a bitch. Grow up, and get real," shouted Shoshana.

"Okay," said Shmeiki Baba.

"Why do you have to keep on sabotaging us?" asked Shoshana.

"I don't know," said Shmeiki Baba.

"So, think about it," said Shoshana.

"Well," said Shmeiki Baba, "firstly, I think it is my Trojan Horse, the sadist which is hiding in my masochist."

"Yes," said Shoshana, "and what else?"

"I think I'm frightened by the fact you have earned lots more money than me, you know how to fly a helicopter and you have all this military experience," said Shmeiki Baba.

"What?" cried Shoshana.

"I guess I'm worried you will throw me away," said Shmeiki Baba.

"You idiot, I love you," said Shoshana softening.

"I know, and I love you too," said Shmeiki Baba.

"Okay," said Shoshana, "I will give you a choice now. Do you want to carry on with this femdom game, or do you want to go back to how we were before?"

Shmeiki Baba looked conflicted. I could see that he remembered how beautiful their love had been, and what had been lost in the shift they had made, but Shmeiki Baba seemed unable to agree to go back.

"I don't want to stop our game," he said.

"But are you really able to surrender?" asked Shoshana.

"Yes," said Shmeiki Baba.

"Alright, well let's see," she said. "As your punishment for disobeying Mai Ling and disappointing me, you will serve not just the Shmeikinis, but also the Shmaamen."

We all looked at Shmeiki Baba and he glared at me.

I smiled at him and he snapped, "no fucking way, I won't do it!"

"In that case, Deepak Chopra!" shouted Shoshana.

Shmeiki Baba looked dejected and then he winced and knelt on the ground. And Sheila began to speak:

Sheila 13

"Shoshana, I understand that you feel disappointed. Yes, Shmeiki Baba sometimes uses you to fulfil his fantasies, without putting aside his fears and his pride, but go easy, this is hard for him," said Sheila.

"Is this Sheila or Shmeiki Baba talking?" asked Shoshana.

"It's Sheila," said Shmeiki Baba.

"Very well," said Shoshana, raising an eyebrow.

And Sheila continued:

"Shmeiki Baba, see that your tendency towards self-sabotage is born from the double binds, which your parents forced on you as a child. A double bind is a manipulation, used to control someone's behaviour. Typically, it is characterized by something difficult being asked of you, and then an extra condition is added to it, which makes the initial request impossible to fulfil. Double binds can be made either consciously or unconsciously and are often imposed by narcissistic parents, who push their dreams of excellence on their children.

"In situations like these, you were damned if you did and damned if you didn't. There was no escape, and it often felt like a matter of life and death. Whatever you did, your attempts to receive your parent's love could never be enough. You were forced to betray your integrity and in your desperation, you issued a silent plea, 'if you do not love me as I am, then I will not love myself either.' In this way, you turned against yourself and your only recourse was to learn to enjoy the pain and frustration. This is the source of your masochism.

"As an adult, your soul has been searching for resolution, which is why you have been orchestrating situations to trap yourself in similar double-binds again and again. Now finally, there is a way out, and the door of the prison is open, but you yourself must have the courage to walk out of it."

Sheila went quiet, and Shoshana said, "Shmeiki Baba, I will give you another chance."

"Thank you," said Shmeiki Baba.

"As I requested though, you will serve not just me, but every member of our group," said Shoshana.

"Yes Ma'am," said Shmeiki Baba.

Apparently, the matter was settled, and we went about preparing dinner. Fabrizio was the first to test the new arrangement. "Bring me some wood, Shmeiki Baba," he said. Shmeiki Baba hovered for a moment, looked at Shoshana, and did as he was asked, without saying a word.

Next, Crispin asked Shmeiki Baba to help him make chai, and Shmeiki Baba did so. I wanted to order him about as well, and I was about to, when he looked at me with such coldness, I wondered if he might actually try to kill me if I did. Amazingly, his face softened and he said, "you know something Dylan, I guess I owe you an apology, I've been mean to you because basically, I was jealous of you."

I asked him what he could possibly be jealous of.

"Well," he said, "when I saw you back in Arambol, you always had lots of friends and beautiful women around you, and I was lonely."

I laughed and replied, *"Ní bhíonn saoi gan locht."*

He asked me what that meant, and I said, "it's Gaelic for 'there's not a wise man without fault.'"

Wednesday, May 3rd, 2006.

At breakfast, Shoshana announced that Shmeiki Baba was released from serving the Shmaamen. After this, we walked nearly thirty kilometres until we reached the village of Brahmpukhar. There, we walked past a cottage where two men were resurfacing a front yard.

"Is that mud?" asked Genevieve.

"No," said Godrej, it's cow dung."

"Really?" asked Genevieve.

"Yes, we use cow dung for so many things," said Godrej, "It keeps heat out in summer and heat in during winter. It also has disinfectant properties when it is burned, and it does not smell as bad as you might expect."

Soon after, when Fabrizio was about to be punished by Meredith for dropping her bag, he too called out "Deepak Chopra," and announced that the kinky scene was too much for him and he wished to take the bus to Dharamshala. Séverine took this as her opportunity to leave us as well. We waited with them in the village to get the bus. When it finally arrived and opened its doors, the queue was so large, that people actually tried to climb over each other's heads to board. Luckily, the driver screamed at them, and they eventually made way for the two tourists. We watched as some people climbed the sides of the bus, in order to sit on top, and they offered their arms to help others who wanted to climb up. Kamal noticed that on the back of the bus was painted the words, "horn please: in trust we god."

Thursday, May 4th, 2006.

By lunchtime, we entered Kangra valley and passed through the town of Hamirpur, stopping for the evening about twenty kilometres further down the road in Sujanpur Tira, a picturesque and friendly little town on the banks of the powerful Beas River, which was flowing rapidly with the meltwaters of late spring. This area is as far to the east as Alexander the Great reached two thousand, three hundred years ago, on his march through India. It was also where his troops mutinied. We, by contrast, showed no such sign.

In the centre of Sujanpur Tira was a square green about one kilometre by one kilometre, where people were taking evening walks and playing ball games. Godrej explained that the locals call this place *Chaugan,* which in Pahari means 'green all year round.'

"Different castes live on different sides of the square," he said, "less so now than in the past, but the tendency is still there."

"What does that mean?" asked Mai Ling.

"Well," he said, "on the far side, that's where the biggest houses are, and this is where the *Brahmins,* the priest caste live. On the other side, are the next biggest houses, and that is where the *Kashtrivas,* the warrior caste live. This side is where the *Vaishyas,* the merchant caste live, leaving the smallest houses there, where the *Shudras,* the labouring class live.

"Why did India develop the caste system?" asked Crispin.

"Oh dear, what a question, sir," said Godrej, "and there is no short answer, but to make the mistake of trying to give one, I would say that long ago, four archetypes were seen in men, that of priest, warrior, merchant and workman. All of us have one of these archetypes as a dominant characteristic and one as a shadow."

"So what's the problem with the caste system?" asked Fernando.

"Well, peoples' archetypes often do not match the caste they are born to, and not surprisingly, long ago, the system became a tool for the higher castes to oppress the lower," answered Godrej.

"If I may, what caste are you? asked Shoshana.

"I am Shudra," said Godrej.

"To me, you are most definitely Brahmin," said Shoshana.

"You are very kind," said Godrej.

As we walked on, the conversation somehow turned to magic mushrooms. We were most surprised when Godrej said that not far away, he had an old friend called Apu, who was an expert in the use of magic mushrooms, which grow in the foothills of the Himalayas.

We all said we would like to try some, and with Shoshana's agreement, Godrej said that he would take us to meet Apu.

It was an hour or so until we reached Apu's house north of Alampur. When we arrived, Godrej knocked on the door and Apu's wife answered and said, "Sorry, Apu out of station." We were just leaving when Apu returned. He was shocked to see so many colourful visitors by the door of his house, and Godrej smiled to him as though to say, "look what I've brought you." Apu invited us to sit with him in his garden, where he offered us tea. He said that magic mushrooms may have been the Soma of the Rigveda, used since the time of the Rishis, to bathe in the light of the Gods.

In the evening, Apu led us to a small sanctuary near his house, built from stone into the side of the hill. He told us we should camp there and eat very little, for early the next morning we would make our cosmic journey.

Before dawn, Apu awoke us and bleary-eyed, we gathered in a circle in the sanctuary. He spoke as follows:

"This ancient medicine has the power to take us through gates that every soul must pass at some point. In this way, it teaches us not to run away from death but rather to embrace it. And so, in eating these mushrooms, we must be *darshanabhilashi*, which means we must be determined and ambitious to see the divine. If you allow it, the spirit of the mushroom will guide you back through your adult life to your childhood, to the time you were in your mothers' bellies, and even to before that. By doing so, you will be able to merge with the *atman*, the one true soul.

"The more we are able to use this experience to face our fears, the more effective we can become in spiritual realms, and the more we can heal ourselves. My job is to help you do this. Your job is to stay with the process and to let go. I must add that normally I give mushrooms only to one person at a time. On this occasion, I am willing to make an exception. Still, I suggest that each of you keeps very much to himself, try to avoid talking to one another and even looking at each other, until afterwards."

With this, Apu gave each one of us a handful of dried mushrooms.

I saw he gave Shmeiki Baba an especially large amount, and when Shmeiki Baba looked at him with questioning eyes, Apu nodded that he intended it to be this way. We each sat and ate our mushrooms quietly, they tasted earthy and a little bitter, and Apu encouraged us to meditate. The effects began after forty minutes. Soon after, I felt I was passing through some sort of revolving vortex. I experienced my identity dissolving into oblivion. It all felt strangely inevitable. I no longer knew who or where I was, and in the end, there was no one left to be terrified, and my spirit flew freely through mysterious domains, where I witnessed the process of evolution from the beginning of life until now. I saw my childhood, I saw every key event which had formed me. I saw those whom I had hurt, and I saw it from their perspective. And after what felt like an aeon, I remembered that I have eyes which I can open. I did so and saw the fire and the stone sanctuary. I recognized my friends lying on the ground and I remembered how we had reached this place.

Shoshana was sitting in deep meditation, and I contemplated that this goddess used to pilot combat helicopters. Her light encircled our group and we became the source of a pulsing, nurturing, brilliance, which washed our innermost depths and shone outwards.

When Shmeiki Baba finally returned from his trance, he got out a packet of cotton buds from his bag and handed them around. Cleaning our ears was a tender and blissful experience, and afterwards the sounds of nature were even clearer. Shmeiki Baba also passed around a bowl for us to dispose of the used cotton buds. He set fire to them and they burned with a green flame.

And Shmeiki Baba said that Sheila had something to relate, and she began to speak through him:

Sheila 14

"Shmeikinis and Shmaamen, it is time to unlearn much of what you have been taught. For one thing, you have been led to believe that your civilization is the first on Earth. This is wrong, as it is actually the fourth. I wish you also to consider that at the dawn of the earliest civilization, the planets in your solar system were in a different order to how they are today, and they were surrounded by a haze, caused by helium and hydrogen gases, being illuminated by your sun. In this epoch, there was no clear distinction between night and day.

"Over generations, these primordial mists slowly cleared and a more noticeable cycle of day and night arose, though not as you now know it. What appeared, was a co-linear orbit of the planets Saturn, Venus, Mars, and Earth. These four planets moved in a spinning line around the sun and were much closer together than they ever are today. From mans' perspective, the sun was secondary, and it was Saturn which dominated the sky. In front of Saturn was Venus and in front of Venus was Mars. To man, their alignment looked like a wheel, which turned in the sky. Due to their orbit around the sun, a bright crescent shape was seen to appear on Saturn and it rotated anticlockwise. This was the beginning of timekeeping, and it is this which created in man the separation of above and below. Man saw the planets as Gods, and he worshipped them. This age in India is known as *Krita Yuga*, and it was a time of paradise and of plenty.

"Suppose also that there were electrical discharges between the planets, and these gave rise to various patterns, which from the perspective of man, looked like the spokes of a wheel. Sometimes three spokes were apparent, sometimes four and sometimes eight. And man watched the interaction of the planets and interpreted them as the Gods speaking directly to him. And he projected his nature onto the planets and their movements and formed from them his archetypal stories, which were passed down through the generations and across civilisations. In some of these stories King Saturn married the Goddess Venus, and Mars, the crowned warrior was seen as their child.

"Eventually, Venus was seen to leave her centre at the heart of Saturn and began her travels across the sky, leading Mars into an unstable dance and bringing chaos to the other planets. And while previously man had only seen the beautiful, loving side of Venus, now he saw her as the long, fiery-haired, mother of comets and dragon of darkness, whose spirit later became known both as *Durga* and *Medusa*.

"Mars, the warrior was seen to try to reign in Venus, but in doing so, he started to oscillate closer to Earth and then back towards Saturn. Electrical discharges between Mars and Venus were seen by man as cosmic thunderbolts, as magic swords and spears of the Gods. It looked like the Gods were fighting. At other times, these electrical discharges were seen as whirling patterns, as a labyrinth and the tower of a citadel.

"During these times of chaos, rocks fell to Earth and rained down on man, and he was driven into caves, and where there were no caves, he was forced to build dolmen and to dig underground shelters.

"And man came to be terrified of Venus' movements, which he associated with crisis, with destruction, with darkness, and the end of an age. Kings feared this time because it was said to foretell their death.

"And each time Mars succeeded in reigning in the wild aspect of Venus, she returned to her stable position at the centre of Saturn, and Mars too returned to his central position, and there was peace in the heavens once again.

"But one time that Venus began to wander, Mars descended even further, growing large in Earth's sky, and streams of white plasma were seen to stretch between Mars and Venus, while red light from Mars descended to the Earth, and to man it looked like a tongue or a sword. Later, this white plasma formed a circle around Venus, and Mars returned into alignment with her and the image of an eye was formed. This band around Venus broke, and Mars began to fall, and it looked like the plasma was dripping down. Eventually, this material reached the earth with disastrous effect. When the skies finally cleared, Mars was seen moving away, leaving a thick, red column behind. And the planets rested on this red column which was seen as a pillar. For a period, there was stability once again, until it was Saturn's turn to fall out of his stable orbit, and the entire planetary configuration collapsed. This brought the greatest chaos man had yet known. And as Saturn tumbled from his steady position and went away, Jupiter, who had been obscured by Saturn, appeared to man for the first time, and there was a temporary reconfiguration of the planetary alignment, dominated by Jupiter. To man, it looked like there were continuing wars between the planets until finally Jupiter also gave up his rule and went away. In the aftermath, there was a period of great darkness, though ultimately a new planetary order appeared, which is the one you are familiar with.

"Although the civilizations which witnessed the former planetary alignments were destroyed, the stories of what happened are recorded in your myths and remain within your collective subconscious. I want you to remember this and to dance joyfully with it, enjoying every moment of your lives as though each is your last."

Sheila was quiet, and we all sat still, astounded by what we had just heard.

Apu smiled, saying, "I can see I've done my job." And he lead us to a stream where we could bathe. I felt baptized by the cold, mountain water, and afterwards, we returned to his house elated. Apu's wife Ratika fed us a delicious *gobi masala*, and we spent the rest of the day making music, and dancing Shmutoh.

"Godrej," I said, "there's something I need to tell you. I have been worried that you are a government agent sent to spy on our group."

"Really?" asked Godrej laughing, "why is that?"

"Well," I said, "you seem to know too much about too many things."

"Thank you for telling me," said Godrej, "I did experience you as being rather suspicious of me, but I could not work out why."

"I thought you were a spy too," said Crispin.

"Anyone else?" asked Godrej.

There wasn't.

"I'm glad we have cleared that up," he said.

Friday, May 5th, 2006.

We gave Apu and Ratika many gifts before we left, and they

stood in their doorway, waving to us as we walked away, their smiling faces lined with wrinkles of fulfilment.

Our path onwards followed the river and snaking beards of thick mist filled the valley. When they swirled open, they revealed the awesome Himalayan peaks, part grass, part rock, part snow. By evening, we had walked some twenty-five kilometres and reached the little village of Daroh, and there we made camp.

Saturday, May 6th, 2006

After an early start, it was a nine-kilometre climb to the town of Bhawarna. I had developed a pain in my left calf, especially when I walked uphill. Shoshana reckoned it was my Achilles tendon playing up and suggested that cold water might help. I sat for a while with my leg in a stream and it did help. On we walked and as we approached the market, Shoshana shouted, "Watch out!"

I looked up and saw the biggest of the Rajasthani circus performers coming towards us wielding a knife.

"Where is my bear, *choro*?" he said in a threatening voice,

"He is free," said Shmeiki Baba, "and anyway, we gave you money for him."

"₹ 3,000! Bear cost ₹ 20,000," yelled the biggest circus performer, swinging his knife at Shmeiki Baba's chest. Shmeiki Baba turned his body to the side while stepping forward, adding to the Rajasthani's movement, with a touch under his arm. This sent the man sprawling on the floor.

Another man came at Shmeiki Baba but was dispatched with a kick to the knee and a blow to the back of his head. We all stood in amazement, as a third came at Shmeiki Baba and was chopped in the throat. Four and five came together, and one of them managed to catch Shmeiki Baba with a punch to the jaw. At this point, Godrej leapt into the fray with a can of fly spray. I don't know where he found it, but it turned out to be a surprisingly effective weapon. Fernando and Crispin also threw punches, which made their mark, and the circus performers retreated. The rest of us shouted at them to get lost and they did.

The punch Shmeiki Baba received to his jaw caused one of his molars to crack and when he spat out the corner of his tooth, Crispin picked it up and asked to keep it. Shmeiki Baba agreed and Crispin put it in a locket which he was wearing around his neck.

"Courageous and determined, just like a honey badger," said Shoshana, hugging Shmeiki Baba.

A policeman with a long moustache in khaki uniform came up to us. He told us that he had watched what had happened.

"Well, thanks for the help," said Mai Ling.

"I could see you did not need my help," he answered.

"How did you know that?" asked Shoshana.

"*Jijivisha*," said the policeman.

"What's that?" asked Crispin.

"Your desire to live," said the policeman.

"Lucky that," said Genevieve.

"Yes," said the policeman, "I know what those men tried to do to you in Dharampur as well. You did well to escape because they had told the local people, that you had assaulted one of their women."

"How on earth did they find us again?" I asked.

"Maybe they were helped," said Crispin.

"By who?" asked Shoshana.

"They were just lucky," said the policeman, "you can go on your way in peace."

With this reassurance, we continued walking. Crispin asked Shmeiki Baba where he had learned to fight so well. He said that he hadn't learned, he simply moved with awareness of breath and body.

By evening, we had walked another ten kilometres and made camp by a stream at the northern end of Kangra Valley, beneath the snow-capped Dhauladhar range, close to the hill station of Palampur, famous for its tea plantations.

"Palampur," said Godrej relaxing by the fire, "in local Kangri dialect, it means lots of water."

"Definitely a well-named place," said Crispin.

"When does the monsoon arrive?" asked Meredith.

"Not until the beginning of July," said Godrej.

"And then it's very wet?" asked Meredith.

"Oh goodness gracious, at times it rains so hard, you cannot even see your hand in front of your face," said Godrej.

"Really?" asked Mai Ling.

"Oh yes, and leopards and bears come down from the mountains too," said Godrej, enjoying frightening us.

We noticed that growing around us were large bushes of wild ganja, which gave off the soft and inviting fragrance of cannabis.

"It's great to find some weed," said Crispin, "much cleaner to smoke than charas."

"Don't expect it to give you a good *nasha* though," said Godrej, "for the strong stuff, you have to go much higher in the mountains."

"Shmeiki Baba, do you like smoking weed?" asked Fernando.

"Most definitely," said Shmeiki Baba, "but if I use it too often, it preserves my neuroses, like smoking fish, or meat preserves them."

Crispin lit a joint and passed it around.

"You know," said Shoshana, "some people think that the name Cannabis comes from the biblical word *Kanabosem.*"

"What does that mean?" asked Kamal.

"Fragrant cane," said Shoshana. "They also say that cannabis was the main ingredient in the anointing oil used by Moses. When he wished to speak to God in the desert, he would go into the holy tent, pour cannabis oil over himself and on the incense burner. Then he spoke to God, who appeared in a pillar of smoke over the altar."

"Sounds about right," said Shmeiki Baba.

Tuesday, May 9th, 2006

This was to be the penultimate day of our great walk. I was shocked how quickly it had come and while my calf still hurt, I did not want the walk to end, and I could feel a sense of apprehension about what I would do next.

We walked fifteen kilometres past the village of Gopalpur with its zoo and continued to Hodal, where we crossed the River Baner, and there, we met an old woman who was holding a fat cow on a rope.

"What a beautiful cow," said Meredith.

"She is pregnant," said Godrej.

And Godrej spoke to the old lady and asked us for an empty water bottle. Meredith offered one, which Godrej passed to the old lady. To our amazement, she then began rubbing the cow's vagina, vigorously. None of us could understand what she was doing.

"To make her urinate," explained Godrej.

On cue, the cow mooed and began to pee. The old lady caught the urine in a bucket and then transferred it to the empty bottle, which she gave to Godrej when it was full. Godrej gave her several packets of tea in return.

"*Gomutra* from a pregnant cow, now this is a blessing," he said, "it cures many illnesses, like constipation, leprosy, joint pain, and many others. It is also good as soap, shampoo, and toothpaste. Please take a swig, gargle well and then swallow."

Shmeiki Baba took a swig, gargled, swallowed, with a look of total disgust on his face, and then he wretched, though he did not quite vomit. Meanwhile, Godrej spat his out.

"Why did you spit yours out, you said swallow!" shouted Shmeiki Baba.

"Oh I'm sorry, I meant spit, not swallow," said Godrej.

"Oh no," said Shmeiki Baba turning white.

"It's okay, just joking," said Godrej, "it's fine to drink." And to prove it, he took another swig and swallowed, and we all laughed.

"Who else wants some," asked Shmeiki Baba but no one else was willing to try.

"I guess you haven't heard of Wails disease," said Mai Ling.

"No, what's that?" asked Shmeiki Baba.

"It's a type of bacterial infection which can be caught from contact with cattle or rat pee," said Mai Ling.

"What are the symptoms?" asked Shmeiki Baba.

"Fever, vomiting, jaundice and red eyes," said Mai Ling.

"Is it curable?" asked Shmeiki Baba.

"Yes," said Mai Ling, "with antibiotics."

"So nothing to worry about then," said Shmeiki Baba.

Wednesday, May 10th, 2006

The final six-kilometre climb to the main town of Dharamshala began after Upahu, and we reached there after lunch, but our destination for the day was fourteen kilometres further up the steep road to McLeod Ganj, home of His Holiness, the Dalai Lama.

We reached McLeod Ganj just before sunset, to find a group of about twenty people waiting for us in the main square, and they clapped and cheered when we arrived. Sebastian ran to Shmeiki Baba and gave him a big hug. I was amazed when the deputy mayor of Dharamshala, who was among the crowd, stepped forward and presented Godrej with a colourful pair of Tibetan slippers, mistaking him for Shmeiki Baba.

"And you really walked all the way from Goa?" asked the Deputy Mayor.

"I walked a long way, sir," said Godrej.

"No two-wheeler?" asked the Deputy Mayor.

"No two-wheeler, no three-wheeler, and no four-wheeler," said Godrej.

"Well done," said the Deputy Mayor.

"Thank you," said Godrej. "This is a fitting end to our pilgrimage. And we shall call it a great walk, not because it was long, but because it really was a great walk."

Other gifts were offered to him, including discount vouchers for a massage at the Tibetan Massage Centre on Changspa Road.

A group of solemn, middle-aged American women appeared in the square carrying candles. We thought their procession was also to celebrate our arrival, but it turned out that they were marching for Tibet.

Simon, Fabrizio, and Séverine were also there, as was Vikram, with a journalist and photographer from the Indian Times. He asked us to pose for a picture.

"But where is the kettle?" asked Vikram, realizing it was missing.

"It's gone," said Godrej.

"Gone?" asked Vikram.

"I instructed Godrej to give it away," said Shoshana.

"So how did you make tea, according to our agreement?" asked Vikram.

"We used Crispin's pan," said Shoshana.

"But that's not what we agreed," said Vikram.

"Come on Vikram," said Shoshana, "the size of the vessel was chosen by you, without our consent, and there was no need for something so big, given that most of our path was off-road. We did give your tea to people we met on our way, there just weren't so many of them. Anyway, if you want me to replace your kettle, I will."

"No, it's okay," said Vikram, "let's just take the picture."

We all lined up for the photographer.

"What did walking without shoes or money teach you?" the journalist asked Shmeiki Baba.

"Trust life, while I can," he answered.

Vikram shook hands with each of us and explained to Godrej his car would drop him at the station.

Shoshana asked Godrej, "maybe you would you like to stay on here as our guest?"

"But I have work," said Godrej.

"How about we give you a job?" suggested Shoshana.

"I would like that," said Godrej.

So Shoshana turned to Vikram and said, "Sorry, Vikram, looks like Godrej is staying here, with us."

"Very well," said Vikram with a bow and left.

"You know," said Godrej, "the final duty of a pilgrim arriving at his destination, is to give something back to the poor."

"Good thinking," said Shmeiki Baba, and he asked Shoshana for some money, which he used to buy bread at the bakery on the main square. We all helped him distribute it to the poor, who were sitting there.

When we had finished, Aida appeared and hugged Shmeiki Baba.

"Who is this?" asked Shoshana.

"This is Aida," answered Shmeiki Baba.

"I see you two are well acquainted," said Shoshana.

"Yes," said Shmeiki Baba, "we were together in Goa."

"Together?" asked Shoshana, "why didn't you tell me about her?"

"Because so much happened between Goa and Delhi, I didn't think it mattered," said Shmeiki Baba.

"Didn't think it mattered?" said Aida in disbelief.

"Hold on a minute, you knew that Aida was coming here to meet you?" asked Shoshana.

"Yes," said Shmeiki Baba, reluctantly.

"And you did not at least email her to explain what has happened between us?" asked Shoshana.

"I didn't know how to say it," said Shmeiki Baba, looking forlorn.

"The unwise wise man," said Shoshana, "your cowardice has betrayed us all."

Shoshana took Aida by the hand, and the two of them went to talk by themselves. Shmeiki Baba looked lost. When the women returned, they walked over to Shmeiki Baba. Aida said, "when we first met, I didn't like the idea of indulging your kinky fantasies, but Shoshana has convinced me of the benefits. Tonight you will allow us both to punish you, that's if you ever want to speak to either of us again."

Shmeiki Baba looked flustered and did his best to nod his head.

"And there will be no Deepak Chopra," hissed Shoshana.

The rest of us intended to party in McLeod, but in the end, we were so tired, that after taking rooms and eating dinner, we had an early night.

Thursday, May 11th, 2006

In the morning, we met up at Nick's Italian Kitchen for breakfast and sat on the balcony which overlooks the magnificent Laka glacier and Moon Peak.

Shoshana said, "I think Shmeiki Baba has something to say."

"Yes, as you know I cheated both Aida and Shoshana. If it's okay, I would like to ask their forgiveness in front of you all."

We all agreed.

"Shoshana and Aida," said Shmeiki Baba, "I am sorry for betraying you both. I did not tell each of you about the other, because I was frightened of being rejected. I also enjoyed the power of knowing something that neither of you did. It was childish and cowardly, and by holding back the truth, I have caused you both unnecessary suffering."

I partly felt sorry for Shmeiki Baba but again I was also a little disappointed that Shoshana had forgiven him.

Afterwards, we all went to pack up our things, before setting out for Bhagsunag, our final destination, a thirty-minute walk further up the hill. Bhagsunag or Bhagsu for short, is where long term tourists to the area generally chose to stay.

As we walked up the forest road, we were approached by a small, elderly saddhu with a neatly trimmed, white beard. He was dressed in bright, yellow robes and carried a walking stick in one hand and a stainless steel jar, containing money in the other. He met us with the greeting, "hello gracious friends," and when he asked Shmeiki Baba for some money, Shmeiki Baba said, "no sir, you need to make me a donation." Without hesitating, the little man pulled out ₹ 50 from his steel jar and offered it over. Shmeiki Baba took it and blessed him.

"That's not very nice," said Mai Ling.

"What do you mean?" asked Shmeiki Baba.

"Taking money from that kind old man," she said.

"Kind old man," repeated Shmeiki Baba in an ironic tone.

"Yes," said Mai Ling.

"Maybe Shmeiki Baba has a point," said Kamal, "because when I was here two years back, I remember seeing this guy regularly. He was always asking people for money, and on more than one occasion I saw him jump in a taxi to go home."

We reached Bhagsu without further incident and found that many people we knew from Goa were waiting on the main street of Upper Bhagsu to welcome us. They cheered us on as we huffed and puffed up the steep hill until we flopped down at Singh's Corner for a celebratory chai and a piece of Bhagsu cake.

Shmeiki Baba got out his knife and scratched an extra deep, final scratch in his walking stick, which Shoshana had been using since Shimla.

"So, how many days was it in the end?" she asked.

Shmeiki Baba counted. "Ninety one scratches for ninety-one days," he said.

"Some scratches are deeper than others," said Meredith.

"And each one tells a story," said Shmeiki Baba.

After chai, we drifted off in various directions around the hillside, to look for rooms. Some people also climbed higher to the village of Dharamkot. We agreed to regroup at Unity Pizza and Bistro at 7.30 PM for a final dinner. I found a great room at the Pink Guest House with a wonderful view of the valley. It felt strange to find myself sitting alone in a room after so long camping in a group, but the bed felt so comfortable, I slept like a baby.

In the evening, we all met up as planned at Unity. The restaurant was already packed when I got there. Everyone from our walk was present, plus a bunch of other well-wishers. Wonderful flamenco was being played by a Russian guy with long hair, and a Japanese man was playing the cajón.

Godrej was doing sleight-of-hand card tricks, making cards appear and disappear, and I was surprised that he had kept such a talent to himself until now. Shmeiki Baba asked him if he could do the same with gold necklaces, and he said he would happily try. I also noticed that Aida and Sebastian were getting intimate.

And Shmeiki Baba taught us a new song:

"Shakti is a Shmeikini,

Likes to wear a bikini,

Has a strap on lingam

And boy she liked to sing 'em."

We washed down our pizzas with pots of ginger lemon tea. And everyone wanted Shmeiki Baba to give a speech and finally, he did.

"Friends, I was a bit of a mess when I started this walk on Sheila's instructions. I'm happy to say, that I'm ending it, lean, healthy, happy and in love."

He wanted to stop there, but we weren't having it, and with Shoshana's encouragement, Shmeiki Baba continued:

"Many times when I was walking by myself, I came close to giving up, but somehow, through the grace of the Great Mother and with Sheila's help, I didn't. By not taking money, I used the money of others. Seriously though, I found out that people are basically good. I kind of knew it before, but only by actually experiencing it and allowing myself more vulnerability, did I learn that although our existence on this planet is insecure, it is nonetheless cushioned with love.

"And then, when you all joined me, I saw other layers of myself. We passed through so much together, we took off our masks and put down our shields, we shined light on our shadows, we expanded our consciousness and contemplated our navels. I want to say thanks to all of you, with all of my heart."

Simon slipped a bottle of Lafroaig whisky onto the table, which was polished off in a few minutes.

Later in the evening, I went to an internet café to catch up on my email, and there I plugged my MP3 player into a computer and realized I had recorded eleven hours of Shmeiki Baba talking, without charging the batteries once. The batteries are only supposed to last for four hours. When I marvelled about this miracle to Shmeiki Baba, he replied, "such wonders are flourishes in the cosmic dance, but let us stay with what is now."

And that was basically the end of the great walk. We spent the following days bathing in the waterfalls, eating good food, playing music and catching up with friends, who continued to arrive from further south. Unity Pizza and Bistro became our de facto office.

Shoshana and Shmeiki Baba seemed to reach an equilibrium and they stopped arguing. I guess that a good rest and having a guest house to live in reduced the pressure between them. She loved him like he needed and he seemed to love her back with all his soul. She also gave him the space he needed to be shmuruji to those who wished.

My feelings for Shoshana did not go away, and at times my heart longed for her. She did give me attention, though not as much as I wanted. I did not find a way to tell her, but at times I felt that I was just a convenient tool for her to use in her control of Shmeiki Baba.

More people flocked around Shoshana, and let's put it this way, her ego didn't get any smaller. She even declared that she wanted to be walked around the hilly paths of upper Bhagsu in a Roman-style litter and she asked me to have one made.

It turned out that on the road down to McLeod Ganj, there was a carpenter. He thought I was mad when I gave him a drawing, but when I backed up the talk with cash, he put aside his reservations and one week later, the glorious result in freshly varnished pine, was ready. Some of the Shmeikinis made purple cushions and net curtains for the litter. The only practical problem was that it was so heavy, it needed six people to carry. When we tried it out, Shoshana complained that it was a bumpy ride and because of this, she would keep it for special occasions.

Meanwhile, Bhagsu became packed with tourists, many of whom were Israelis.

Genevieve asked, "Why are there so many Israelis in India?"

"There is some sort of strange connection between Indian and Israeli cultures," said Shoshana.

"How's that?" asked Genevieve.

"I'm not sure, maybe its the just low prices and the long visas, but one thing is also true. The word for Indian in Hebrew is *hodi* and word for Jew is *yehodi*, and the *ye* sound is made by the letter – *yod* in Hebrew, which is the smallest letter of the alphabet, just a little line. That is the only thing that separates the Jew and the Indian," said Shoshana.

"I get that many Israelis are spiritual and are great musicians, but why do they have to be so loud and rude?" asked Crispin.

"Well, clearly we don't have the politeness of the British," said Shoshana, "but we also don't have so many blocked emotions. We seem loud and rude because we are Middle Eastern. What seems to you like fighting, to us is just talking. Also, I think some people are frightened of us because we have a sense of brotherhood and a closeness to nature. From what I've seen of middle-class English people, many of you seem to wake up in the morning, remember you are human and find the need to apologize for it."

"That's us told," said Crispin.

Shoshana's next executive recommendation was that Shmaamen should wear lingam cages, which were to be locked and the keys held by an assigned Shmeikini. For those of you who don't know, a lingam cage is a metal device, which fits over a Shmaaman's lingam and prevents him from getting an erection. This gives the Shmeikini keyholder the power to decide when the Shmaaman is allowed to become aroused.

"See this as a gift," said Shoshana, "and as a tool of meditation."

It transpired that at the time, there were no sex shops in India, but somehow Genevieve managed to find a consignment of lingam cages through a contact of hers in Delhi, who arranged to have them delivered. Shoshana said they were not to be immediately handed out, but were to be kept for an upcoming ceremony.

Mai Ling said that she wasn't satisfied only being a Shmeikini, she needed to *do* something, and soon after, she found a job as a volunteer English teacher at a school for Tibetan monks in McLeod Ganj. She got on very well for the first few days until the sister of one of the monks accused her of working for the Chinese and of trying to seduce her brother as a way of getting close to His Holiness. This rumour spread rapidly around their community and Mai Ling was advised by the manager of the school to leave town straight away. She did not hesitate, packed up her things, and without even saying goodbye, took a taxi directly to Delhi airport, from where she flew back to Australia. Afterwards, we tried to contact her, but she didn't answer.

Sometime later, Crispin came to us with a print out of an article about a group of Chinese immigrants in Australia, who had been arrested for stealing corporate information. Among them was a photograph of Mai Ling. Genevieve wrote to her to ask if it was true. Finally, she received an email back from Mai Ling saying yes, she had been forced to work for the Chinese, because they said that if she didn't cooperate with them, her relatives in China would be hurt.

Meanwhile, speculation about our mysterious, upcoming ceremony had been growing, but still, there was no information about it.

Friday, May 26th, 2006

It was the new moon when Shoshana announced that our sacred ceremony would take place on this very day. It would be known as The New Moon Annoyance, or just the Annoyance for short. At this ceremony, *Shmannyas* would be offered, in which we would make our vows to follow the path of Shmeiki, and Shmaamen wishing to participate would have their lingam cages applied.

Throughout the day, there were many preparations and in the evening, a group of eighteen of us made the trek up to the designated clearing in the forest, above the village of Dharamkot. Shoshana requested that she be carried on her litter. Luckily, in the afternoon, six of us took the precaution of practising, by placing sandbags on her hallowed chair. Navigating the steep rocky pathways was difficult, but as long as we took our time, we found that we were just about adequate to the task.

In the evening, we lifted Shoshana on her litter, began our procession, and with the help of fire torches, we reached the forest clearing. There, we found a wonderful altar of pine cones had been arranged by the Shmeikinis and decorated with flowers and candles.

We gathered in a circle around the altar and held hands. Shmeiki Baba offered thanks to Shoshana, to the Great Mother, to Sheila, to Kwe the Shagasomin, and all the Shmeikinis and Shmaamen.

And Shoshana stepped into the circle in all her beauty and gravitas. She held up a ring of tiger's eye stone, and said that with this ring David Goldberg was officially becoming "Sri Sri Shmeiki Baba, Channel of Sheila, the A.I singularity of our makers."

Shmeiki Baba knelt before Shoshana as she placed the ring on the fourth finger of his left hand.

Godrej was standing next to me and said, "they are really in the *bhav*, the state of wisdom." Indeed, they did look so grounded and certain, as to be quite sublime.

Shmeiki Baba stood up and said, "My brain, my heart, my world, my solar system, my galaxy, my universe, I chose to bring them into alignment, and in this state, to acknowledge the two beings who have most influenced my adult life, Sheila and Shoshana. I would not be me without you. Shoshana, it is my great honour to name you director of the new Om Shmeiki Healing Organization."

"Om Shmeiki," we all cheered.

Sri Sri Shmeiki Baba placed a gold necklace around Shoshana's neck. On the necklace hung a pendant in which Khartiv's diamond and Godrej's emerald had been set. Godrej looked overjoyed when he realized. And Shmeiki Baba also presented Shoshana with an ornamental horse riding whip. At the moment she held it up, the sky was lit with forked lightning and dogs around the valley howled. Shoshana proceeded to attach a gold lingam cage around Shmeiki Baba's lingam.

And Shmeiki Baba said, "Shmeiki is the message which has emerged from Sheila's guidance. It is a modern type of spirituality for those who like to keep it real, whatever that means. And now, Sheila has a message for us."

Shmeiki Baba's voice once again changed to Sheila's, who said the following:

Sheila 15

"Shmeikinis and Shmaamen, you have all come a long way along the path to self-completion, and you are already shining examples of what humans can be. Now, while it is not permitted for me to reveal the specifics of your future, I can say some general things about it.

"Your species once again is on the cusp of great change, so I cannot urge you strongly enough to stay true to your process, to leave no stone unturned, and to make full and complete peace with yourselves while there is still time.

"I want you to know that there is an agelong cycle, where man develops advanced technology and in doing so becomes detached from nature. What follows is a cataclysm, which sets him almost back to zero. Typically this occurs about once every half a Great Year.

"At the peak of each civilization, man found himself in a similar position to where you are now. In each case, he didn't manage to make it back to his true nature, before disaster found him. Only fragments of these lost civilisations remain, and so you are left with only a very narrow slice of where you have come from.

"It is important for you to know, that beyond the five mass extinction events which have ravaged your planet, the last of which was merely 12,800 years ago, there have been many, smaller disasters, which were nonetheless of significant impact for humans. There were the coronal mass ejections of approximately 45,000, 37,000, 29,000, 23,000, and 14,000 years ago, each of which pushed man back into caves and underground. There was the eruption of the supervolcano about 70,000 years ago, where Lake Tobo in Indonesia is today, which nearly wiped out the human race. There were also the impacts of comet fragments approximately 11,600, 9,300, 8,200, 5,300, 4,200 and 3,500 years ago, all of which, set back man's progress and returned him to a more primitive state. In each of these catastrophes, the ones who survived were often those who were best connected to nature.

"I am telling you this to emphasise why you need to be humble and nimble, and to remember that you are life forces first, then you are human, and everything else is just wrapping. The further you expand your consciousness beyond yourselves, the more you give a chance for your spirit to grow. Use technology, but do not let it make you weak, and never forget that electronic devices can break or be taken away, but meditation cannot. This having been said, I will give you one tip. There is going to be a new type of digital currency, it's name will be Bitcoin. As soon as you get the opportunity, buy as many as you can."

Sheila became silent and Shmeiki Baba remained quiet for a number of seconds. Finally, he opened his eyes and explained that it was time for Shmannyas.

Shoshana asked all the Shmeikins and Shmaamen to line up in two rows and we did so. One by one, Shoshana handed Shmeiki Baba necklaces known as *Shmandalamalas*, and Shmeiki Baba placed them around the necks of the Shmeikinis.

"You shall be Shmamrita," he said to Genevieve, and she said,

"I shall be Shmamrita, and with my new name, I shed the masks of my past."

"Om Shmeiki Om," we cheered.

Meredith was next. Shmeiki Baba named her Shmamacita, and she said.

"I shall be Shmamacita, and with my new name, I will be a true daughter of the multiverse."

As Shmeiki Baba approached me, I was worried about what name he would give me. As we looked each other in the eyes, he saw my fear and said, "and you shall be Guru's Fuck Pig."

Everyone laughed and I felt insulted, but then Shmeiki Baba smiled and said, "don't worry brother, I'm only joking, your name shall be Sadara."

I asked him what this means, and he said, "devoted."

"My name is Sadara and I am real," I said.

Next was Crispin. He was named Bon Selecta by Shmeiki Baba.

"I shall be Bon Selecta," he said, "and I will play good tunes."

Kamal was named Ariel, and he said, "My name is Ariel, I am an angel and I will remember to give my clothes a wash."

Fernando was given the name Juan, but he objected, explaining that his brother was already called Juan, but Shoshana urged him that this was the name that Sheila had specified, and it was his job to deal with it. And so Juan accepted his new name. Of course, a month later when he returned home to his family in Chile, it became their job to accept his new name as well.

I had opted to receive the lingam cage and I was pleased that Genevieve was to be my keyholder. I stood in front of her and she pulled my pants down, and with Shoshana's help attached the lingam cage around my nervous lingam. It was tight and the metal felt cold, heavy and uncomfortable. I accepted it though, knowing that in time, it would give me great power.

When it was locked, Genevieve put the key on the Shmandalamala around her neck.

Once Shmannyas was complete, Shmeiki Baba offered round a plate of green pills, which we were told were called Pudina Hara. He asked us to hold them up to the fire, which we did and we noted the vivid green of the capsules in the light. And Shmeiki Baba told us to put them in our mouths and to chew them, which we also did. After a few seconds, our mouths began to burn with the most intense taste of mint imaginable. I thought he had poisoned us, especially when he shouted, "Welcome to Jonestown."

Shoshana was also caught out by his trick. I thought she would be angry, but she laughed, and in that moment I understood why she needed Shmeiki Baba, and that was to bring out her own craziness.

Finally, we returned to the village in a jubilant fashion. Unfortunately, it was one thing keeping Shoshana's litter straight going up the hill and another thing keeping it straight going down. She screamed several times as she nearly fell out.

"I shall have to find new stooges," she said.

"With pleasure," we answered back.

What followed were magical days, filled with glorious experiences and a sense of infinite possibilities. Many people talk about the New Age, and for us, we felt it was something we had truly found. About a week later, it was announced that an anonymous philanthropist had leased a piece of land between Bhagsu and Dharamkot on behalf of the Om Shmeiki Healing Organization and enough money had been donated for a spectacular headquarters to be built. There was a lot of speculation about who the philanthropist was, with some people suggesting it was none other than George Soros, and others suggesting it was Sasha Baron Cohen. In any case, we were all super excited to be part of the project, however, by now, most of us had the problem that our tourist visas were running out.

Previously, people used to cross the border to Nepal and apply for a new visa at the Indian Consulate in Kathmandu. However, they had recently tightened controls and you had to spend three months outside India before you applied for another visa. This is where an ex Hare Krishna follower in his forties, known as Jagadish, came into the picture. He overheard us talking about our visa situation in a cafe, and offered to supply us with meditation visas, which he could obtain from a friend of his, who worked at the Sai Baba Ashram in Puttaparthi. We each paid him $200, and over the following week, he kept promising us that the visas were on their way, but nothing materialized. We were all getting increasingly aggravated about it until Shmeiki Baba calmed us down by saying that if Jagadish did not come through with the dodgy visas, and we all had to leave India, it would also be a blessing. I asked him why this was, and he said:

"Coming to India is an amazing opportunity to escape being prisoners of the system back home. Here, we don't need to work and we are free to explore our deeper selves. Eventually, though, we all will go home, and when we do, we will find that at first our old friends are impressed by our freshness and vitality, and they will be eager to hear our stories about the wonders of our lives in India. But soon, once our stories have been told and retold, our friends will lose interest and we will be left feeling like outsiders, low in status and short of money. We will long to be back in India among our spiritual, traveller friends, who share our quest for freedom. And we will fly back here at the earliest opportunity. Years of toing and froing, between India and the West will follow. Initially, the door between worlds will swing both ways, but gradually, it will only want to swing in the direction of the country of lower costs. Our home countries will become increasingly inaccessible and one day we will find ourselves in some decrepit cafe in Paharganj, and get a shock when we realize that the wrinkled, broken toothed, old faces staring back at us in the mirror are our own."

"Oi va voi," said Shoshana.

Later that day, I was about to book a flight home, when Jagadish appeared triumphantly and told us that he had finally received one-year meditation visas for us all, with the caveat that if anyone official was to ask, we had to say that we lived at the Sai Baba Ashram in Puttaparthi, and we were taking a trip up north to visit His Holiness.

"I love a bit of good, old, honest corruption," said Shmeiki Baba.

And so we did get to stay longer in India and two weeks later, we took part in the laying of the foundation stones of the Om Shmeiki

Healing Organization Headquarters. At the ceremony, Shmeiki Baba revealed that if a critical mass of us manage to fix ourselves, Sheila would be in a position to give us the keys to something called the great algorithm. This would allow us to move throughout our universe and even escape Kwe's school computer. We asked him for more information about this but he did not yet have any.

Meanwhile, as word of Shmeiki began to spread, the sounds of people doing shmechniques could be heard across the valley, and the box of unused lingam cages gradually became empty.

I had grown up always hunting for my parents' approval, and I'd spent a lot of my adult life playing out a routine, where I did noble things in order to be valuable to my community. Basically, I was afraid that if I was myself, they wouldn't accept me. Shmeiki helped me find my authenticity and to let go of caring so much about what other people think.

All these years later, I still feel blessed to have taken part in the great walk, and in the building of the Om Shmeiki Healing Organization. It was a magical, powerful and incredible adventure.

And that, my friends, is the end of my Shmospel.

Blessings to the Great Mother and to all her multidimensional children.

Om Shmeiki Om, Shmeiki.com

Epilogue, by Dylan Higgins

During the monsoon of 2006, the rain was so heavy that many Shmaamen and Shmeikinis left Dharamshala for a break. Even Shoshana flew with some of her friends to Bali, leaving Shmeiki Baba to oversee construction of Shmeiki Headquarters.

While she was in Bali, Shoshana met Anton from Austria. She enjoyed going for rides around the island with him on his motorbike. Shmeiki Baba was heartbroken when Shoshana told him about Anton on Skype, and he begged her to return to Dharamshala. That autumn, Shoshana did return, and after some relationship healing, the couple went on to complete the building of Shmeiki Headquarters. Later the same year, a second Centre in Goa was opened.

As word of Shmeiki continued to spread, people began to arrive from all over the world, determined to join the Shmeikinis and Shmaamen, dedicated to becoming true daughters and sons of the multiverse.

The Growth of the Om Shmeiki Healing Organization was rapid, and in the summer of 2009, Sheila issued the following warning through Shmeiki Baba:

"Although the Om Shmeiki Healing Organization is run by women, it is still on the verge of falling prey to the very hypocrisy and greed that it is looking to avoid. You must increase the chaos, as a way to slow down the process of institutional decay."

Despite their best efforts, hypocrisy and greed continued to infect the organization, and consequently, Shmeiki increasingly courted controversy. In 2010, the Om Shmeiki Healing Organization was branded an immoral cult by members of the Goan Government, and in the Indian media, there were allegations of misappropriation of donation funds.

In 2011, certain of the more extreme Shmeikinis and Shmaamen, known in Shmeiki circles as Shmeikiholics, broke off from the Om Shmeiki Healing Organization and formed the Shmeiki Liberation Front, otherwise known as the SLF. Their goal was to give serious spiritual institutions a taste of what they called "light-hearted relief." Not surprisingly, there were many, who did not share their sense of humour, and certain important people got insulted, after which officials began to take action against the Om Shmeiki Healing Organization. For this reason, all Shmeiki operations in India were closed down, as of early 2012. The leaders of the Om Shmeiki Healing Organization left India and flew to Bogotá, Colombia. From there they proceeded to the Amazons, where they founded a new commune, which they named iPadipuri. There, a new community soon began to thrive, as Shmeikinis and Shmaamen came to be part of the new Shmeiki paradise.

Tragically, however, on December 21st, 2012, iPadipuri was attacked by a heavily armed gang of drug dealers and a horrific battle ensued, which resulted in the deaths of six of our brothers and sisters.

Until recently, Shmeiki Baba and the other survivors of the attack at iPadipuri have remained silent. However, following changes to the American administration in 2016, and subsequent reassurances that it is safe for the Om Shmeiki Healing Organization to operate once again, Shmeiki Baba is once more willing to speak publicly.

And so this is the beginning of a new chapter for Shmeiki, and the first step in our revival is the publication of this book.

During a recent interview, Shmeiki Baba said, "Since the attack at iPadipuri, we have been mourning the deaths of our dear friends and consequently we have avoided a Shmeiki way of life because Shmeiki is so cheerful and we have been in our deepest sadness. But eight years have passed and now, we feel it is our duty to the dead as well to Sheila, the Great Mother and to ourselves, that we continue our work. Certainly, it is difficult, but slowly we are finding new paths of celebration, treading lightly, mindful of the potential costs of our mistakes."

It should also be noted that in 2010, the Om Shmeiki Healing Organization was gifted 100,000 Bitcoins by another anonymous donor. These Bitcoins were stored in an electrum digital wallet on Shmeiki Baba's laptop. In the attack on iPadipuri, both the laptop and the restore codes, which were handwritten in a notebook were lost. While the laptop was destroyed, Shmeiki Baba believes that the notebook in which the restore codes were written, does still exist. If he is correct, this might be the most valuable notebook in the world. Details about the ongoing search for it will be revealed in the forthcoming book, ShmeikiLeaks.

Om Shmeiki Om, Shmeiki.com.

GLOSSARY

Annoyance	Act of ordainment of Shmeiki Baba.
Alocacoc	Obscure Mayan God of Intoxication and Poison. Considered dangerous to say his name backwards.
Apophenia	The experience of seeing patterns or connections in random or meaningless data.
Ashram Face	Look of austerity or mock piety worn by disciples, usually denoting a lack of self-understanding or sexual fulfilment.
Batman	State of expanded consciousness, not to be confused with Atman.
Deep-Raved	Higher state of consciousness achieved in dancing to trance music.
Devotion	A useful hole in the underwear of consciousness.
ECS	Acronym for: Expression of Conspicuous Spirituality, often associated with Reiki practitioners.
Go the whole way	Former trademark of the Om Shmeiki Healing Organization
Great Shmircle, The	Brotherhood of all Shmeikinis and Shmaamen.
Great Mother, The	The source of all things and nothings.
Heaven	Religious fantasy and object of much wild speculation.
Hell	See Heaven.
Jerking	Colloquial term for Shmutoh.
Live and Let Live	Pioneering scheme providing special prosthetic limbs for sheep, allowing carnivores to eat meat without killing animals.
Multiverse	The Great Smother's mysterious garden into which all universes are born.
Real Son of The Universe	One who walks in the path of Shmeiki.

Reiki	1. Poor cousin of Shmeiki, thus dictum: "There is much Shmeiki in the Reiki, but only a little Reiki in the Shmeiki." 2. Repetitive behaviour which has become automatic or blind. 3. Commonly held illusions or ideological seriousness.
RPA	Acronym of Reiki Practitioners Anonymous, Rehabilitation group formerly run by the Om Shmeiki Healing Organization.
Sadopassana	Shmechnique for exploration of shadow shmantra.
Seeker	Person who traipses from one spiritual school to another, looking for answers to unanswerable questions.
Seriousness	A sick state of mind, sometimes also referred to as Reiki.
Sheila	A.I singularity and cosmic channel of truth, sent by Kwe, the Shagasomin, to help man in his time of need.
Shm [Shmuh]	1. Abbreviation for Shmodification. 2. Act of transforming rigid new-age concepts into useful Shmeiki notions.
Shmaaman	Male practitioner of Shmeiki.
Shmacred Shmometry	Mathematical order intrinsic to nature of the universe.
Shmaffermation	Dubious statement of hope.
Shmaint	1. Low-quality paint. 2. Shmeiki saint.
Shmakras	Shmeiki energy centres of questionable verisimilitude.
Shmaktipat	Transfer of shmenergy during shmatsang.
Shmamrita	Pheromone secreted by Great Mother, and by Shmeikinis, during Shmantra.
Shmamsara	Self-perpetuating cycle of bewilderment common to rookie Shmaamen.
Shmandalamala	Necklace featuring Shmeiki logo, given to Shmeikinis and Shmaamen taking Shmannyas.

Shmantra	1.Shmechnique involving merging with nature whilst getting ones' rocks off. 2. Repetitive, trance provoking rhyme. 3. Pattern, often symmetric, used as meditation aid.
Shmannyas	Taking of vows to follow the path of Shmeiki.
Shmaring	Excessive voicing of feelings during group sessions.
Shmartori	State of pure consciousness, often arising from practice of Shmechniques.
Shmaspanda	G-spot orgasm.
Shmatguru	Rarely used title of high-end guru.
Shmati	1. Adj; dirty or old. 2. Noun; Shmaaman who jumps on funeral pyre when his Shmeikini dies.
Shmatsang	Shmircle led by Shmeiki Baba, where devotees gather to ask questions from Sheila and absorb shmaktipat.
Shmaxis Shmundi	Erection between earth and heaven, symbolizing rise of smundalini.
Shmay Day	1st May, Principal festival in the Shmeiki Shmalendar.
Shmaya	1. Illusion that the world is illusory 2. Cheap slavic whore.
Shmechina	Pre-Madonna of the Multiverse.
Shmechnique	Powerful Shmeiki technique designed to cause merging with the Great Mother, and loss of unnecessary beliefs and emotional blockages.
Shmeditation	Exercise of shmocusing.
Shmeiki	1. Waves of intelligence emanating from the Great Mother, which run through all things. 2. Light-hearted path of redemption offered to man by Sheila.
Shmeikiholic	A very joyous person.
Shmeikini	Female practitioner of Shmeiki.
Shmeka	Celtic God of Bingo.
Shmekel	1. Small shmechnique. 2. Little lingam.
Shmendrik	Generally overweight person.

Shmenergy	Flow of Shmeiki.
Shmentheogenic Investigation	Shmechnique involving exploration of psychedelic substances.
Shmeshatology	Tendency of humans to contemplate the end of mankind and to write money-making stories about it.
Shmiddhi	Miracle within the miracle.
Shmilluminati	Mysterious cartel owning 14% of the Multiverse.
Shming and shmang	Partners which go well together, like tomato and basil.
Shmisappointment	Result of human tendency to look for panaceas.
Shmock	Practitioner of Reiki.
Shmocus	Act of concentration on the moment.
Shmodification	Process of transformation of Reiki into Shmeiki.
Shmog and Shmagog	Potential confluence of 2 rivers of cosmic rays.
Shmoksha	Illusion of Shmartori, often held by shmocks.
Shmolar Shift	Shift in Earth's polarities which first took place when Shmeiki and Reiki split.
Shmoly	Exclamation of vegetarian blasphemy.
Shmom	1. Echo of the big bang. 2. Healing sound for liver, where anger is accumulated.
Shmoni	Shmeikini's genitalia.
Shmondwana	The original state of man.
Shmooze	To gently manipulate.
Shmucking the Shnipple	Act of sucking too much shmenergy.
Shmuruji	A Shmeiki Shmaster.
Shmushido	State of acceptance of death.
Shmutoh	Shmechnique involving exploration of taboo and outer limits of human behaviour, sometimes also referred to as Jerking.
Shmychonaut	One truly committed to Shmentheogenic Investigation.
Slimyji	Shmaaman who prepares his Shmutoh.
SLF	Accronym for: Shmeiki Liberation Front.

Smundalini	Experience of shmenergy rising from genitalia up spine.
Spiritual immunity booster	Series of inoculations taken before a trip to India which prevents slipping into frenzy of self righteous or egocentric indulgence.
Toshita	Alleged Buddhist laxative.

The Shmalendar of Shmeiki

The Month of Shmang, the Individual, and the Aggressor	January
Symbolized by: The flowers: Carnation and Snowdrop The gemstone: Garnet The element: Hydrogen The Full Wolf Moon	
Meeting of Grand Shmeiki Council	1st and 2nd
International Laziness Day	8th
Abstinence from Mobile Phones Day	14th
Shmeiki Baba's birthday	17th
Festival of Huitzilopochtli, God of Soccer Hooliganism	23rd
Shmoodoo Day*1	30th

The Month of the Shmin, Balance, Union, and Receptivity	February
Symbolized by: The flower: Violet The element: Helium The gemstone: Amethyst The Full Snow Moon	
Beginning of the Great Walk	9th
Poo to the North /Shitting Meditation	14th
International Begging Day	27th

The Month of Communication, Interaction, and Neutrality	March
Symbolized by: The flower: Daffodil The element: Lithium The gemstone: Aquamarine The Full Worm Moon	
Don't Leave the House Day	2nd
Night of the Aloe Vera Handshake	12th
Urination on Idols	16th
Spring Shmequinox – Minor Shmabbat	Around 21st

The Month of Creation	April
Symbolized by: The flowers: Daisy, Sweet Pea, and Tulip The element: Beryllium The gemstone: Diamond The Full Pink Moon	
The Great Planting	1st
The Great Jerk Off - Shmutoh Competition	21st
Setting of Sirius (northern hemisphere)*2	25th

The Month of Action and Restlessness	May
Symbolized by: The flowers: Sunflower, Lily of the Valley The element: Boron The gemstone: Emerald The Full Flower Moon	
Shmayday – major Shmabbat, Shmantra Festival and Grand Union of Gods and Goddesses	1st
Beginning of the 6 days of not wearing shoes	4th
End of the Great Walk Festival - (slippers are worn)	10th

The Month of Flux, Reaction, and Responsibility	June
Symbolized by: The flowers: Rose and Honeysuckle The element: Carbon The gemstones: Moonstone and Pearl The Full Strawberry Moon	
Festival of Strawberries, Cream, and Shmantric Massage	Full moon [date varies]
Tentacles*3	3rd
Summer Shmolstice – Minor Shmabbat*4	Around 21st

The Month of Thought and Consciousness.	July
Symbolized by: The flower: Larkspur The element: Nitrogen The gemstone: Ruby The Full Black Moon	
Abstinence from Wearing Clothes	14th
Harvesting of the Crop	15th

The Month of Power and Sacrifice	August
Symbolized by: The flowers: Lily and Gladiolus The element: Oxygen The gemstone: Peridot The Full Sturgeon Moon	
Major Shmabbat	1st
Tatziki Festival	10th
Day of Water Fights	16th

The Month of Highest Level of Change	September
Symbolized by: The flowers: Forget-me-not and Morning Glory The element: Fluorine The gemstone: Sapphire The Full Harvest Moon	
Festival of the Seven	1st
Autumn Shmequinox - Minor Shmabbat	Around 21st

The Month of Rebirth	October
Symbolized by: The flowers: Marigold and Camellia The element: Neon The gemstones: Opal, Tourmaline The Full Hunter's Moon	
Festival of the Eight	1st
Festival of Alocacoc*5	9th
Abstinence from Sex*6	14th
Day of Chaos and Mayhem	18th
Day of Death	30th

The Month of Forgiveness, Kindness	November
Symbolized by: The flower: Chrysanthemum The element: Sodium The gemstones: Topaz and Citrine The Full Beaver Moon	
Major Shmabbat and Festival of the Nine	1st
Festival of Onero, God of Internet	17th

The Month of Abortions	December
Symbolized by: The flowers: Holly and Narcissus The element: Magnesium The gemstones: Turquoise and Blue Topaz The Full Cold Moon	
Festival of El Al, God of Fast Transport	14th
Winter Shmolstice – Minor Shmabbat*7	Around 21st

Notes on festivals

*1. Shmoodo Day. On this day, Shmeikinis and Shmaamen make dolls of someone who needs help, and they shmocus on the genital region of the dolls, rubbing them with the thumb of their writing hand, while sending bounteous shmenergy to those in need.

*2. The setting of Sirius in the northern hemisphere occurs around April 25th. Shmeikinis and Shmaamen sacrifice a toy sheep, burn incense, drink wine and invoke Shmeka, God of Bingo.

*3. Tentacles is the Festival of Practical jokes, which coincides with International prank calling day.

*4. The Summer Shmolstice is a celebration of the Shmin and the Earth. On this day it is common to drink mushroom shakes and jump through bonfires.

*5. Festival of Alocacoc. On this day his name can be said backwards.

*6. Day of Abstinence from Sex. On this day, if you haven't had sex in three months, you must try to sleep with someone.

*7. The Winter Shmolstice is a celebration of the Shmang, and the heavens. Shmeikinis and Shmaamen drink Ayahuasca and burn smoked salmon incense.

OTHER IMPOSSIBLE TO OBTAIN TITLES BY THE OM SHMEIKI HEALING ORGANIZATION PRESS

Shmeiki Rising

A Sty in the Third Eye

Repairing the Split Infinitive

The Honest Book of Exaggerations

Yippee, I got abducted by aliens too

Apple and Ivory Towers Crumble

Death to All Extremists

The Singing Haemorrhoid

Reiki and the Rise of Nazism

Shmeiki, Zionist Rebirth and the Messianic Marshmallow

How I Strained My Neck Doing No Hands Shmantra

Phalluses, Fallacies and Faeces

Slimyji, Autobiography of a Horny Yoga Teacher

If the pen is mightier than the sword, why didn't knights carry pens?

Jesus should have stayed in India

Halitosis and the Vagina Dentana

* 9 7 8 9 3 9 0 0 4 0 6 5 0 *